旅遊英語
TOURISM 必備指南

金利 主編

還在為出國旅行不知道如何開口向外國人說話而困擾嗎？
還在為搭飛機、入住飯店時手忙腳亂而煩惱嗎？
不要懷疑，你缺的就是這本《旅遊必備英文指南》！

快樂旅行，說走就走。你準備好了嗎？

崧燁文化

目錄

Chapter 1
搭乘飛機

Chapter 2
下榻飯店

chapter
3
出行交通

Chapter
4
觀光娛樂

Chapter
5
購物

Chapter
6
餐飲

Chapter
7
突發狀況與其他場景

前言

　　這是一個全民開口說英語的時代。為了提升溝通品質，盡享旅行樂趣，變身面試達人，促成大筆交易，你必須能說一口漂亮的英文！本書是專門為英語學習愛好者打造的叢書，囊括了必備詞彙及道地表達，旨在幫助讀者在實際情境中將英語運用自如。

　　和老外交流時，我們通常會先想到中文，然後再去想對應的英文表達。這是我們學習英語的思維方式。比如訂機票時，我們肯定先想到單程票，再去想對應的英文說法。本書在編排單字和句子時，都是先提供中文，後提供英文。並且按照這種思維方式，本書設計為詞→句→會話的學習流程。針對每一情景，設定了必備表達、句句精彩、情景模擬三個部分，讓讀者由淺至深、循序漸進、環環相扣地進行學習，打牢基礎！

1. 必備表達

　　我們歸納了旅遊場景中經常使用的中文說法，整理出單字和片語，引導讀者學習對應的英語表達，並加以解析。

2. 句句精彩

　　與單字理解方式一樣，我們整理了旅遊場景中經常使用的中文句子，將其放入對話場景，提供對應的英語表達，並對重難點問題加以解析。

3. 情景模擬

　　本書針對每一個情景，設計了情景會話。這部分用於實戰演練。我們提供了中文表達的句子，要求讀者說出對應的英文。這些內容均在之前的環節學習過，旨在為讀者提供一個鞏固與提高的機會。這樣，讀者既可以鞏固所學知識，又可以自我檢測，力求做到學以致用。我們相信，透過將單字、句子與會話合為一體，一定能為讀者帶來意想不到的收穫。

　　透過閱讀本書，你將體會到只要方法用對了，想要流利地開口說英語將不再是難題。

　　快樂旅行，說走就走。你準備好了嗎？

Chapter

1

搭乘飛機

Scene 1 預訂機票

Step 1 必備表達

預定	make a reservation：reservation 預定。
單程票	one-way ticket：one-way 單程的。
往返票	round-trip ticket：round-trip 往返的。
直達航班	direct flight：也可用 nonstop flight 來代替。
轉機航班	connecting flight：也可用 transfer flight 來代替。
再次確認航班	reconfirm a flight：reconfirm 再次確認。
頭等艙	first class：class 可表示（飛機、車輛等）的艙位。
商務艙	business class：商務艙是大部分交通工具的第二等級艙位。
經濟艙	economy class：經濟艙是座位等級較低的一個艙位，該艙票價便宜，座位設在客艙中間到機尾的地方，占機身空間的四分之三或更多。
起飛時間	departure time：departure 離開，出發。

Step 2 句句精彩

① 有 10 月 15 日去紐約市的航班嗎？

A：Are there any flights to New York City on October 15th? 有 10 月 15 日去紐約市的航班嗎？

B：Yes. We have a flight leaving at eleven o'clock. 有，11 點有趟航班。

Tips

■ Are there any flights to London this evening? 有今天晚上去倫敦的航班嗎？

■ There's a ten fifteen flight on that day. 那天有趟 10 點 15 分的航班。

② UA978 號航班還有空座位嗎？

A：Any seats left on flight UA978? UA978 號航班還有空座位嗎？

B： No, they are all booked. 沒有，都訂完了。

Tips

> UA978 是航班號，其中字母代表不同的航空公司，如：聯合航空 (UA) United Airlines；美西航空 (HP) America West Airlines。

■ We have a few seats in business class. 我們的商務艙還有些座位。

All the seats on European flights are booked up for tonight. 今天晚上去歐洲各地的航班座位全都訂完了。

③ 我不要夜間航班。

A： I don't want a night flight. Is there any other flight available? 我不要夜間航班，還有其他的航班嗎？

B： Sorry, there is none for today, sir. 對不起，先生，今天的沒有了。

Tips

> night flight 又稱 red-eye flight，即「夜航」或「紅眼航班」，指夜間飛行的航班。乘客乘坐這種航班抵達後大都睡眼惺忪，故此得名「紅眼航班」，通常票價較低。
>
> I prefer a morning flight to New Delhi. 我想訂去新德里的早班機票。
>
> Would you like the morning flight, afternoon flight or red-eye flight? 您喜歡乘坐上午、下午還是夜間航班？

④ 明天從北京飛往紐約的第一趟航班是什麼時候？

A： When is the earliest flight tomorrow from Beijing to New York? 明天從北京飛往紐約的第一趟航班是什麼時候？

B： It'll depart at 7 a.m. 早上 7 點起飛。

Tips

> depart 離開，起飛
>
> When is the next available flight? 下一趟航班是什麼時間呢？
>
> Then when is the earliest direct flight available to Beijing? 那最早什麼時間有到北京的直達航班？

⑤ 從北京到華盛頓的單程票價是多少？

A： How much is the one-way ticket from Beijing to Washington? 從北京到華盛頓的單程票價是多少？

B： It costs 3,000 yuan. 需要 3,000 元。

Tips

- Single ticket or return ticket? 單程還是往返票？
- Economy fare for single ticket from Beijing to Shanghai is 500 yuan. 從北京到上海的單程經濟艙票價是 500 元。
- How much is a round-trip ticket to Seoul? 飛往首爾的往返機票是多少錢？

⑥ 我需要再次確認一下我的機票。

A： I need to reconfirm my flight. 我需要再次確認一下我的機票。

B： OK, please give me your PNR number. 好的，請告訴我您的預訂號。

Tips

- PNR number 的全稱是 Passenger Name Record number，也就是「預訂號」的意思。預訂號既包括數位又包括字母，一般是 5 位元或者 6 位。在確認和驗證機票時，一般航空公司都會需要這個號碼。
- May I reconfirm my flight? 可以再次確認下我的航班嗎？
- I'd like to reconfirm my flight to New York next Thursday. 我想再次確認我下週四到紐約的航班。

⑦ 中途要停留嗎？

A： Will there be any layovers? 中途要停留嗎？

B： There's a one-hour layover in HK, China. 在香港會停留一小時。

Tips

- layover 表示中途短暫的停留，也可用 stopover 來代替。stopover 這一動詞片語也表示「中途停留」的含義。
- You have to stop over in Boston. 您需要在波士頓短暫停留。
- No. It is a non-stop. 不用，這是直飛航班。

Step 3　情景模擬

① 詢問航班詳情

A： Are there any flights to New York City on October 15th? 有 10 月 15 日去紐約市的航班嗎？

B： Yes, there's a ten fifteen flight tomorrow morning. 有的，明天上午 10 點 15 分有

趙航班。

A： Will there be any layovers? 中途要停留嗎？

B： Yes, you need to transfer in Bangkok. 是的，您需要在曼谷轉機。

A： What time will it arrive in New York? 幾點能到紐約？

B： At about twelve. 大概 12 點。

② 櫃檯預訂機票

A： Any seats left on flight UA978? UA978 號航班還有空座位嗎？

B： Yes, we have a few seats in business class. 有的，我們的商務艙還有些座位。

A： OK, I'll need one with an open return. 好的，我要一張回程時間不定的往返機票。

B： American Airlines has a flight leaving at 9:25 a.m. 美國航空公司有一趟航班，在早上 9 點 25 分起飛。

A： I guess that's OK. What time should I check in? 我覺得這個可以，我應該什麼時候去辦理登機手續？

B： You have to be there two hours before departure time. 你必須在飛機起飛前兩小時到達那裡。

③ 詢問票價

A： How often is there a flight to Paris? 去巴黎的航班多長時間一趟？

B： We have flights to Paris every hour. 我們每小時都有去巴黎的航班。

A： Then, at what time does the next plane leave? 那下一趟航班幾點起飛？

B： The next one is flight 10 at 10:45 a.m. 下一趟航班是 10 號航班，上午 10 點 45 分起飛。

A： How much is the one-way ticket? 單程票多少錢？

B： 638 dollars, including the tax. 638 美元，含稅。

A： Then one ticket, please. 那請訂一張給我。

Scene 2　登機手續

Step 1　必備表達

機場	airport：世界上比較著名的機場是：亞特蘭大（ATL）、洛杉磯（LAX）、法蘭克福（FRA）、巴黎戴高樂（CDG）、阿姆斯特丹(AMS) 等。
辦理登機櫃檯	check-in counter：check in 辦理登機手續；counter 櫃檯。
機票	airline ticket：也可用 plane ticket 或 passenger ticket 來表示。
護照	passport：護照通常分為普通護照、外交護照、公務護照等。
簽證	visa：「落地簽」就是 landing visa。
登機牌	boarding pass：機場為旅客提供的登機憑證。
行李推車	trolley：超市中的購物車就是 shopping trolley。
安檢門	security gate：security 安全。
登機門	boarding gate：boarding time 登機時間。
隨身行李	carry-on：也可以用 carry-on bag 來代替。
廣播	announcement：announce 通知。
航站樓	terminal：也可以用 terminal building 來代替。

Step 2　句句精彩

① 乘客應該在飛機起飛前兩小時辦理登機手續。

A：When should I check in for my flight? 我應該在什麼時候辦理登機手續？

B：Passengers should check in at least two hours before the departure time. 乘客應該至少在飛機起飛前兩小時辦理登機手續。

Tips

■ 在機場裡，check in 常用來表示「辦理登機手續」；在飯店裡 該片語就表示「登記入住」。

■ departure time 表示「起飛時間」，除此之外還可以表示「出發時間」。其中 departure 是動詞 depart 的名詞形式，表示「離開，離去」。

(2) 登機門在哪裡？

A： Where is the boarding gate? 登機門在哪裡？

B： Go along this way; then turn left at the first corner. The boarding gate is on your right. 一直向前走，然後在第一個轉角處向左轉。登機門就在您的右側。

Tips

  Would you please tell me where the boarding gate is? 請告訴我登機門在哪裡？

  Can you show me the way to the boarding gate? 能告訴我登機門在哪裡嗎？

  How can I get to the boarding gate? 我怎樣才能找到登機門？

(3) 這是辦理航班登機手續的地方嗎？

A： Is this where I can check in for my flight? 在這裡可以辦理登機手續嗎？

B： Yes, sir. Please show me your ticket and passport. 是的，先生。請出示您的機票和護照。

Tips

  Is this the right counter to check in for my flight? 是在這裡辦理登機手續嗎？

  Can I check in for my flight at this counter? 能在這個櫃檯辦理登機手續嗎？

  How do I go through customs? 如何辦理通關手續？

(4) 請出示您的機票和護照，好嗎？

A： May I have your tickets and passports, please? 請出示您的機票和護照，好嗎？

B： Here you are. 給您。

Tips

  May I see your passport? 能看一下您的護照嗎？

■ Here are your tickets and your boarding pass. 這是您的機票和登機牌。

  Can you show me your boarding pass? 能看看您的登機牌嗎？

(5) 我能隨身帶多少行李？

A： How many carry-on bags can I have? 我能隨身帶多少行李？

B： You are permitted two carry-on bags. You can check the others. 你可以隨身攜帶兩件行李。其他的可以托運。

Tips

  You'll have to check that big bag. 你需要托運那個大件行李。

■ What should I take as my carry-on? 登機時我要帶哪些東西？

■ You need to check the other bags. 您的其他行李必須托運。

⑥ 這趟航班開始登機了嗎？

A： Has this flight already started boarding? 這趟航班開始登機了嗎？

B： Not yet. We are delayed about half an hour. 還沒有。航班晚點大約半小時。

Tips

■ delay 意為「延期；耽擱」，在這裡表示航班「延誤」。

■ When is the boarding time for this flight? 這趟航班的登機時間是什麼時候？

■ Has this flight begun boarding? 這趟航班開始登機了嗎？

⑦ 飛往巴黎的 606 航班晚點了。

A： Why can't we board now? We have been here for one hour. 為什麼現在還不能登機？我們已經在這等了一個小時。

B： Sorry. Flight 606 to Paris has been delayed. 對不起。飛往巴黎的 606 航班晚點了。

Tips

■ How long is this flight going to be delayed? 這班飛機會晚點多久？

■ I'm sorry to announce that we are canceling flight 905 due to severe weather in New York. 很抱歉，由於紐約天氣惡劣，我們要取消 905 航班。

Step 3　情景模擬

① 詢問起飛時間

A： When does the flight leave? 何時起飛？

B： 5:45 pm. 下午 5 點 45 分。

A： When should I check in for my flight? 我應該在什麼時候辦理登機手續？

B： Passengers should check in at least two hours before the departure time. 乘客至少應該在飛機起飛前兩小時辦理登機手續。

A： OK. I see. 好的，我明白了。

B： Don't forget your ticket and passport. 別忘記帶機票和護照。

A： Sure. Thank you. 當然。謝謝。

② 辦理登機手續

A： When do I need to check in for the flight? 我應該什麼時候辦理登機手續?

B： Two hours before departure. 起飛前兩小時。

A： Is this where I can check in for my flight? 這是辦理登機手續的地方嗎?

B： Yes. But you should show your ticket and passport first. 是的, 但是您得先出示機票和護照。

A： Here you are. 給你。

B： OK. This way, please. 好的。請走這邊。

③ 開始登機

A： Has this flight already started boarding? 這趟航班開始登機了嗎?

B： Yes, sir. 是的, 先生。

A： Where is the boarding gate? 登機門在哪兒?

B： Go down that way, and you can find it on the right. 沿著那條路走, 登機門就在右手邊。

C： May I see your passport? 請出示您的護照。

B： Here it is. 給您。

Scene 3　在飛機上

Step 1　必備表達

安全帶	seat belt：也可以說成 safety belt、life belt 或者 safety harness。
機艙	cabin：cabin class 二等艙；passenger cabin 客艙。
靠走道的座位	aisle seat：aisle 通道，走道。
中間的座位	middle seat：in the middle of 在……中間。
靠窗座位	window seat：飛機窗戶的「遮光板」是 sun shade。
頭頂置物艙	overhead compartment：compartment 隔間，baggage compartment 行李艙，cargo compartment 貨艙。
使向後傾斜	recline：表示將座椅放倒，就可以用這個詞。
起飛時刻	departure time：還可以說成 time of departure。
窗簾	blind：window blind 百葉窗。
機長	captain：飛行期間，機長在與飛行有關的所有事情上有最終決定權，並承擔相關責任，所以也可以用 pilot in command 表示。
駕駛艙	cockpit：近義詞有 compartment、enclosure。cockpit crew 則是「機組人員」。

Step 2　句句精彩

① 乘客在機艙內不允許抽菸。

A： Can I smoke here? 我能在這裡抽菸嗎？

B： Sorry. Passengers are not allowed to smoke in the cabin. 對不起。乘客在機艙內不允許抽菸。

Tips

■ All domestic flights are nonsmoking. 所有國內航班都禁菸。

■ You can't smoke on any domestic flights. 您在國內的航班上都不能抽菸。

■ Smoking is prohibited on all domestic flights. 國內航班禁止吸菸。

② 飛機起飛前乘客必須關閉手機。

A： Passengers should power off cell phones before the plane takes off. 飛機起飛前，乘客必須關閉手機。

B： Sorry. I'll turn it off right now. 對不起。我馬上就關機。

Tips

power off 關機

Please turn off your mobile phone before the plane takes off. 飛機起飛前請關閉手機。

■ Please make sure that your cell phone has been powered off. 請確認您的手機已關閉。

③ 一定要繫好安全帶。

A： Do I have to keep my seat belt on at all times? 我需要一直繫著安全帶嗎？

B： Yes. Make sure to fasten your seat belt. 是的。一定要繫好安全帶。

Tips

Can you tell me how to fasten the seat belt? 你能告訴我怎麼繫著安全帶嗎？

Do I have to keep the belt fastened all the time? 我得一直繫著安全帶嗎？

When can I unfasten the safety belt? 什麼時候才能解開安全帶？

④ 你坐在我的位子上了。

A： You're sitting in my seat. The seat is 5C. 你坐在我的位子上了。這個座位是 5C。

B： Oh, really? I'm sorry. 哦，是嗎？我很抱歉。

Tips

Excuse me. You have my seat. 不好意思，你坐在我的位子上。

I think that's my seat. 我以為那是我的座位。

I'm afraid you are on the wrong seat. 恐怕您坐錯位置了。

⑤ 您介意和我換位置嗎？

A： Would you mind trading seats with me? 您介意和我換位置嗎？

B： No, not at all. 不，不介意。

Tips

mind 表示「介意」，「介意做某事」可以使用 mind doing sth. 這個片語來表達。比如，I don't mind helping you fasten your safety belt. 我不介意幫您繫安全帶。

■ Can I change seats with you? 我可以跟你換位子嗎？

■ Would it be possible for us to trade seats? 能和我們換個座位嗎？

⑥ 我是否可將座位向後放倒？

A： May I recline my seat? That will be more comfortable. 我能將座位向後放倒嗎？那樣舒服些。

B： Sure. That's OK. 當然。沒有問題。

Tips

■ recline 使向後傾斜，也可以用 lower the back of the seat 表示。

■ Could you put your seat up, please? 請豎直椅背，好嗎？

⑦ 上面的置物箱都滿了，我該把行李放哪呢？

A： What can I do for you? 您需要幫忙嗎？

B： The overhead compartments are all full; where can I put my baggage? 上面的置物箱都滿了，我該把行李放哪呢？

Tips

■ You can put the baggage in the overhead compartments.
您可以將行李放在上面的置物箱裡。

■ What can I do with my baggage? 我的行李怎麼辦呢？

Step 3　情景模擬

① 對號入座

A： Is there anything wrong? 有什麼問題嗎？

B： You're sitting in my seat. 你坐在我的位子上了。

A： Oh, I'm really sorry. 哦，真對不起。

B： Is this the first time that you take plane? 這是你第一次坐飛機嗎？

A： Yes. Well, my seat is 5A, but I don't know where it is. 是的。嗯，我的座位是5A，可是我不知道它在哪。

B： Your seat is on the next row. 您的座位在後面那排。

② 座位調換

A： Can I help you? 需要幫忙嗎？

B： I want to change seats. I don't like an aisle seat. 我想換座位。我不想坐靠近走道的位子。

A： OK, let me see if there are any other seats available. How about this window seat? 好的，讓我看看是否還有空位。這個靠窗的位子行嗎？

B： That's great. Thank you. 太好了。謝謝。

A： Have a happy journey. 祝您旅途愉快。

B： Thank you for your help. 感謝你對我的幫助。

③ 放置行李

A： What can I do for you? 有什麼能為您效勞的嗎？

B： The overhead compartments are all full. Where can I put my baggage? 上面的置物箱都滿了，我該把行李放哪呢？

A： Don't worry. Let me see. How about the compartment over there? Is it big enough? 別擔心。讓我看看。那邊的置物箱怎麼樣？夠大嗎？

B： Let me have a try. Be careful, there are breakable items in it. That's OK. 讓我試試。小心，這裡面有易碎品。就這樣吧。

A： Is there anything else that I can do? 我還能為您做些什麼？

B： No, thanks a lot. 沒有了。多謝。

Scene 4 機 上 服 務

Step 1 必 備 表 達

機上電影	inflight movie：inflight 飛機上發生的。航空公司為了緩解旅客的疲勞，經常會在飛機上播放一些電影或宣傳片，供旅客觀看，以消磨時間。
電影頻道	movie channel：channel 頻道，encoded channel 加密頻道，discovery channel 探索頻道。
電子設備	electronic device：由於電子設備發射的無線電頻率可能對飛機造成干擾，因此在飛機起飛和降落時通常要求關閉電子設備。
耳機	earphone：飛機上使用的耳機一般有三種，一種是導氣孔式的，一種是單插孔式的，一種是雙插孔式的。
素食	vegetarian food：vegetarian 素食主義者。
牛肉	beef：beef steak 牛排，beef jerky 牛肉乾，beef noodles 牛肉麵。
提供晚餐	serve dinner：serve 為……服務；提供。
煎蛋捲	omelet：western omelet 西式煎蛋捲，oyster omelet 蚵仔煎。
橙汁	orange juice：大部分航空公司會提供免費飲品。
枕頭	pillow：air pillow 空氣枕，pillow cover 枕套，throw pillow 抱枕。
空服人員	flight attendant：航班機上人員一般包括一名機長、兩名副駕駛、一名或兩名空保，以及五名機上空服人員。

Step 2 句 句 精 彩

① 可以幫我把行李放上去嗎？

A： Could you please help me put my baggage up there? 可以幫我把行李放上去嗎？

B： Sure. Leave it to me. 當然可以。交給我吧。

Tips

■ Could you please help me get my baggage? 可以幫我把行李拿下來嗎？

　Would you please put my baggage up there? 請幫我把行李放上去，好嗎？

② 能再給我一個枕頭嗎？

A： Could I get one extra pillow? 能再給我一個枕頭嗎？

B： Wait for a minute. I'll fetch one for you. 請稍等。我去給您拿一個。

Tips

　Could you give me one more blanket? 請再給我一條毯子，好嗎？

　One extra pillow, please. 請再給我一個枕頭。

③ 對不起，我不知道如何打開閱讀燈。

A： Excuse me. I don't know how to turn on the reading light. 對不起，我不知道如何打開閱讀燈。

B： Don't worry. Let me help you. 別著急。我來幫您。

Tips

　Do you have any newspapers or magazines? 你們有報紙或雜誌嗎？

　Do you have Chinese newspapers? 你們有沒有中文報紙？

④ 什麼時候可以使用電子產品？

A： When can I use my electronic devices? 什麼時候可以使用電子產品？

B： Please wait for a moment. I'll announce you later. 請稍等會兒。一會兒我會通知您。

Tips

　The earphones didn't work. Can I get another pair? 耳機壞了，能給我換一副嗎？

　This headphone is not working. Can I have a new one? 這副耳機壞了，麻煩給我一副新的。

⑤ 機上電影什麼時候開始播放？

A： What time does the flight movie start? 機上電影什麼時候開始播放？

B： In a few minutes. 幾分鐘後。

Tips

　Which is the movie channel? 電影頻道是哪個？

■ I mostly like action movies. 我通常喜歡動作片。

⑥ 飛機上供應午餐嗎？

A：Will we be served lunch? 飛機上供應午餐嗎？

B：Yes. We will serve you lunch at 11:30. 是的。我們會在 11 點半為您提供午餐。

Tips

■ What kind of drinks do you have? 機上提供哪些飲料？

■ When do you start to serve dinner? 請問晚餐幾點開始供應？

■ What would you like to drink? 你想喝點什麼呢？

⑦ 請給我牛肉飯。

A：What would you like, sir? 先生，您吃點什麼？

B：I'd like rice with beef, please. 請給我牛肉飯。

Tips

■ Orange juice, please. 請給我橙汁。

■ Beef or pork? 請問您要吃牛肉還是豬肉？

■ Can I have a soda with lemon chips? 可以給我一杯加檸檬片的汽水嗎？

Step 3　情景模擬

① 使用電子產品

A：Excuse me. When can I use my electronic devices? 打擾一下。什麼時候可以使用電子產品？

B：You can't use them when the plane is taking off. When it is possible to use. 飛機起飛時，您不能用電子設備。等到可以用的時候，我會告訴您。

A：All right. This headphone is not working. Can I have a new one? 好吧。這副耳機是壞的，麻煩給我一副新的。

B：Please wait for a moment. I'll get a new one. 請稍等。我去拿副新的。

A：Thanks a lot. 非常感謝。

B：Not at all. 不客氣。

② 閱讀報刊

A： Would you please give me the morning edition, please? 請把晨版的報紙給我好嗎？

B： Sure. Here you are. 好的。給您。

A： Excuse me. I don't know how to turn on the reading light. 對不起，我不知道如何打開閱讀燈。

B： Let me help you. 我來幫您。

A： Thank you for your help. 感謝你對我的幫助。

B： It's my pleasure. 不客氣。

③ 娛樂時間

A： What time does the inflight movie start? 機上電影什麼時候開始？

B： In a few minutes. 幾分鐘之後。

A： What's it about? 是關於什麼的？

B： It's a love story between a rich girl and a poor boy. It will last about an hour and a half. 關於一個富家女和窮小子之間的愛情故事。差不多持續一個半小時。

A： OK. Thank you. 好的。謝謝。

B： Have a good time. 祝您旅途愉快。

Scene 5 身體不適

Step 1 必備表達

洗手間	lavatory：不允許在飛機起飛、降落前使用洗手間，途中幾乎都可以。但是遇到強對流雲層（強烈顛簸時）時不可以。
亂流	turbulence：亂流和海洋中的渦流、大浪一樣，嚴重影響飛機等飛行器的航行安全。
（洗手間）有人使用	occupied：occupy 占領，使用。
（洗手間）沒人使用	vacant：這個詞還可以表示飯店的空房，如：vacant room。
嘔吐	vomit：還可以用 throw up 來表示。
暈機	airsickness：「暈車」就是 car sickness，而「暈船」就是 sea sickness。
耳鳴	ringing in the ears：也可以用 tingling 代替 ringing。
嘔吐袋	airsick bag：在機艙裡，有時會有一些乘客因為暈機或身體不適而嘔吐。大部分航空公司備有嘔吐袋，以防乘客在機上嘔吐；另外，嘔吐袋還可以用於裝垃圾。
堵塞	block up：block 阻塞。
在（船，火車，飛機）	on board：「乘船，乘火車，乘飛機」還可以表達成 by boat、by 上 train、by plane。
傾斜	tilt：飛機傾斜可以用 tilt 表示。

Step 2 句句精彩

① 還有別的洗手間嗎？我等不了了。

A：Are there any other lavatories? I can't wait. 還有其他洗手間嗎？我等不了了。

26

B： Sure. This way, please. 當然有。請跟我來。

Tips

The bathroom is out of toilet paper. 洗手間沒有衛生紙了。

Where's the rest room? 洗手間在哪兒？

② 我覺得有些不舒服。

A： What's wrong with you, sir? 先生，您怎麼了？

B： I feel a little sick. 我覺得有些不舒服。

Tips

I don't feel well. 我覺得不舒服。

I'm feeling under the weather. 我覺得不舒服。

Are you feeling sick? 你感覺不舒服嗎？

③ 亂流之後，我感覺快要吐了。

A： I feel like I might throw up after the turbulence. 亂流之後，我感覺快要吐了。

B： Here is an airsick bag. 這裡有嘔吐袋。

Tips

■ Get me an airsick bag, please. 請給我一個嘔吐袋。

I feel like vomiting. 我想吐。

I feel dizzy. 我頭暈目眩。

④ 我耳鳴。

A： My ears are all blocked up. 我耳鳴。

B： Never mind. It's normal. You'll be better later. 沒關係。這是正常現象。一會兒就好了。

Tips

I have a stomachache. 我肚子疼。

I have a throbbing pain. 我感到劇痛。

I have a bit of a fever. 我有點兒發燒。

⑤ 可以給我一些暈機藥嗎？

A： Can I have some medicine for airsickness? 可以給我一些暈機藥嗎？

B： Please wait for a moment. 請稍等。

Tips

■ Do you have anything for airsickness? 你們有暈機藥嗎？

■ She seems to be airsick. 她好像暈機了。

■ Do you have anything for a headache? 你們有治頭痛的藥嗎？

(6) 我感覺身體缺水。

A： I don't feel very well. My body is in lack of water. 我覺得不太舒服。我感覺身體缺水。

B： Drink more water. 多喝點水吧。

Tips

■ It's too dry. 太乾燥了。

■ My skin feels uncomfortably tight. 我覺得皮膚很緊繃。

(7) 當飛機傾斜的時候，我覺得不舒服。

A： You look pale. What's wrong? 你看起來臉色不太好。怎麼了？

B： I feel uncomfortable when the flight tilts. 當飛機傾斜時，我覺得不舒服。

■ Is everything all right? 你還好吧？

■ You don't look well. 你好像不太舒服。

■ I feel better now. 我覺得好多了。

Step 3　情 景 模 擬

(1) 身體不適

A： May I help you? 請問需要什麼嗎？

B： I feel a little sick. I need an airsickness bag. 我覺得有些不舒服。麻煩給我一個嘔吐袋。

A： Yes, madam. There's one in the seat pocket. Here you are. 好的，女士。嘔吐袋在椅背裡的口袋，給你。

B： Thank you. 謝謝。

A： Should I bring you some water? 需要喝點水嗎？

B： Yes, please. 好的。

② 索取藥品

A： What can I do for you, sir? 先生，有什麼能為您效勞的嗎？

B： I feel like I might throw up after the turbulence. Can I have some medicine for airsickness? 亂流之後，我感覺自己快要吐了。可以給我一些暈機藥嗎？

A： OK. Please wait a moment. 好的，請稍等一下。

A： (after a while)Here is some water and the medicine for you. （過了一會兒）給您水和藥。

B： Thank you. 謝謝。

③ 機上補水

A： When will we be landed? 我們什麼時候能降落？

B： I guess it'll take another four hours. 我猜還得四個小時。

A： I don't feel very well. My body is in lack of water. 我覺得不太舒服。我感覺身體缺水。

B： Drink more water. 多喝點水吧。

Scene 6 準備降落

Step 1 必備表達

降落	descent：動詞形式為 descend，表示「下來，向下傾斜」。
海關申報表格	customs declaration form：海關是在沿海、邊境設立的執行進出口監督管理的國家行政機構。
所有物	belongings：possessions 也表示「所有物」。
當地時間	local time：local 當地的，地方的。
地面溫度	ground temperature：也可以用 surface temperature 表示。
攝氏度	Centigrade：攝氏度是目前使用比較廣泛的一種溫標，用符號℃表示。另外，華氏溫度 (Fahrenheit) 也比較常用，用符號表示。
高度	altitude：altitude 一般指海拔高度。
時差	time difference：兩個時區的標準時間（即時區數）相減即得到時差。
國際日期變更線	the international date line：該線位於太平洋中的 180 度經線上，作為地線球上「今天」和「昨天」的分界線，因此被稱為「國際換日線」。
轉移	divert：「改變航線」可以用 divert the plane 表示。
時差	jetlag：「倒時差」可以用 suffer jetlag 表示。

Step 2 句句精彩

① 機長說我們即將開始降落。

A：The captain said we would start our descent shortly. 機長說我們即將開始降落。

B：That's great. I've had enough. I'm so exhausted. 太好了。我受夠了。我累死了。

Tips

■ The plane circled the airport before landing. 飛機在著陸之前在機場上空盤旋。

The airplane flies at 900 kilometers an hour. 飛機以每小時 900 公里的速度飛行。
■ The pilot will land the plane safely. 駕駛員將使飛機安全降落。

② 我們得在下飛機之前填好這些海關申報表格。

A： What should we do before we get off? 下飛機之前我們要做什麼？

B： We have to fill out these customs declaration forms before getting off the plane. 我們得在下飛機之前填好這些海關申報表格。

Tips

declaration 的意思是「申報單」。此外,「危險貨物申報單」可以說成 dangerous declaration form,「出口報單」可以說成 declaration for exportation。
Do you have anything to declare? 有什麼東西要申報嗎？
Please fill out your customs declaration form. 請填寫你的海關申請單。

③ 請各位乘客回到座位上,並豎直椅背。

A： Can I stand here for a moment? 我能在這站會兒嗎？

B： Sorry. Please go back to your seat and put your seatbacks in the upright position. 對不起。請各位乘客回到座位上,並豎直椅背。

Tips

For your own safety, please go back to your seats and fasten the seat belts. 為了您的自身安全,請回到您的座位上,並繫好安全帶。
We are experiencing some turbulence. Please return to your seat and fasten your seat belt. 我們即將經過亂流。請回到座位上並繫好安全帶。
The plane is going to land. Please return your seat to an upright position. 我們即將降落,請回到座位上,並把椅背立直。

④ 別忘了帶好您的物品。

A： Don't forget to take your belongings. 別忘了帶好您的物品。

B： Thank you for informing me. 謝謝提醒。

Tips

It slipped my mind. 我忘了。
Aren't you forgetting something? 沒忘了什麼東西吧？

⑤ 本趟航班正接近北京首都國際機場，當地時間為下午 3 點，地面溫度是 23 攝氏度。

A： Where are we now? 我們現在在哪兒呢？

B： We are approaching Beijing Capital International Airport; the local time is 3:00 p.m. and the ground temperature is 23 degrees Centigrade. 本趟航班正接近北京首都國際機場，當地時間為下午 3 點，地面溫度是 23 攝氏度。

Tips

■ centigrade 攝氏

■ What is the local time now? 現在當地時間是幾點？

■ What time is it? 現在幾點？

⑥ 由於空中交通繁忙，本次航班將於 10 分鐘後才能降落。

A： Why haven't we landed? 我們怎麼還沒降落？

B： It will be another 10 minutes before we can land due to the heavy air traffic. 由於空中交通繁忙，本趟航班將於 10 分鐘後才能降落。

Tips

■ Our plane was delayed by fog. 我們的飛機因大霧而誤點了。

■ The aircraft was flying above thick fog. 飛機在濃霧上方飛行。

■ The plane crashed, killing all its passengers and crew. 飛機失事了，所有乘客和機組人員都遇難了。

⑦ 向各位乘客致歉，由於紐約的天氣狀況，本趟航班必須轉降曼哈頓機場。

A： We are sorry to inform you that due to the weather conditions in New York, we have to divert our fight to Manhattan Airport. 向各位乘客致歉，由於紐約的天氣狀況，本趟航班必須轉降曼哈頓機場。

B： That's terrible. 真糟糕。

Tips

■ We have to transfer in HK, China, and we have a two-hour wait. 我們會在香港轉機，而且要等兩個小時。

■ I'll change planes in Amsterdam and continue on to Beijing. 我要在阿姆斯特丹轉機到北京。

Step 3　情景模擬

① 海關申報

A： Ladies and gentlemen, we'll arrive at our destination. If you have any questions, please tell me. 女生們，先生們，我們馬上就要到達目的地了。如果有什麼問題，請告訴我。

B： We have to fill out these customs declaration forms before getting off the plane. But I can't quite understand this item. 我們得在下飛機之前填好這些海關申報表格。不過我不太明白這一條。

A： Let me see. If you have nothing to declare, just write 「No」. 我看看。如果您沒有物品要申報，直接填「無」。

B： That's all? 就這樣？

A： Yes, it's very easy. 是的，很容易。

B： OK. Thank you. 好的。謝謝。

② 準備降落

A： Ladies and gentlemen, We are approaching Beijing Capital International Airport; the local time is 3:00 p.m. and the ground temperature is 23 degrees Centigrade. 女士們，先生們，本趟航班正接近北京首都國際機場，當地時間為下午 3 點，地面溫度是 23 攝氏度。

B： That's great. We are in Beijing now. 太棒了。我們現在到北京了。

A： Please go back to your seat and put your seatbacks in the upright position. 請各位乘客回到座位上，並豎直椅背。

B： Would you please give me a hand? I can't deal with it. 能幫我一下嗎？我搞不定了。

A： Sure. Pay attention to your hands. 當然。小心您的手。

B： Thanks a lot. 非常感謝。

③ 溫馨提示

A： Ladies and gentlemen, we will land in 10 minutes. Don't forget to take your belongings. 女士們，先生們，我們 10 分鐘後就要降落了。別忘了帶好您的物

品。

B： Would you please help me take my bag later? I can't reach it. 一會兒能麻煩你幫我拿一下包嗎？我勾不到。

A： No problem. You can call me later. 沒問題。一會兒您叫我。

B： Thank you. 謝謝。

A： Is there anything else that I can do? 還有其他事嗎？

B： No, thanks. 沒有了，謝謝。

Scene 7　安全落地

Step 1　必備表達

入境卡	disembarkation card：通關時需要填寫兩份表格，一份是海關申報單，一份是出入境證明單。海關官員會檢查這兩份表格，決定您是否可以入境以及停留多長時間。
轉機候機室	transit lounge：transit 中轉的。
行李提領證	baggage claim tag：claim 的常用含義是「聲稱，斷言」，在這裡表示「認領」。
入境櫃檯	immigration counter：immigration 移民。
通關	get through customs：customs 海關。
行李傳送帶	luggage carousel：carousel 是「圓盤傳送帶」的意思。
行李遺失招領處	Lost and Found Office：lost and found 是「失物招領」的意思。
免稅的	duty-free：-free 是「免受……」、「無……」的意思，如 side-effect free 免受副作用。
報稅	declare：向稅務部門申報並辦理有關納稅手續。

Step 2　句句精彩

① 你有簽證嗎？

A： Do you have your visa? 你有簽證嗎？

B： Certainly. Here you are. 當然。給您。

Tips

■ Passport and disembarkation card, please. 請出示您的護照和入境登記表。

■ I'm applying for the American Embassy for studying. 我正在向美國大使館申請留學簽證。

■ I was granted a visa. 我獲得了入境簽證。

② 你來訪的目的是什麼？

A： What is the purpose of your visit? 你來訪的目的是什麼？

B： I come here to study. 我來這裡學習。

Tips

■ Why are you going to America? 你為什麼去美國？

■ The primary purpose of this trip is business. 此行的主要目的是商務洽談。

■ What reasons do you have for going to America? 請告訴我去美國的原因。

③ 你好，請問行李領取處在哪？

A： Excuse me, where is the baggage claim area? 你好，請問行李領取處在哪？

B： Baggage claim is downstairs. 到樓下領取行李。

Tips

■ Where can I pick up my baggage? 我要到哪裡取行李？

■ Where can I find a baggage trolley? 哪裡有行李推車？

④ 我有個行李箱沒到。我該怎麼辦？

A： One of my suitcases didn't make it. What should I do? 我有個行李箱沒到。我該怎麼辦？

B： Don't worry. Put your address on this form and we'll ship it to you when we find it. 別擔心。把你的地址寫在表上，我們找到後會寄送給你。

Tips

■ make it 在對話中表示「及時抵達」的意思。

■ My luggage is missing. 我的行李丟了。

■ My baggage hasn't shown up in the baggage claim area. 行李領取處沒有我的行李。

⑤ 我必須為此繳稅嗎？

A： Must I pay duty on this? 我必須為此繳稅嗎？

B： Sure. It's twenty dollars in total. 當然。一共 20 美元。

Tips

■ How much do I need to spend in order to get a tax rebate? 花多少錢才可以辦理退稅？

■ I would like to buy some duty-free goods. 我要買免稅商品。

■ Does the price on the tag include the tax? 標籤上的價格含稅嗎？

⑥ 您有什麼東西要申報嗎？

A： Have you got anything to declare? 您有什麼東西要申報嗎？

B： Yes, I need to declare one. 是的，我有一件要申報。

Tips

- ■ You can follow the yellow lines if you have something to declare. 如果您有東西需要申報，請走黃色通道。
- ■ Everything needs to be included on the customs declaration. 你必須在報關單上填上所有的東西。
- ■ Everything you have with you should be declared. 您攜帶的所有物品都要申報。

⑦ 所有轉機的旅客，請前往 7 號登機門。

A： I need to change planes. Where should I go? 我需要轉機。怎麼走？

B： All connecting passengers are requested to proceed to Gate 7. 所有轉機的旅客，請前往 7 號登機門。

Tips

- ■ proceed to 有「向某地進發」的意思，其中 to 是介詞。
- ■ Will I need to change planes? 我需要轉機嗎？
- ■ When will the transit flight take off? 轉接航班什麼時候起飛？

Step 3　情景模擬

①　簽證

A： Do you have your visa? 你有簽證嗎？

B： Sure. I experienced great difficulty in getting a visa. 當然。我申請出國簽證，困難重重。

A： What's the problem? 有什麼問題？

B： They didn't think I have enough money. 他們認為我沒有足夠的資金。

A： But now everything seems OK. 但是現在似乎沒問題了。

B： Thank god. 謝天謝地。

② 行李丟失

A： Which carousel is the Chicago flight's baggage on? 從芝加哥來的行李在哪個傳送帶上？

B： Carousel 4. 4 號傳送帶。

A： One of my suitcases didn't make it. What should I do? 我有個行李箱沒到，我該怎麼辦？

B： OK, let me see what I can find out. 好，我來找找看。

B： Sorry, I didn't find out your baggage. Please put your local address on this form and we'll ship it to you when we find it. 對不起，我沒找到您的行李。請把您的地址寫在表上，我們找到後會寄送給您。

A： All right. Thank you all the same. 好吧。還是謝謝你。

③ 物品申報

A： Should I go through the green channel? 我可以走綠色通道嗎？

B： If you have nothing to declare, you can. Have you got anything to declare? 如果你沒有物品申報的話就可以。您有什麼東西要申報的嗎？

A： Yes, I need to declare one. 是的，我有一件要申報。

B： Then you should go through the red channel. This way, please. 那麼您得走紅色通道。請走這邊。

A： Thank you very much. 非常感謝。

B： You are welcome. 不客氣。

下榻飯店

Scene 8　預訂房間

Step 1　必備表達

預約	reservation：其動詞形式是 reserve，表示「預約」的意思，固定搭配有 make a reservation 預訂。
空房	vacancy：其形容詞形式為 vacant，表示「空缺的」，可用在席位或房間未被預訂的情況。
三人間	triple room：triple 三方的，三倍的。
套房	suite room：suite 一套；組合成套的房屋，一般帶有獨立的洗手間或浴室。
住宿費	accommodation：英語中表示「費用」的詞還有：affair、cost、expense, charge。
折扣	discount：discounting 打折扣，make a discount 也有打折的意思。
雙人房	double room：飯店酒店的標準房間。
服務費	service charge：charge 作名詞時表示「費用」，作動詞時表示「索價、收費」的意思。
豪華客房	deluxe room：deluxe 高級的，豪華的；還可以用 deluxe suite 表示「高級套房」；deluxe edition「豪華版」。
附加費	extra charge：extra 額外的，關於 extra 的固定搭配還有：extra time「額外的時間」；extra money「額外的錢」；extra work「加班」。
單人房	single room：single 單一的；「單程道」可以說 single pass。

Step 2　句句精彩

① 我想訂一間雙人房。

A：Reservations. How can I help you? 這裡是客房預定部。請問您有什麼需要？

B：I'd like to book a double room. 我想訂一間雙人房。

Tips

■ Do you have a double room for tonight? 今晚還有雙人房嗎？

Can I book a single room? 我能預定一個單人間嗎？

Could you reserve a single room for me? 能給我預定一個單人間嗎？

② 我想要能觀景的房間。

A： What kind of room would you like? 你要什麼樣的房間？

B： I'd like a room with a view. 我想要一個能觀景的房間。

Tips

It has a wonderful sea view. 在那裡可以看到美麗的海景。

I need a room with a double bed. 我要一間有雙人床的客房。

Could I have a smoking room, please? 我能要一個可吸菸的房間嗎？

③ 我沒有預訂房間。你們有空房嗎？

A： I don't have a reservation. Do you have any vacancies? 我沒有預訂房間。你們有
空房嗎？

B： I'm sorry. We're fully booked for the night. 對不起，今晚房間都訂滿了。

Tips

Could you check for me whether it has any vacant rooms for tomorrow? 能不能幫我查一下
明天有空房嗎？

Are there any open rooms for tomorrow? 明天有空房嗎？

④ 抱歉，先生，沒有房了，現在都客滿了。

A： Do you have any rooms for tonight? 今天晚上有空房間嗎？

B： I'm afraid not, sir. We're booked solid right now. 抱歉，先生，沒有房了。現在都
客滿了。

Tips

■ be booked solid 相當於 be booked up solid，表示「充滿著、全滿」的意思。

I'm sorry, we're fully booked. 對不起，我們這裡已經客滿了。

Sorry, all the rooms are taken at the moment. 對不起，我們客滿了。

⑤ 住一晚多少錢？

A： How much is it per night? 住一晚多少錢？

B： It's $75 per night. 每晚 75 美元。

Tips

■ What is the rate? 住宿費是多少？

■ What does a single room cost? 單人間的費用是多少？

■ How much is a single room? 單人間多少錢？

⑥ 有沒有便宜一點的房間？

A： Do you have less expensive rooms? 有沒有便宜一點的房間？

B： Sorry, this is the cheapest one. 對不起，這是最便宜的房間了。

Tips

■ Could you give me a discount if I stay for four nights? 如果我住四個晚上，有沒有折扣？

■ Does a Golden Card give me any kind of discount? 金卡能打折嗎？

■ What's the discount if I own a membership card? 會員卡的折扣是多少？

⑦ 這個價格包含服務費嗎？

A： Does it include service charge? 這個價格包含服務費嗎？

B： Yes. It also includes housekeeping and use of the gym facilities. 是的。費用還包括房間整理費和健身器械使用費。

Tips

■ housekeeping 家政；家務管理，在對話中表示「房間整理」的意思。

■ The room rate includes three full meals. 住宿費包括三餐膳食費。

■ Do you charge for phone calls? 打電話收費嗎？

Step 3　情 景 模 擬

① 預訂房間

A： I don't have a reservation. Do you have any vacancies? 我沒有預訂房間，你們還有空房嗎？

B： Just a moment. I'll check. I'm afraid not, sir. We're booked solid right now. 稍等。我確認一下。抱歉，先生，沒有空房了。現在都客滿了。

A： Can you check for me if there are any vacancies tomorrow? 你能不能幫我查一查

明天有沒有空房？

B： Yes. We have only one left. 有。我們只剩下一間了。

A： Can you hold it for me? 你能不能為我保留這個房間？

B： OK. Can you tell me your phone number? 好的。能告訴我您的電話號碼嗎？

A： Please take a note of it. 7-4-5-6-2-1. 請記一下。7-4-5-6-2-1。

② 房間要求

A： Which kind of room would you like? 您想要什麼樣的房間？

B： Could I have a smoking room, please? 我能要一個可吸菸的房間嗎？

A： I'm sorry, sir. All of our rooms are non-smoking. 對不起，先生。所有的房間都禁菸。

B： Then, I'd like a room with a view. 那麼，我想要能觀景的房間。

A： How about this one? 這間怎麼樣？

B： Great. The scenery is attractive. 太棒了。景色宜人。

③ 住宿費用

A： Can you tell me the rate for a single room, please? 請問單人間的費用是多少？

B： Our single room runs between $80 and $95. 一個單人間要花 80 ～ 95 美元。

A： Do you have less expensive rooms? 有沒有便宜一點的房間？

B： I've got a Golden Card for the hotel. Will you give me some discount? 我有飯店的金卡。能打折嗎？

A： Actually yes. We'll take 10% off. 是的。我們可以讓您打九折。

B： That's terrific. 太好了。

Scene 9 住宿登記

Step 1　必備表達

辦理住宿登記	check in：在旅館辦理住宿、在機場辦理登機手續都需要 check in。此外，它還有「簽到、報到上班」的意思。
登記	register：registered 註冊的，已登記的。
登記表	registration form：registration 登記，註冊。
押金	deposit：on deposit（錢款）存著的。
身分證明	identification：identification card 身分證。
門卡	key card：旅店房間的門口有打卡的地方。按照箭頭，打一下卡，紅燈會變綠，即可開門。進門後，一般在門的旁邊也有一個打卡的地方。把卡插進去就會有電。退房時一定要把卡拔出來，關好門再走。
核實	check on：check 檢查，核對。
付錢	pay for：大部分飯店以中午 12：00 為分界線。客人十二點後入住，次日十二點前結帳。
旅客登記表	traveler's form：form 表格，此外還有 traveler's check「旅行支票」這一表達。
拼寫	spell out：spell 拼寫。
旅社	hostel：多指青年旅社，相比飯店會更加便宜。做動詞時的意思是「宿於招待所或旅社」。
旅館	inn：通常用來表示小旅館、小客棧。

Step 2　句句精彩

① 打擾一下。我可以在這裡辦理入住手續嗎？

A：Excuse me. Can I check in here? 打擾一下。我可以在這裡辦理入住手續嗎？

B： Yes. Please show me your ID card. 可以。請出示您的身分證。

Tips

> I'd like to check in. 我想辦理入住手續。
> I want to check into my room. 我想辦理入住手續。

② 您的姓名是？

A： May I have your name, please? 請告訴我您的姓名。

B： Bill White. 比爾•懷特。

Tips

> Could you spell out your name? 請問您的姓名怎麼拼？
> Can you tell me your name? 能告訴我您的名字嗎？
> How to spell your name? 您的名字怎麼拼？

③ 我查一下您的預訂記錄。

A： I need to check in. The name's Gregory. 我要入住。我叫葛列格里。

B： I'll check on your reservation. 我查一下您的預訂記錄。

Tips

> ■ Sorry, there's no reservation under this name. 對不起，沒有用這個名字預定的客房。
> Sorry, we don't have anyone under that name with a reservation. 對不起，沒有用這個名字預定的房間。

④ 你能登記一下嗎？

A： Am I all set? 我可以入住了嗎？

B： Will you sign the register, please? 你能登記一下嗎？

Tips

> Will you fill in this registration form, please? 請填寫這張登記表，好嗎？
> Would you mind filling in this form, please? 請填一下這張登記表，好嗎？

⑤ 需要先付押金嗎？

A： Do you need a deposit? 需要先付押金嗎？

B： Yes, we need a deposit of 100 dollars. 是的，我們需要 100 美元的押金。

Tips

■ How much do I need to pay for the deposit？我需要支付多少押金？

■ Do you require a deposit? 需要先付押金嗎？

⑥ 你有身分證明嗎？

A： I need to check in and my last name is Harrison. 我要入住，我姓哈里森。

B： Please show me your identification. 請出示您的身分證。

Tips

■ Show me your ID card, please. 請出示您的身分證。

■ Can I see your ID? 能出示下您的身分證嗎？

■ Do you have ID on you? 您帶身分證了嗎？

⑦ 一定是出錯了。我訂了一間單人房。

A： There's no reservation under this name. 這裡沒有以這個名字預訂的客房。

B： There must be a mistake. I have reserved a single room. 一定是出錯了。我訂了一間單人房。

Tips

■ You have a reservation for a single room for today, is that right? 您預訂了一間今天的單人房，對嗎？

■ The registration record is that you reserved a double room. 飯店登記記錄顯示你預訂了一間雙人房。

■ Your booking is for 3 days from tonight to next Monday, a single room, right? 您預訂了一間今晚到下週一共三天的單人間，對嗎？

Step 3 　情景模擬

① 辦理入住

A： Excuse me. Can I check in here? 打擾一下。我可以在這裡辦理入住手續嗎？

B： Yes. What name is the reservation under? 可以。您預訂時的名字是什麼？

A： Tom Cruise. This is my ID card. 湯姆·克魯斯。這是我的身分證。

B： I'll check on your reservation. Sorry, there's no reservation under this name. 我查一下您的預訂記錄。對不起，這裡沒有以這個名字預訂的客房。

A： There must be something wrong. I have reservations for tonight. 一定是出了什麼問題。我在你們旅館預訂了今晚的房間。

B： Let me check again. 讓我再查一遍。

② 預約登記

A： Do you have a reservation with us? 您在我們這裡預訂客房了嗎？

B： Yes, I booked a single room for today. 是的。我預訂了一個今晚的單人間。

A： Will you sign the register, please? 你能登記一下嗎？

B： Sure. What should I do? 當然。我需要做什麼呢？

A： Have you got any identification? 你有身分證嗎？

B： Yes, I have. Here you are. 有的，給你。

③ 押金支付

A： How much for a single room? 單人間多少錢？

B： It's $75 per night. 每晚 75 美元。

A： Do extra beds cost more? 外加床鋪要付錢嗎？

B： Yes. It will be an additional $25 per bed. 是的。每張床多加 25 美元。

A： Do you need a deposit? 需要先付押金嗎？

B： Yes. 50 dollars. 是的。50 美元。

Scene 10　酒店設施

Step 1　必備表達

電梯	elevator：即常用的升降電梯，與其同義的還有 lift 這個單字。
吹風機	hair dryer：dryer 烘乾機，乾燥機。
保險箱	safe：這個單字還有「安全的」意思。
內線電話	internal call：內線電話之間相互撥打是免費的。
外線電話	external call：external 外面的、外部的。
上網	get access to the Internet：get access to 表示「可以使用；獲得；接近」。
網球場	tennis court：court 表達的是「（網球、手球、籃球）場地」的意思。
暖氣	heater：heat 熱度，高溫。
淋浴間，蓮蓬頭	shower：take a shower 洗澡。
馬桶	toilet：還可以用 bathroom 來表達這個意思。
無線網路	Wi-Fi：是一種可以將個人電腦、手持設備等終端以無線方式互相連接的技術。

Step 2　句句精彩

① 請問電梯在哪裡？

A： Excuse me. Where is the elevator? 請問電梯在哪裡？

B： Go along, then turn left. 一直走，然後左轉。

Tips

■ Can you show me the way to the elevator? 能告訴我電梯在哪兒嗎？

■ Do you know where is the elevator? 您知道電梯在哪兒嗎？

② 你們提供吹風機嗎？

A： Do you provide hair dryer? 你們提供吹風機嗎？

B： Yes. But you need to pay an extra fee. 提供。但是您得額外付費。

Tips

What's the charge for your laundry service? 洗衣服務怎麼收費？

Can we have laundry done here? 能在這裡洗衣服嗎？

Do you have laundry service? 你們提供洗衣服務嗎？

③ 房間裡的保險箱怎麼用？

A： How do I use the safe in my room? 房間裡的保險箱怎麼用？

B： Please read the instructions on it. 請閱讀上面的說明。

Tips

I want to put some things in a safety deposit box. 我想把物品放在保險箱裡。

Can I leave my valuables here? 能把貴重物品放在這兒嗎？

Is there a place I can store valuables? 有地方放貴重物品嗎？

④ 請問怎麼打內線電話？

A： How do I make internal calls? 請問怎麼打內線電話？

B： Here is a form on the wall. 牆上有電話表。

Tips

Can I make outside calls with the phone in the room? 房間裡的電話能打外線嗎？

How do I make external calls? 請問外線電話怎麼打？

⑤ 我能在房間裡上網嗎？

A： Can I get access to the Internet in my room? 我能在房間裡上網嗎？

B： Sure. But you should pay more. 當然可以。但是得另外收費。

Tips

You can go to the Entertainment Center on the second floor for Internet service. 您可以去二樓的娛樂中心上網。

■ Your room is facilitated with free Internet. 你房間備有免費上網的設施。

⑥ 房客可以免費使用網球場嗎？

A： Is the tennis court free for guests? 房客可以免費使用網球場嗎？

B： Yes. From 2 o'clock to 4 o'clock in the afternoon.
可以。下午兩點到四點可以使用。

■ What kind of entertainment do you have? 你們都提供哪些娛樂項目？

■ What sort of amusement do you serve? 你們提供哪些娛樂項目？

⑦ 我房間裡的暖氣壞了。

A： What can I do for you? 我能為您做些什麼？

B： The heater in my room doesn't work. 我房間裡的暖氣壞了。

■ There is something wrong with my heater. 我房間裡的暖氣有問題。

■ The airconditioner doesn't work. 空調壞了。

■ I don't have any soap in my bathroom. 我的洗手間裡沒有肥皂了。

Step 3　情景模擬

① 客房服務

A： Room service, please. 我需要客房服務。

B： What can I do for you? 您需要什麼？

A： Where are the airconditioner switches? 空調的控制開關在哪裡？

B： They are beside the door. 在門的旁邊。

A： Do you provide hair dryer? 你們提供吹風機嗎？

B： Yes. I will fetch one for you. 是的。我去給您拿一個來。

② 房間設施

A： I want to put some valuable things in a safe. Can you offer me one? 我想把貴重物品放在保險箱裡。能給我一個嗎？

B： Your room has been equipped with one. 您的房間已經備有一個了。

A： How do I use the safe in my room? 房間裡的保險箱怎麼用？

B： Just press your code on the safe. 把保險箱上輸入密碼就行了。

A： Thank you. 謝謝。

B： If there is anything wrong, please call us. 如果有問題，請打電話給我們。

③ 娛樂設施

A： Can I get access to the Internet in my room? 在房間裡可以上網嗎？

B： Sure. It's a service we offer to our guests for free. 當然。這是我們為客人提供的一項免費服務。

A： Is the tennis court free for guests? 房客可免費使用網球場嗎？

B： Yes. And we have a professional coach to teach you. 是的。而且我們還有專業的教練為您提供指導。

A： That's great. 太棒了。

B： Have a good time. 祝您玩得愉快。

Scene 11 清 潔 服 務

Step 1 必 備 表 達

衛生紙	toilet paper：類似表達還有 tissue paper 衛生紙。
肥皂	soap：hand sanitizer 洗手液；mildy wash 洗面乳。
洗髮精	shampoo：shampoo 還 有 動 詞 形 式，意 為「洗 髮」；hair conditioner 護髮素。
沐浴露	shower gel：gel 凝膠，凍膠，定型髮膠。
浴缸	tub：作動詞時，意思是「洗盆浴」；此外，bath 也可表示浴盆、浴缸；shower 表示淋浴，shower nozzle 噴頭，淋浴蓬蓬頭。
床單	bed sheet：也可用 sheet 來代替。
枕套	pillowcase: 同義表達還有 pillow slip；pillow 枕頭。
洗衣服務	laundry service：laundry 洗衣店，洗衣房；洗好的衣服。
毛毯	blanket：quilt 被子；棉被。
汙點	stain：stainless 無汙點的。

Step 2 句 句 精 彩

①　我的房間需要立刻打掃一下。

A：I want to have my room cleaned right away. 我的房間需要立刻打掃一下。

B：Of course, right away. 當然，馬上就來。

Tips

■ Can I get my room serviced? 能打掃一下我的房間嗎？

■ Will you have housekeeping come to clean my room? 能找人打掃一下我的房間嗎？

■ Can you arrange for someone to clean the room? 請找人打掃一下我的房間，可以嗎？

②　請換一下床單和枕套。

A：What can I do for you? 我能為您做點什麼？

B： Please change the sheet and the pillowcase. 請換一下床單和枕套。

Tips

　I need my sheets changed. 請把我的床單換掉。

　Can I get some clean sheets? 能換些乾淨的床單嗎？

■ Will you have someone change the bed sheet? 能找人換一下床單嗎？

(3) 我的沐浴露用完了，可以給我再拿些過來嗎？

A： I have run out of shower gel. Would you bring some more here? 我的沐浴露用完了。可以給我再拿些過來嗎？

B： Sure. How about this brand? 當然可以。這個牌子怎麼樣？

Tips

　run out of 用完

　My bathroom is out of shower gel. 我浴室裡的沐浴露用完了。

　There is no shower gel in my bathroom. 我洗手間裡沒有沐浴露了。

(4) 浴缸不乾淨。能請人來清理一下嗎？

A： The tub is not clean. Can you arrange for someone to clean it? 浴缸不乾淨。能請人來清理一下嗎？

B： Sorry. We'll send someone to deal with it right now.
對不起。我們馬上派人來處理。

Tips

　deal with 處理

　Could you clean my tub a little earlier? 你能早點來清理我的浴缸嗎？

　Is it possible to have my tub cleaned earlier? 早點來清理我的浴缸，可以嗎？

(5) 你們提供洗衣服務嗎？

A： Do you have laundry service? 你們提供洗衣服務嗎？

B： Sure. Just put the items you want to be washed in the laundry bag and the housekeeper will pick it up from your room. 當然。把要洗的衣服放到洗衣袋裡，房間服務人員會去您房間裡取。

Tips

　laundry service 洗衣服務；valet service 洗熨服務。

■ Where can we have our laundry done? 衣服送哪裡洗啊？

■ Can we have laundry done here? 這裡有洗衣服務嗎？

⑥ 我什麼時候能取回洗好的衣服？

A： When can I have my laundry back? 我什麼時候能取回洗好的衣服？

B： If we pick them up in the morning, you can have your laundry back in the afternoon before 5 o'clock. If we pick them up in the afternoon, you can get them back on the next morning before 10 o'clock. 如果我們早上取走了衣服，您下午五點之前就能拿回衣服。如果我們下午取走了衣服，那麼您第二天早上十點之前能拿到。

Tips

■ Can I have my suit pressed? 能幫我把西裝熨好嗎？

■ I need my suit pressed; can you take care of that? 我的西裝需要熨，你能幫我嗎？

■ Is there somewhere I can have my suit pressed? 在哪兒能把我的西裝熨平？

⑦ 洗衣服務怎樣收費？

A： How is laundry service charged? 洗衣服務怎樣收費？

B： Regular laundry is free of charge, with an extra charge for dry cleaning. 普通洗不收費，乾洗要額外收錢。

Tips

■ be free of 沒有……的；be free of charge 免費。

■ What are your rates of laundry service? 洗衣服務如何收費？

■ What's the charge for your laundry service? 你們的洗衣服務如何收費？

■ How much does it cost to have laundry done? 洗衣的費用是多少？

Step 3　情 景 模 擬

① 打掃房間

A： Do you need any help? 你需要幫忙嗎？

B： I want to have my room cleaned right away. 立刻打掃一下我的房間。

A： Sure. I will do it right now. 好的。馬上就來。

B： I hope you could do our room earlier next time. 我希望你們下次能早點打掃我們的房間。

A： Of course. Sorry. 當然。抱歉。

B： Please change the sheet and the pillowcase. 請換一下床單和枕套。

A： OK. I'll get a new one. 好的。我去拿一套新的。

② 物品短缺

A： I'm calling for room service. 我需要客房服務。

B： I'm honored to serve you here. What can I do for you? 很榮幸能為您服務。我能為您做些什麼？

A： Could you send up some champagne and strawberries please? 請給我們送些香檳和草莓，好嗎？

B： Of course. 當然。

A： Thank you. By the way, I have run out of shower gel. Would you bring some more here? 謝謝。另外，我的沐浴露用完了，可以給我再拿些過來嗎？

B： No problem. I'll be back in a few minutes. 沒問題。幾分鐘就到。

③ 衛生環境

A： What can I do for you? 我能為您做點什麼？

B： I just checked in, but I find that the tub is not clean. Can you arrange someone to clean it? 我剛剛入住，但是我發現浴缸不乾淨。能否請人來清理一下？

A： Sorry. It's our fault. 對不起。這是我們的錯。

B： I paid a lot for this room; I hope that it won't happen again next time. OK? 我已付了高額的房費，希望這樣的事情不要再發生，好嗎？

A： Sure. It won't happen again. We will pay attention to this. 當然。這樣的事情不會再發生了。我們會注意的。

B： Thank you. 謝謝。

Scene 12　維修服務

Step 1　必備表達

維修部	Maintenance Department：maintenance 維修，保養。
空調	air conditioner：conditioner 調節器；fan 風扇。
燈泡	light bulb：bulb 電燈泡；lamp 燈。
燒壞	burn out：burn 燃燒；burn off 燒盡。
沖洗	flush：作動詞時，表示「沖洗；被沖洗」；作名詞時，可表示「奔流」。
檢查	check out：這個片語還有「結帳退房」的意思。
不穩定的	unsteady: steady 穩定的。
處理	take care of：除了「處理」，還有「照顧」的意思；deal with 也可表示「處理」。
插座	outlet/socket：plug 插頭。
水龍頭	water tap：tap 水龍頭；作動詞時，意思是「輕敲」。

Step 2　句句精彩

① 請問這裡是維修部嗎？

A： Is this the Maintenance Department? 請問這裡是維修部嗎？

B： Yes. What can I do for you? 是的。能為您做什麼嗎？

Tips

■ This is the Maintenance Department. 這裡是維修部。

■ Is that the Maintenance Department? 請問是維修部嗎？

② 我房間的空調壞了。

A： What's wrong with you? 怎麼了？

B： The air conditioner in my room doesn't work. 我房間的空調壞了。

Tips

■ The water heater is broken again. 熱水器又壞了。

☐ It's on the fritz. 它出故障了。

③ 燈泡燒壞了。

A： The light bulb has burned out. 燈泡燒壞了。

B： I'll change a new one for you right now. 馬上為您換新的。

Tips

☐ Ah, I'm afraid there's something wrong with the TV. 啊，電視機好像出問題了。

☐ The water tap drips all night long. 水龍頭整夜都在滴水。

☐ The TV doesn't work in my room. 我房間的電視壞了。

④ 馬桶不能沖水。

A： What's wrong, sir? 先生，出什麼問題了？

B： The toilet does not flush. 馬桶不能沖水。

Tips

☐ There seems to be something wrong with the toilet. 抽水馬桶好像出了點毛病。

■ The drain is blocked again. 下水道又堵了。

☐ There's something clogging the drain. 下水道堵了。

⑤ 麻煩你們來檢查一下好嗎？

A： Could you check it out, please? 麻煩你們來檢查一下，好嗎？

B： Don't worry. Let me see. 別擔心。讓我看看。

Tips

☐ The water heater isn't working again. Can you fix it? 熱水器又壞了。你能修一下嗎？

☐ Could you send someone to fix it? 能派人來修一下嗎？

⑥ 桌子有時會晃動，恐怕需要修理一下。

A： Where are you now? The desk is a little bit unsteady and it seems to need fixing. 你現在在哪兒？桌子有些晃動，恐怕需要修理一下。

B： OK. I'll be there in a few minutes. 好的。我很快就到。

Tips

☐ The chair is broken; it needs fixing. 椅子壞了，該修了。

■ Can you fix it? 您能修理一下嗎？

⑦ 我馬上處理這件事。

A： I'll deal with it immediately. 我馬上處理這件事。

B： I'm here waiting for you. 我就在這兒等著你們。

Tips

■ We can have it repaired. 我們能找人修理它。

■ I'll send for an electrician from the maintenance department. 我派人去請維修部的電工過來。

■ We'll send someone to repair it immediately. 我們馬上派人來修。

Step 3　情 景 模 擬

① 維修部

A： Is this the Maintenance Department? 請問這裡是維修部嗎？

B： Yes. Can I help you? 是的。能為您提供什麼幫助？

A： The air conditioner in my room doesn't work. 我房間的空調壞了。

B： Can you tell us your room number? 能告訴我們您的房間號嗎？

A： Room 308. 308 房間。

B： OK. We will be there right now. 好的。馬上就到。

② 設施壞了

A： May I come in? 我能進來嗎？

B： Come in, please. 請進。

A： What's the trouble? 遇到什麼麻煩了？

B： The toilet does not flush. 馬桶不能沖水。

A： Let me see. Oh, it's clogged...It's all right now. You may try it. 讓我看看。哦，堵了……現在好了。你試試。

B： Yes. It's working now. Thank you. 是的。現在好了。謝謝。

A： You're welcome. Anything else? 不客氣。還有別的事嗎？

B： The water tap drips all night long. I can hardly sleep. 水龍頭一整夜都在滴水。我無法入睡。

A： I'm very sorry, sir. Some part needs to be replaced. I will be back soon. 對不起，先生。有些零件需要更換。我馬上就回來。

③ 請求幫助

A： The desk is a little bit unsteady and it seems to need fixing. Could you check it out, please? 桌子有時會晃動，恐怕需要修理一下。麻煩你們來看一下好嗎？

B： No problem. But we don't have anyone available right now. Can you wait a moment, please? 沒問題。可是這裡現在沒有人手。您能等一下嗎？

A： All right. But you should promise to send someone here as soon as possible. 好吧。但是你們得承諾盡快派人過來。

B： I promise. 我保證。

A： OK. Otherwise, I have no other choice. 好吧。反正我也沒有別的選擇。

B： Thank you for your understanding. 謝謝您的理解。

Scene 13 額外服務

Step 1 必備表達

門房	doorman：可指門童；bell boy 行李員，門童。
易碎品	fragile items：fragile 易碎的。
早上叫醒服務	morning call：還可用 wake-up call 來代替。
收傳真	receive a fax：fax 傳真；send a fax 發傳真。
小費	tip：小費還可以用 fee 來表示。
換房間	change to another room：change 改變，更換。
客房服務	room service：room reservation service 客房預訂服務；room service attendant 客房服務員。
訂早餐	order breakfast：order 訂購。
喚醒	wake-up：wake 叫醒；wake-up call 叫醒服務。
要求	request：by（或 on）request 應（某人）請求。
班車	shuttle bus：主要指在短距離之間往返的巴士；shuttle 短程穿梭運行的飛機、火車或汽車。

Step 2 句句精彩

① 你能幫我把行李拿上去嗎？

A： Could you have my baggage sent up? 你能幫我把行李拿上去嗎？

B： Of course. 當然可以。

Tips

■ Will you have my baggage sent up to my room? 請派人把我的行李送到我的房間，好嗎？

■ Will you have someone bring my bags up to my room? 請派人把行李送到我的房間 好嗎？

■ Will someone carry my bags up for me? 有誰能幫我提下東西嗎？

② 小心，我的行李箱裡有易碎品。

A： Be careful with my luggage. There are fragile items in it. 小心，我的行李箱裡有易碎品。

B： OK. 好的。

Tips

    fragile items 易碎品；fragile 易碎的；item 物品

    Don't leave my things like this. 別這樣亂放我的東西。

■ Please take care of my luggage. 請顧一下我的行李。

③ 可以把晚餐送到我房間來嗎？

A： You're all set, sir. Will there be anything else? 您可以入住了，先生。還有別的事情嗎？

B： Can I have my dinner brought up? 可以把晚餐送到我房間來嗎？

Tips

    What time do you serve breakfast? 你們幾點提供早餐？

    Will you bring my breakfast when it's ready? 可以把早餐送到我房間來嗎？

    I'd like to have my breakfast delivered to my room. 我希望早餐能直接送到房間裡來。

④ 我需要早上叫醒服務。

A： I'd like to request a wake-up call, please. 我需要早上叫醒服務。

B： Alright, what time? 好的，幾點？

Tips

    I need a wake-up call. 我需要叫醒服務。

    Will you call and wake me up at six? 請六點叫醒我好嗎？

⑤ 你可以幫我寄這封信嗎？

A： Can you mail this letter for me? 你可以幫我寄這封信嗎？

B： Sure. Leave it to me. 好的。交給我吧。

Tips

    Would you please send these post cards for me? 能幫我寄一下這些明信片嗎？

    Can you send this letter for me? 能幫我寄一下這封信嗎？

6 這個房間太吵了，我無法入睡，可以換間房嗎？

A： The room is too noisy for me to sleep. May I change to another room? 這個房間太吵了，我無法入睡，可以換間房嗎？

B： Sorry. We don't have any room available now. 對不起。我們現在沒有空房了。

Tips

■ no room available 沒有空房；be full up 客滿；spare room 空房。

■ Which way is my room? 怎樣去我的房間？

7 從飯店到機場，有班車嗎？

A： Do you have a shuttle bus between the hotel and the airport? 從飯店到機場，有班車嗎？

B： Of course. It will take you half an hour. 當然。半小時就能到機場。

Tips

■ I would like a limo at 8:00. 我需要一輛豪華轎車，八點出發。

■ I'd like to be picked up at 8:00 in a limo. 我八點需要一輛豪華轎車。

Step 3　情 景 模 擬

1 搬運行李

A： Where is the key card? 電子門卡在哪裡？

B： I don't know. You had it last. 我不知道。之前是你拿著呢。

A： Could you have my baggage sent up? 你能幫我把行李拿上去嗎？

B： All right. 好的。

A： Be careful with my luggage. There are fragile items in it. 小心，我的行李箱裡有易碎品。

B： Don't worry. I'll be careful. 別擔心。我會小心的。

2 送餐服務

A： When is breakfast served? 早餐幾點提供？

B： From 6 to 9 in the morning. Would you like your breakfast served in your room? 早上六點到九點。您要在房間裡用早餐嗎？

A： No, we'll have it downstairs in the dining room. 不，我們下樓去餐廳吃。

B： How about your dinner? 那晚餐呢？

A： Can I have my dinner brought up? 可以把晚餐送到我的房間來嗎？

B： Sure. 當然可以。

③ 提出要求

A： What's the problem, sir? 有什麼問題嗎，先生？

B： The room is too noisy for me to sleep. May I change to another room? 這個房間太吵了，我無法入睡，可以換間房嗎？

A： Sorry, there is no room available now. 對不起，現在沒有空房了。

B： What should I do, then? I couldn't fall asleep the whole night. 那怎麼辦呢？我整晚都沒睡著。

A： I'm really sorry. I will change one for you as soon as possible. 真的對不起。我會盡快為您換房間。

B： Thank you. 謝謝。

Scene 14　酒店投訴

Step 1　必備表達

櫃檯接待員	receptionist：reception 接見，接待；reception desk 接待處；reception room 接待室，會客室。
不禮貌	impolite：polite 的反義詞；polite 有禮貌的；be polite to sb. 對……有禮貌。
打擾	disturb：disturbance 打擾，擾亂；disturbing 煩擾的。
收拾	tidy up：tidy 整齊的；tidy away 收拾起來。
用光	run out：run 跑；run short 短缺，不足。
噪音	noise：noiseless 沒有噪音的；noisemaker 喧鬧的人；noisy 嘈雜的，喧鬧的。
糟糕的	awful：awful weather 氣候惡劣；awfulness 莊嚴。
投訴	lodge a complaint：lodge 提出；complaint 抱怨。
保全部門	Security Department：security 安全；public security 公共安全。
無禮的	rude：rudely 無禮地，粗暴地。

Step 2　句句精彩

① 我放在桌子上的手錶不見了。

A：My watch which I put on the table is missing. 我放在桌子上的手錶不見了。

B：I am sorry. You should have deposited valuables with the reception. 非常抱歉。你應該把貴重物品寄存在接待處。

Tips

■ deposite 存放；valuable 作名詞時，表示「貴重物品」。

■ He lost his credit card. 他的信用卡丟了。

■ My passport is missing. 我的護照丟了。

② 這裡的櫃檯接待員很沒禮貌。

A： You seem unhappy. What's wrong? 你看起來不太高興。怎麼了？

B： The receptionist here is very impolite. 這兒的櫃檯接待員很沒禮貌。

Tips

■ You have an attitude problem. 你的態度有問題。

■ Your service has been really appalling. I'd like to talk to your manager. 你們的服務很糟糕，我想跟你們的經理談談。

■ I'm so pissed off with his attitude. 我對他的態度非常反感。

③ 隔壁房間的客人很吵，我不能休息。

A： The guest next door makes so much noise that disturbs me. 隔壁房間的客人很吵，我不能休息。

B： OK, I will deal with that. 好的，我會去處理這個問題。

Tips

■ Can you change the room for me? It's too noisy. 能給我換個房間嗎？這兒太吵了。

■ My wife was woken up several times by the noise the baggage elevator made. 運送行李的電梯發出的噪音吵醒了我妻子幾次。

■ The room is too cold for me. I feel rather cold when I sleep. 這間房太冷了。我睡覺時感覺很冷。

④ 我在這等了很長時間，可還是沒人來打掃我的房間。

A： I have been waiting here for a long time, but still no one comes to tidy up my room. 我在這等了很長時間，可還是沒人來打掃我的房間。

B： I'm awfully sorry, sir. 非常對不起，先生。

Tips

■ She swept the floor clean. 她把地板掃乾淨了。

■ Help me clean up the house. 幫我打掃打掃屋子。

⑤ 我洗澡剛洗了十分鐘就沒有熱水了。

A： I ran out of hot water in the middle of a 10-minute shower. 我洗澡剛洗了十分鐘就沒有熱水了。

B： Sorry, sir. I'll solve the problem for you as soon as possible. 很抱歉，先生。我將盡快為您解決這個問題。

Tips

■ There is no hot water. 沒有熱水。

■ Sorry, we'll send someone to fix it. 抱歉，我們馬上派人去修理。

⑥ 送餐太慢了，食物也很差勁。

A： What about this hotel? 這家飯店怎麼樣？

B： The room service is too slow and the food is awful. 客房服務效率低下，食物也很差勁。

Tips

■ The quality of service in this restaurant has improved a lot. 這個飯店的服務品質已經有了很大改善。

■ She said it was too much for her. 她說這使她難以忍受。

⑦ 新換的被罩上還是有汙跡。

A： What's the matter, madam? 有什麼事嗎，女士？

B： There is still a stain on the newly changed quilt cover. 新換的被罩上還是有汙跡。

Tips

■ quilt cover 被罩

■ Please get me a clean one. 請給我換個乾淨的。

Step 3　情景模擬

① 物品丟失

A： I need to issue a complaint. 我要投訴。

B： Please take it easy. Can you tell me what happened? 別急。能告訴我發生什麼了嗎？

A： My watch which I put on the table is missing. 我放在桌子上的手錶不見了。

B： Please, sir, calm yourself. I'll try to help you. Are you sure it's on the table when you left? 先生，請冷靜一下。我會盡力幫您的。您確定您離開時，它在桌子上嗎？

A： Quite sure. 非常確定。

B： OK. We'll try our best to solve the problem. 好的。我們盡力為您解決問題。

② 服務態度

A： I'd like to file a formal complaint. 我要投訴。

B： Can you tell me why you are so angry? 能告訴我您為什麼這麼生氣嗎？

A： The receptionist here is very impolite. 這裡的櫃檯接待員很沒禮貌。

B： I'm sure the waiter didn't mean to be rude. Perhaps he didn't understand you well. 相信服務員並不是有意冒犯您。他可能沒有了解您的意思。

A： He understood me quite well. 他很明白我的意思。

B： I'm sorry, sir. I will investigate it and give you an explanation. 對不起，先生。我會調查此事，再給您一個解釋。

③ 房間環境

A： What can I do for you? 我能為您做點什麼？

B： The guest next door makes so much noise that disturbs me. I want to change a room. 隔壁房間的客人很吵，我不能休息。我想換個房間。

A： I do apologize to you. We'll manage it, but we don't have any spare room today. Could you wait till tomorrow? 我向您道歉。我們會盡力辦到，但是今天我們沒有空房。等到明天好嗎？

B： Can you make promise? 你能保證嗎？

A： Of course. 當然。

B： I hope we'll be able to enjoy our stay in a quiet suite tomorrow evening and have a sound sleep. 希望明晚我們能住在一個安靜的套房裡，睡個好覺。

A： Sure, sir. Thank you for your understanding. 當然，先生。謝謝您的理解。

Scene 15　退房結帳

Step 1　必備表達

退房結帳	check out：check in 入住登記。
延長／縮短逗留時間	extend/shorten one's stay：extend 延伸，擴大；extend to 達到，延伸到；shorten 縮短。
錯誤	mistake：by mistake 錯誤地；make a mistake 犯錯。
迷你吧台	mini bar：bar 酒吧。
付款	settle account：settle 解決；account 帳目，帳單；close an account 結算。
付款方式	method of payment：method 方式，方法。
總金額	grand total：grand 宏偉的，豪華的。
信用卡	credit card：debit card 借記卡。
支票	cheque：check 也有「支票」的意思。
帳單	bill：bank bill 銀行匯票；itemized bill 明細帳單。

Step 2　句句精彩

① 我要退房。

A：I want to check out. 我要退房。

B：OK, what's your room number? 好的，您的房間號是多少？

Tips

■ I want to settle my account. 我想結帳。

■ I want to pay my bill. 我要結帳。

■ We'd like to check out. Our room is number 116. 我們要退房了。房間號是 116。

② 我想續住一晚。

A：It's time to check out, sir. 先生，該退房了。

B： I want to extend my stay for one more night. 我想續住一晚。

Tips

Can I extend check-out time by just a few hours? 我可以延遲幾小時退房嗎？

■ Can we check out just a few hours later? 我們可以延遲幾小時退房嗎？

I'd like to stay one more night. 我要續住一晚。

③ 如果我想縮短住宿時間，需要支付費用嗎？

A： If I want to shorten my stay, will I be charged? 如果我想縮短住宿時間，需要支付費用嗎？

B： No extra charge. 不會額外收費。

Tips

Is there a charge for late checkout? 過了退房時間，會收我們罰金嗎？

Is there a late checkout charge? 過了退房時間，會收我們罰金嗎？

④ 帳單上有一處錯誤。

A： What's wrong, madam? 女士，有什麼問題嗎？

B： There is a mistake on the bill. 帳單上有一處錯誤。

Tips

What is this item on the bill for? 帳單上的這一項用作了什麼？

I need a detailed list of my room expenses. 我需要一張住房費用明細單。

The bill doesn't seem right. Could you double check it? 帳單好像有誤，能再算一次嗎？

⑤ 您使用過迷你吧台嗎？

A： Did you use the mini bar? 您使用過迷你吧台嗎？

B： Yes. I had a bottle of beer from the mini bar. 是的。我喝了迷你吧台的一瓶啤酒。

Tips

That's for the extra bed. 這是加床費。

I didn't make any overseas calls. 我沒有打過國際長途電話。

I'd like to charge my meal to my room. 請把餐費記在我的房費上。

⑥ 你打算如何付款？

A： How are you going to settle your account? 你打算如何付款？

B： In cash. 用現金。

Tips

■ Can I pay by credit card? 我可以用信用卡支付嗎？

■ Will you be paying in cash? 您用現金結帳嗎？

■ Sorry, we don't accept personal checks. 對不起，我們不收個人支票。

⑦ 總金額是多少？

A： What's the grand total? 總金額是多少？

B： 201 dollars. 201 美元。

Tips

■ I'd like a receipt, please. 請給我開張收據。

■ Can I get a receipt? 能給我開張收據嗎？

■ Can you print me a receipt? 能給我列印一張收據嗎？

Step 3　情景模擬

① 退房結帳

A： I want to check out. 我要退房。

B： Sure, let me get your bill. Wait a moment. 好的，我看看您的帳單。稍等。

B： Did you use the mini bar? 您使用過迷你吧台嗎？

A： Yes. I had a bottle of beer last night. 是的。昨天晚上我喝了瓶啤酒。

B： OK. Here's your bill. 好的。這是您的帳單。

A： Thank you. 謝謝。

② 短暫停留

A： What is the latest check-out time? 退房最遲幾點？

B： 11:00a.m. 上午 11 點。

A： Can we check out just a few hours later? 我們可以延遲幾個鐘頭退房嗎？

B： I'm afraid I'd have to charge you for that. 那樣的話，恐怕要收費的。

A： That will be OK. I want to extend my stay for one more night. 沒關係，我想續住一晚。

B： OK. Let me deal with it. 好的。我來辦理吧。

③ 帳單錯誤

A： Can you give me an itemized bill? 能給我看看帳單明細嗎？

B： What's the matter? 怎麼了？

A： There is a mistake on the bill. What is this for? 帳單上有一處錯誤。這是用於什麼的錢？

B： This charge was for your external calls. 這是您打外線電話的錢。

A： I didn't make any external calls. I always use my own mobile phone. 我沒有打過外線電話。我一直在用自己的手機。

B： Don't worry. Let me have a check. 別擔心。我來查一下。

chapter

3

出行交通

Scene 16 乘坐地鐵

Step 1 必備表達

地鐵	subway：英式英語也可用 underground 表示。
地鐵站	subway station：地鐵站通常會設有多個出入口。行人不用穿過馬路即可由此進入車站，非常方便。
方便的	convenient：名詞形式為 convenience，常說的「便利店」就是 convenience store。
驗票回轉閘門	ticket turnstile：驗票閘門通常一次僅限一人通過，且為單向通行。其中 turnstile 指「十字轉門」。
換乘	transfer：「換乘站」為 transfer station。
出口	exit：相對應的「入口」則是 entrance。
地鐵線路圖	subway map/legend：地鐵站和地鐵車廂內均張貼地鐵線路圖，以便乘客查詢線路。
遮罩門	screen door：又作 shielding door，設在地鐵站內，以防止乘客跌落。
運行	operate：也可用 run 來表示。
日以繼夜	day and night：也可用 day in and day out 來表示。
自動售票機	ticket vending machine：通常設在地鐵站進站口處，方便乘客自行購買車票。其中 vending machine 也可以指出售零食飲料的「自動售貨機」。
線路	line：乘客可根據目的地選擇換乘線路。

Step 2 句句精彩

① 從這裡坐地鐵去廣場方便嗎？

A：Is it easy to get to the square from here by subway? 從這裡坐地鐵去廣場方便嗎？

B： Yes, it is. You can take subway line 1 and get off at square. 方便。你可以乘坐地鐵一號線，在廣場下車。

Tips

> Is it convenient to the railway station from here by subway? 從這裡坐地鐵去火車站方便嗎？
>
> I don't think so. Taking a bus is more convenient. 我不這樣認為，乘坐公車去會更便捷。
>
> Yes, it is. And you can take a bus as well since it is cheaper than the subway. 方便。你還可以乘坐公車去。公車的票價比地鐵便宜。

② 你知道最近的地鐵站在哪嗎？

A： Do you know where the nearest subway station is? 你知道最近的地鐵站在哪嗎？

B： Yes. Go straight this road and then turn right. It is on the opposite of the hospital. 知道。順著這條路直走右轉，就在醫院的對面。

Tips

> Sorry, I am a new comer here, too. 不好意思，我也是初來者。
>
> I am afraid you have to take a bus there. Because it is three blocks away from here. 恐怕你要乘坐公車過去。地鐵站離這裡有三個街區的距離。
>
> Is there a subway station nearby? 這附近有地鐵站嗎？

③ 從哪裡可以看到地鐵線路圖呢？

A： Where can I see a subway map? 從哪裡可以看到地鐵線路圖呢？

B： Go downstairs to the platform and you can see subway maps on the pillar. 下樓到月台上，就能看見柱子上張貼著地鐵線路圖。

Tips

> The subway map is on the back side of your ticket. 車票的背面就有地鐵線路圖。
>
> I am not sure. You can ask the staff near the ticket turnstile. 我不是很清楚。你可以問一下驗票回轉閘門旁邊的工作人員。

④ 地鐵全天候運行嗎？

A： Does the subway operate day and night? 地鐵全天候運行嗎？

B： No, it doesn't. It operates from 5:45 to 23:30. 不是。從早上五點四十五分到晚上十一點半運行。？

> 片語 day and night 就指「日以繼夜」，此外還可以用 day in and day out 來表達此意。

■ When will the last subway to the shopping mall leave? 到購物中心的末班地鐵幾點發車？

■ Yes, it is. But the interval time of the train will last long at night. 是全天候運行。但是夜班車的間隔時間較長。

⑤ 到圖書館應該走哪個出口？

A： Which exit should I take to go to the library? 到圖書館應該走哪個出口？

B： Exit A. A 出口。

Tips

■ Which exit is closest to the library? 哪個出口離圖書館最近？

■ I think it is exit B. But you'd better ask the staff to confirm. 我認為是 B 出口。但你最好向工作人員確認一下。

■ How can I get out of the station after getting off the subway? 我下地鐵後，該怎麼出站？

⑥ 這條線是去動物園的嗎？

A： Is this the right line to the zoo? 這條線是去動物園的嗎？

B： Yes, it is. 是的。

Tips

■ No, it isn't. You have to go to the other side. 不是。你得到對面去乘車。

■ No. You have to transfer to line 2 and you will see a sign there. 不是。你需要換乘 2 號線，那裡會有指示牌。

■ What line do I take to get to downtown? 哪條線去市區？

⑦ 你能告訴我怎麼使用自動售票機嗎？

A： Can you tell me how to use the ticket vending machine? 你能告訴我怎麼使用自動售票機嗎？

B： Sure. There are several buttons on the left side and you need to press the number of ticket that you want to buy and then press the confirm button. Then insert coins or bills into the machine and you will see the tickets and changes on the bottom of the screen. 好的。左邊有一排按鈕，你需要選擇購票的張數，並按下確認按鈕。之後往機器裡投入硬幣或紙幣。車票和找零的數額就會出現在螢幕的下方。

Tips

■ Sorry, I have never used it before. 對不起，我以前從來沒用過自動售票機。

■ Can I get change from the ticket machine? 自動售票機會找零錢嗎？

Step 3　情景模擬

① 詢問地鐵站

A： Do you know where the nearest subway station is? 你知道最近的地鐵站在哪嗎？

B： Yes, I do. It is just in the shopping mall behind you. 知道。就在你身後的購物中心裡。

A： Can I see it when I go into the mall? 我進去之後能看見地鐵站嗎？

B： No, you have to go downstairs by elevator. 不能。你需要坐電梯去樓下。

A： Thank you. 謝謝你。

B： You are welcome. 不客氣。

② 查詢地鐵線路圖

A： Excuse me. Where can I see a subway map? 打擾一下，從哪裡可以看到地鐵線路圖呢？

B： You can find it on the walls of each exit. 每個出口處的牆上都張貼著線路圖。

A： But I have already come into the station. I can not see the map there. 但是我已經進站了，看不到出口處的地圖。

B： OK then. You can go downstairs to the platform and there are maps on the pillar on both sides. 那這樣吧，你可以去樓下的月台看看，月台兩側的柱子上有線路圖。

A： Thank you. 謝謝。

B： You can ask the staff there if you can not find the map. 如果找不到，你可以詢問工作人員。

③ 自動售票機買票

A： Can you tell me how to use the ticket vending machine? 你能告訴我怎麼使用自動售票機嗎？

B： Sure. How many tickets do you want to buy? 當然。你要買幾張票？

A： Two. 兩張。

B： Press button 「two」 on the left side and press confirm button in the middle. 先按

左邊的「兩張」鍵，然後按下中間的「確認」鍵。

A： Where do the tickets and changes come? 車票和找零從哪裡出來？

B： On the bottom of the screen. 在螢幕的下方。

Scene 17　搭乘公車

Step 1　必備表達

公車線路圖	bus route map：route 路線，旅途中的旅遊路線即 travel route。
首／末班車	first/last bus：last 最後的；first 第一的。
終點	final stop：final 最終的；stop 是「網站」的意思，用來指公車站。
高峰時段	peak times：peak 高峰，最高點，「旅遊旺季」可以表示成 peak season。
非高峰時段	off-peak time：off-peak 非高峰的。
月票	monthly pass：公車公司推出月票可以說成 launch a monthly pass。
公車票錢	bus fare：fare 票價，費用，表示「車費」時，多用複數。
找錢	give change：change 零錢，換零錢是 change into small bills。
雙層巴士	double-decker：double 雙重的，兩倍的；「雙層巴士」還可以說成 decker bus；「城市觀光巴士」則是 city sightseeing bus。
轉乘卡	transfer card：transfer 是「換乘」的意思，地鐵的換乘站也可以用 transfer station 表示。
公車卡	bus pass：pass 原指「通過」，在這裡是「通行證」的意思；公車卡還可以用 bus card 表示，旅客公車卡則是 tourist ticket。

Step 2　句句精彩

① 哪路車去國家圖書館？

A：Which bus goes to the National Library? 哪路車去國家圖書館？

B：You can take bus 123. 你可以坐 123 路公車。

Tips

■ Which bus goes to the Forbidden City? 哪路車去紫禁城？

■ You have to take BRT(Bus Rapid Transit) 1 and then transfer to bus 5 at Qianmen Station. 你需要先乘坐快速公車 1 路，然後在前門站換乘 5 路公車。

■ Bus 55 has to deviate from its usual route because of the road repour. 因為修路，55 路車需繞行。

② 讓我看看公車路線圖。

A： How can we get to the Great Wall? 我們怎樣才能到長城？

B： Let me have a look at the bus route map. 讓我看看公車路線圖。

Tips

■ Is this the right bus to the Summer Palace? 這趟公車是去頤和園的嗎？

■ Can you tell me the way to the Great Wall? 你能告訴我去長城怎麼走嗎？

■ Sorry, I'm new here. I don't know how to get there.
對不起，我也剛來，不知道怎麼去那裡。

③ 去機場的末班車是幾點？

A： When is the last bus to the airport? 去機場的末班車是幾點？

B： The last bus is at eleven o'clock. 機場末班車十一點鐘發車。

Tips

■ I'm afraid you've missed the last bus. 恐怕你已經錯過了末班車。

■ The last bus to the airport comes at eleven thirty. 去機場的末班車十一點半來。

■ You missed it. The last bus just departed two minutes ago. 你沒趕上車。末班車兩分鐘前剛走。

④ 坐到終點需要多長時間？

A： How long will it take to arrive at the final stop? 坐到終點需要多長時間？

B： It takes about one and a half hours. 大約一個半小時左右。

Tips

■ How long will it take to reach the final stop? 到達終點需要多長時間？

■ I can't tell you the exact time now since there is traffic control up there. 前方交通管制，我現在也無法告訴你準確時間。

■ One hour and twenty minutes, including the time of traffic jam. 算上堵車時間一共是 1 小時 20 分鐘。

⑤ 103 路公車多久一趟？

A： How often does No. 103 bus run? 103 路公車多久一趟？

B： It runs every five minutes. 每隔五分鐘一趟。

Tips

■ 「How often...?」是詢問頻率時使用的句型。

■ Bus 887 runs every three minutes at peak times and every eight minutes at off-peak times. 887 路公車在高峰時段每隔三分鐘一趟，非高峰時段每隔八分鐘一趟。

■ Strictly speaking, bus 887 runs every five minutes, but you might wait for ten minutes and see two buses come together in rush hours. 嚴格來說，887 路公車每隔五分鐘一趟，但是在上下班高峰期你可能會等上十分鐘，然後發現兩輛一起來了。

⑥ 到動物園多少錢？

A： How much is the bus fare to the Zoo? 到動物園的車票價格是多少？

B： One dollar each person. 每人一美元。

Tips

■ For children, the fare is halved. 兒童票半價。

■ How much will it cost to go to the Zoo? 到動物園多少錢？

■ You will get a 60% discount if you own a bus pass. 如果你使用公車卡，那麼車費可以打四折。

⑦ 我坐過站了，可以在這下車嗎？

A： I missed my station. Can I get off here? 我坐過站了，可以在這下車嗎？

B：I am afraid not. The bus can only stop at bus stops. 恐怕不行。公車只能在車站停。

Tips

■ Yes, you can. But I can't change to another lane right now, so you have to wait. 可以。但是我現在換不了車道，你得等一等。

Step 3　情景模擬

① 詢問公車路線

A： Which bus goes to the National Library? 哪路車去國家圖書館？

B： There is no bus going to the National Library directly from here. 沒有直接從這兒

去國家圖書館的公車。

A：Then how can I get there? 那我該怎麼去呢？

B：You have to take bus 456 to the People's Hospital Station and transfer to bus 522. 你需要先乘坐 456 路公車，然後在人民醫院站換乘 522 路公車。

A：Will the conductor call out the stops? 售票員會報站嗎？

B：Yes, of course. 會的，當然會。

② 詢問發車間隔

A：How often does No. 648 bus run? 648 路公車多久一班？

B：Strictly speaking, bus 648 runs every five minutes. 嚴格來說，648 路公車每隔五分鐘一趟。

A：But what is the fact? 那麼實際情況呢？

B：You might have to wait for more than ten minutes and there come two buses together because of the traffic jam. 因為堵車，你可能需要等上十多分鐘，然後兩輛車一起到站。

A：I guess I have to wait for a while. Thanks a lot. 我估計我要等一陣子了。非常感謝。

B：You are welcome. 不客氣。

③ 詢問票價

A：到動物園的車票價格是多少？ How much is the bus fare to the Zoo?

B：Do you have a bus pass or monthly pass? 你有公車卡或月票嗎？

A：Yes, I have a bus pass. 是的，我有公車卡。

B：Forty pence. 四十便士。

A：But my friend doesn't have. How much is the fare in cash? 但是我朋友沒有。如果付現金，票價是多少？

B：One dollar per person. 一美元一位。

Scene 18　乘坐計程車

Step 1　必備表達

計程車候車處	taxi stand：stand 停車候客處。
計價器	meter：除了常用的「米」之外，這個詞還有「器、計、表」的意思，如：water meter 水表；electric meter 電表。
後車箱	trunk：trunk lid 後車箱蓋，在美式英語中還可以用 boot 表示後車箱。此外它還有「皮箱，行李箱」的意思。
前座乘客	front-seat passenger：front-seat 前座，passenger 乘客；後座是 backseat。
捷徑	shortcut：也可用 cut 表示，走捷徑是 take a short cut。
額外費	surcharge：也可用 extra fee、extra charge 來表示。
電話叫車服務	dispatch taxi service：dispatch 是「派遣，調度」的意思。
不用找零	keep the change：這個在收銀時非常常用，表示「不用找了」。
單行道	one-way traffic：one-way 單行的；雙向道就是 two-way。
塞車	traffic jam：jam 擁擠，堵塞；還可用 traffic block 來表示。

Step 2　句句精彩

① 請派一輛計程車到 CDD 公司來。

A： Please send a taxi to the CDD Company. 請派一輛計程車到 CDD 公司來。

B： No problem. The driver will be on his way soon. 沒問題。司機馬上就出發。

Tips

■ Sorry, sir. Now is the peak time. Can you wait for 15 minutes? 先生，不好意思。現在是高峰時間，您能不能等十五分鐘？

■ The taxi will arrive around 5:30. Please enjoy your trip. 計程車將於 5 點 30 分左右到達。祝您旅途愉快。

② 計程車候車處在哪裡？

A： Where is the taxi stand? 計程車候車處在哪裡？

B： Go along this road and you will find a taxi stand on the street corner. 順著這條路直走，你在街角就可以看到計程車候車處。

Tips

- Can you point the direction of the taxi stand? 你能指一下計程車候車處的方向嗎？
- There is one in front of each hotel gate. 每個飯店門前都有計程車候車處。
- There is no taxi stand here. I think you can call for dispatch taxi service. 這裡沒有計程車候車處。我認為你可以使用電話叫車服務。

③ 我們按照計價表收費。

A： How much is the fare to the airport? 到機場要多少錢？

B： It depends on the meter reading. 我們按照計價表收費。

Tips

- reading 在這裡是儀錶的「讀數」。
- How much will it cost to get to the airport? 到機場多少錢？
- The meter will read your fares. 計價器會顯示您的車費。

④ 麻煩打開後車箱，好嗎？

A： Could you please open the trunk? 麻煩打開後車箱，好嗎？

B： My pleasure. The trunk is already opened. 好的。後車箱已經打開了。

Tips

- Can you give me a hand and put my baggage into the trunk? 你能幫我把行李放進後車箱嗎？
- Do you need help with the luggage? 需要幫忙搬行李嗎？
- Do not forget your luggage after getting off. 下車後不要忘記拿行李。

⑤ 司機和前座乘客必須繫上安全帶。

A： Buckle up, please. The driver and the front-seat passenger are required to wear safety belts. 請繫上安全帶。司機和前座乘客必須繫好安全帶。

B： No problem. Thanks for reminding me. 好的，多謝提醒。

Tips

- Please wear your belts before driving. 開車前請繫好安全帶。
- If you refuse to wear belts, it's regarded as violating the traffic regulations. 如果你不繫安全帶，將被視為違反交規。
- Be sure that you have fastened the safety belt. 確認下你已經繫好了安全帶。

(6) 請抄近路走。

A： Please take a shortcut. 請抄近路走。

B： Sorry, sir. That way is one-way traffic. 先生，不好意思。那條路是單行道。

Tips

- Sit steadily. Here we go! 坐穩了。出發了！
- We can't go. That road is for bus only. 不行，那條是公車專用道。

(7) 夜間乘車要多付 15% 的費用。

A： There's a 15 percent surcharge on night rides. 夜間乘車要多付 15% 的費用。

B： I guess I have to accept it since I have no choice at this time. 在這個時間我別無選擇，所以我不得不接受這個價錢。

Tips

- If you take a ride during nights, you will be surcharged. 如果你在夜間乘車，你要多付一些費用。
- That is OK. Let's go! 沒問題，走吧！
- Do you have any receipt of the surcharge? 額外的費用有票據嗎？

Step 3　情 景 模 擬

(1) 叫車服務

A： Please send a taxi to the CDD Company. 請派一輛計程車到 CDD 公司來。

B： No problem. We will dispatch one for you. 沒問題。我們會為您派一輛車過來。

A： How much is the fare? 車費多少錢？

B： You'll be charged according to the meter reading. 我們按照計價表收費。

A： Well, how long should I wait for? 好的，我需要等多久？

B： At most ten minutes if the traffic is smooth. 交通暢通的話，最多十分鐘。

② 打開後車箱

A：Could you please open the trunk? 麻煩打開後車箱好嗎？

B：Sure. Do you need help with your luggage? 當然。需要幫你搬行李嗎？

A：Thank you. I appreciate that. 謝謝，非常感激。

B：It is my pleasure. And do not forget your luggage after getting off. 這是我的榮幸。下車別忘記了拿行李。

A：Let's go to the museum. 我們去博物館。

B：Here we go. 這就出發。

③ 抄近路

A：Please take a shortcut. 請抄近路走。

B：Sorry, madam. That way is one-way traffic. 女士，對不起。那條路是單行道。

A：I am going to be late for work. Can you please make an exception? 我上班要遲到了。你能不能通融一下？

B：Are you serious? We may die if there is a car accident. 你開什麼玩笑？如果發生車禍，我們都將失去生命。

A：Fine. Please take me to my destination as soon as possible. 好吧。請盡快將我送到目的地。

B：Sure. 當然。

Scene 19　乘坐火車

Step 1　必備表達

火車站	railway station：railway 鐵路，鐵道。
月台	platform：除了月台的意思外，它還有「講台，平台」等意思。
慢車；區間車	local train：local 局部的。
火車時刻表	timetable：railway timetable 或 train schedule 也可以表示火車時刻表。
售票口	ticket window：還可以用 wicket 來表示。
列車員	conductor：還可以用 train attendant 來表示。
票根	ticket stub：stub 存根。
臥鋪	sleeper：還可以用 sleeping berth 來表示。
直達車	nonstop train：nonstop 直達的，不停的。
頭等車廂	first-class compartment：compartment 指「隔間，車廂」。
高鐵	high-speed rail：high-speed 高速的，快速的。

Step 2　句句精彩

① 還有去紐約的票嗎？

A： Are there any seats available for New York? 還有去紐約的票嗎？

B： Yes, there are a few tickets left. 有的。還剩幾張票。

Tips

■ Sorry. All tickets were sold out. 不好意思，票全都賣完了。

■ Tickets for standing room only. 只剩下站票了。

■ Yes, there are still a plenty of tickets. Which class do you want? 有的，還有很多票。你想要幾等車廂的票？

② 兒童票多少錢？

A： What's the fare for children? 兒童票多少錢？

B： Children less than 1.5 meters can get the ticket at half price. 身高低於 150 公分的
兒童可以買半價票。

Tips

■ Children shorter than 1.2 meters are for free. 身高低於 120 公分的孩子不用買票。

■ How much do you charge for the children? 兒童票多少錢？

■ Your son is over 1.5 meters so he needs to buy a full price ticket. 你兒子的身高已經超過
150 公分，因此需要購買全價票。

③ 我要三張軟臥下鋪。

A： What can I do for you? 有什麼能為您效勞的嗎？

B： Three bunks in a soft sleeper, please. 我要三張軟臥票。

Tips

■ bunk 鋪位。

■ One upper bunk in a hard sleeper, please. 我要一張硬臥上鋪。

■ Soft sleepers were all sold out. Now we have hard berths, soft seats and hard seats. 軟臥票都
已售出。現在還有硬臥、軟座和硬座票。

④ 火車准點嗎？

A： Is the train on schedule? 火車準點嗎？

B： Yes, the train is on schedule. 是的，火車準點運行。

Tips

■ Is the train K123 on schedule? K123 次列車準點嗎？

■ Train K123 is half an hour late because of the snowstorm. 因為有暴風雪，所以 K123 次列
車晚點 30 分鐘。

■ The train is on schedule now. But it might be late due to the terrible weather. 列車現在正點
運行。但由於天氣惡劣，可能會晚點。

⑤ 我要搭快車，而非慢車。

A： I want to take an express train, not a local train. 我要搭快車，而非慢車。

B： Sorry. I will change the ticket for you now. 不好意思。我現在就給你換票。

Tips

I prefer express trains to local trains. 比起慢車，我更願意搭快車。

You didn't make yourself clear just now, so you have to pay 10% of the ticket fees to return the ticket. 你剛才沒有說清楚，因此你需要支付 10% 的退票手續費。

Sorry, sir. There is no express train ticket left. 先生，不好意思。快車的票都賣完了。

⑥ 火車什麼時候開？

A：What time does the train leave? 火車什麼時候開？

B：The train leaves at seven o'clock. 火車七點鐘開。

Tips

What's the departure time? 發車時間是幾點？

The departure time is 5:26. 發車時間為 5 點 26 分。

The train should be leaving at a quarter to ten. 火車 9 點 45 分離開。

⑦ 請問車上有賣食物的小推車嗎？

A：Do you have a food trolley on the train? 請問車上有賣食物的小推車嗎？

B：Yes, it has. And it also offers boxed meal. 有的，有小推車，還賣便當。

Tips

Is the train equipped with food trolley? 請問車上有賣食物的小推車嗎？

The food trolley is coming every other hour. 小推車每隔一個小時過來一次。

You have to buy food at the fixed place. 你應在固定的場所買食物。

Step 3　情景模擬

① 詢問車票

A：Are there any seats available for New York? 還有去紐約的票嗎？

B：Yes. Do you want an express train ticket or a local train ticket? 有的。你想要買快車還是慢車的票？

A：I want an express train ticket. 我買快車的票。

B：Which class do you want? 你想要幾等列車？

A：I want a second-class. 二等。

B：OK. Here is your ticket. 好的。這是您的票。

② 詢問兒童票價

A： Excuse me. What's the fare for children? 打擾一下。兒童票多少錢？

B： Well, how tall is your child? 嗯，你的孩子有多高？

A： I have two children. One is 1.1 meters and the other is 1.4 meters. 我有兩個孩子。一個 110 公分，另一個 140 公分。

B： Children shorter than 1.2 meters are free of charge. 身高在 120 公分以下的兒童不用買票。

A： How about the other? 那另一個呢？

B： Children between 1.2 meters and 1.5 meters can buy tickets at half price. 身高在 120 公分至 150 公分之間的兒童可以半價購票。

③ 購買車票

A： Three lower bunks in a soft sleeper, please. 我要三張軟臥下鋪的票。

B： All soft sleepers are sold out. Now we have hard sleepers only. 軟臥票已賣完。現在只有硬臥票。

A： Do you have three bunks in the same compartment? 有在同一個隔間裡的三張臥鋪票嗎？

B： Let me see... yes, we have two lower bunks and one upper bunk. 讓我看看⋯⋯有的，我們有兩張下鋪和一張上鋪。

A： OK. That's great. I'll take them. 好的。那太好了。就要這三張。

B： Please wait for a minute. 請稍等一會兒。

Scene 20　乘坐輪船

Step 1　必備表達

上船	embark：board 也有「上船」的意思。
出發	set out：start off，depart，start from 都有「出發」的意思。
港口	port：常用搭配有：coastal port「沿海港口」；closed port「關閉的港口」。此外還可以用 harbor 表示「海港」。
保險	insurance：常見保險險種有：medical insurance「醫療保險」；life insurance「人壽保險」；travel insurance「旅遊保險」。
暈船	seasickness：這個詞由 sea 和 sickness 構成，類似結構的詞還有 homesickness「思鄉之情」。
甲板	deck：相關表達有 on deck「在甲板上」，引申為「準備就緒的」；upper deck 表示「上層甲板」。
船票	steamer ticket：steamer 汽船，direct steamer 直達船。
碼頭	pier：bridge pier 是「橋墩」的意思，pier foundation 是「墩基」。
航行	sail：常用搭配為 set sail「起航」。
上岸	go ashore：ashore 表示「在岸上；向岸」，drift ashore 就是「漂向岸邊」。
輪渡	ferry：cross-channel ferry 橫跨海峽的輪渡；by ferry 乘輪渡。

Step 2　句句精彩

① 什麼時候開始登船？

A： When will the ship start embarking? 什麼時候開始登船？

B： It is around 12:45. 12 點 45 分左右。

Tips

■ The ship starts embarking at 2 a.m. and leaves at 3 a.m. 凌晨兩點開始登船，凌晨三點起航。

■ The ship will embark passengers at New York port. 船將在紐約港載客。

② 什麼時候輪船出發去青島？

A： When will the ship leave for Qingdao? 什麼時候輪船出發去青島？

B： The ship leaves for Qingdao one hour later. 去青島的輪船一小時以後出發。

Tips

■ When will the ship depart? 輪船什麼時候出發？

■ What time will this ship set out for Qingdao? 什麼時候輪船出發去青島？

③ 輪船的終點是哪？

A： What is the destination of this ship? 目的港在哪裡？

B： The destination of this ship is Dalian. 目的港是大連。

Tips

■ What is the destination port? 目的港在哪裡？

■ The destination of this ship is Sanya and it is by way of Shenzhen. 目的港是三亞 途經深圳。

④ 去倫敦要停靠幾個港口？

A： How many ports do we call at on our passage to London? 我們去倫敦一路要停靠幾個港口？

B： Three in total — Rotterdam, Amsterdam and London. 總共停靠三個港口——鹿特丹、阿姆斯特丹和倫敦。

Tips

■ call at 有「(車，船) 停靠，停留」的意思。

■ How many ports do we call at on our passage from Dalian to Lianyungang? 從大連到連雲港一路，我們要停靠幾個港口？

■ We don't call at New York port. 我們在紐約港不停。

⑤ 請問我怎麼才能到甲板上呢？

A： Excuse me. How can I get to the deck? 請問我怎麼才能到甲板上呢？

B： Turn right after you go outside the room and walk along the passage. Go up two storeys and you will be on the deck. 出房間後右轉，沿著走廊一直走。上兩層你就到甲板上了。

Tips

■ You just need to go upstairs over there and you will see the deck. 你只需要順著那邊的樓梯走上去，就能看到甲板。

It is too dangerous to get to the deck because of the rainstorm outside there. 外面下著暴雨，現在到甲板上去太危險了。

⑥ 我需要買保險嗎？

A： Do I need to buy insurance? 我需要買保險嗎？

B： The insurance fee is already included in your ticket fare. 保險費用已經包含在車票費用中了。

Tips

It is your choice. 你可以自己選擇。

It is voluntary. 這是自願的。

In my opinion, it's very essential to buy insurance when travelling by ship. 在我看來，搭船買保險非常有必要。

⑦ 當輪船進港時，我想觀賞風景。

A： I would like to have some sight-seeing while the ship is in port. 當輪船進港時，我想觀賞風景。

B： You only have one and half hours, then we will set out again. 你只有一個半小時的時間，然後我們就要再次起航了。

Tips

in port 表示「進港；停泊」的意思。

Take your time, sir. I don't think we can set out until tomorrow morning since we need to overhaul the ship. 先生，您不用著急。輪船需要檢修，我覺得明天上午才能起航。

Sorry, sir. Only passengers who arrive at their destination have permission to land. 先生，不好意思。只有到達目的地的乘客才允許登陸。

Step 3 情景模擬

① 詢問停靠港口

A： How many ports do we call at on our passage to London? 去倫敦一路要停靠幾個

港口？

B：Two alternatives can be chosen. One is a nonstop ship and the other needs to call at four ports. 有兩種選擇。一種是直達，另一種需要停靠三個港口。

A：Which one is cheaper? 哪一個更便宜？

B：The latter one. 後者更便宜。

A：Which three ports does the ship call at? 這艘船都停靠哪些港口？

B：Rotterdam, Amsterdam and London. 鹿特丹、阿姆斯特丹和倫敦。

② 登甲板

A：Excuse me. How can I get to the deck? 請問我怎麼才能上甲板呢？

B：It is too dangerous to get to the deck because of the rainstorm outside there. 外面下著暴雨，你現在上去太危險了。

A：But I am seasick and I need some fresh air. 但是我暈船了，需要呼吸新鮮空氣。

B：There is a clinic on the second floor. You can get some pills there. 二層有一個醫務室，你可以去買些藥。

A：Is the clinic open for 24 hours? 醫務室是 24 小時開放嗎？

B：Yes, it is. 是的。

③ 購買保險

A：Do I need to buy insurance? 我需要買保險嗎？

B：It is your choice. 你有選擇權。

A：What is the difference if I buy it or not? 買與不買有什麼區別呢？

B：If you buy the insurance, you will get compensation from both our company and the insurer if you had an accident. 如果你購買了保險，一旦你發生意外，你會得到我們公司和保險公司的雙份賠償。

A：So I will buy. How about you? 那我會買。你呢？

B：I will buy one, too. 我也買一份。

Scene 21　租車自駕

Step 1　必備表達

租車	rent a car：rent 租賃，名詞形式為 car rental。
國際駕照	international driving permit：driving permit/license 表示「駕照」。
租車合約	rental agreement：agreement 合約。
自排車	automatic car：automatic 自動的。
手排車	manual car：manual 手動的，用手操作的。
押金	security hold：還可以用 deposit、antecedent money 來表達。
刮痕	scrape：這個詞可以表示汽車的刮痕，而 dent 是「凹痕」。
試車	test drive：租車的時候可以先試駕，再檢驗一下車況。
全險	full coverage：coverage 範圍，覆蓋規模，在這裡指「保險覆蓋範圍」。
檢視車輛	walk-through：還可以用 vehicle inspection 來表示。
運動型多功能車	SUV：其全稱為 sport utility vehicle。

Step 2　句句精彩

① 我想要租兩天汽車。

A： I want to rent the car for two days. 我想要租兩天汽車。

B： What kind of car do you want? 你想租哪種車？

Tips

■ We have multiple types of cars. What type do you prefer? 我們這裡有各種車型的汽車。你喜歡哪種？

■ How many seats do you want the car have? 你想要幾座車？

■ For yourself or others? 你自己開還是別人開？

② 你想要什麼車型？

A：What type do you have in mind? 你想要什麼車型？

B：I'd like to rent a compact car. 我想要租一輛小型車。

Tips

■ Do you have any type in mind? 你想要什麼車型？

■ I want to rent an automatic car. 我想租一輛自排車。

■ I think SUV is comfortable and stable. I'd like to rent one. 我覺得運動型多功能車既舒適，開起來又很穩，我想租一輛。

③ 一天的租金是多少？

A：What is the rate for the car per day? 這種車一天的租金是多少？

B：It depends on your choice and the days you rent. 這取決於你選擇的車型和租車的時間。

Tips

■ How much is the daily rental? 一天的租金是多少？

■ The daily rental is 80 dollars, plus a deposit. 每天的租金是 80 美元，另外還要交押金。

■ The rental fee is 70 dollars per day. And other fees such as gas and parking fee will be on clients. 每天的租金是 70 美元。其他的費用，如油費和停車費由乘客支付。

④ 你要不要買保險？

A：Do you want insurance? 你要不要買保險？ B：Full coverage, please. 我要全險。

Tips

■ Would you like to buy insurance? 你要買保險嗎？

■ Accident insurance only. 只上意外保險。

■ I don't want any kind of insurance, thanks. 我不想要任何形式的保險，謝謝！

⑤ 開車的里程數有限制嗎？

A：Is there any mileage limit? 開車的里程數有限制嗎？

B：Yes, there is. 250 miles at highest per day. 有，有限制。每天最高 250 英里。

Tips

■ Is there any limitation of mileage? 開車的里程數有限制嗎？

■ 230 miles for common members. 350 miles for golden card members and no limit for platinum card members. 普通會員每天最高 230 英里；金卡會員每天最高 350 英里；白金卡

會員沒有限制。

■ We don't have any limitation on mileage, but you have to pay the petrol fees. 我們對於里程數沒有限制，但是你需要自己付汽油費。

⑥ 我還車時需要把油加滿嗎？

A： Do I have to fill up when I return the car? 我還車時需要把油加滿嗎？

B： Yes. That would be in the contract. 是的。這個會寫在合約上。

Tips

■ fill up 填補；裝滿

■ Do I need to fill up the tank when I return the car? 我還車時需要把油加滿嗎？

■ It is up to you. If you don't want to bother, then we can deduct the gas fee from deposit. 這個由您決定。如果您不想麻煩，我們就從押金中扣除油錢。

⑦ 我覺得這輛車不太好，可以換一輛嗎？

A： I don't think this car is in very good conditions. Can I change one? 我覺得這輛車不太好，可以換一輛嗎？

B： Of course. Anyone you want. 當然可以。隨你喜歡。

Tips

■ Can I change a car during the rental period? 我能在租賃期間換車嗎？

■ These four cars are of the same type. You can try them one by one if you want. 這四台車是同款的。如果你願意，可以逐一試駕。

■ Sorry. We only have one car of this type left. Do you consider other types? 不好意思，這款車就這一台了。你考慮其他款型嗎？

Step 3　情 景 模 擬

① 租車諮詢

A： I want to rent the car for two days. 我想要租兩天汽車。

B： What kind of cars do you want to rent? 您想租什麼車型？

A： I want a 7-seat car. 我想租一輛七座的車。

B： We have multiple types of cars. Do you have any preferences? 我們這裡有各種車型。您有什麼偏好嗎？

A： No. As long as it is an automatic car, it's OK. 沒有，只要是自動擋的車就行。

B： OK. I suggest Touran. 好的。我推薦途安。

② 詢問租金

A： What is the rate for the car per day? 這種車一天的租金是多少？

B： The rental fee is 80 dollars per day. 每天的租金是 80 美元。

A： Do you charge a deposit? 需要交押金嗎？

B： Yes. The deposit is 200 dollars. 需要。押金是 200 美元。

A： Can I use my credit card? 我能用信用卡嗎？

B： Of course. 當然可以。

③ 里程限制

A： Is there any mileage limit? 開車的里程數有限制嗎？

B： If you are not our member, 200 miles at highest. 如果你不是我們的會員，最多只能開 200 英里。

A： I am your golden card member. Is there any preferential treatment? 我是你們的金卡會員。有什麼特別的優惠嗎？

B： Yes. 360 miles if you are our golden card member. 有的。如果你是金卡會員，可以開 360 公里。

A： How can I be your platinum card member? 我怎麼樣才能成為你們的白金卡會員？

B： You have to rent five cars added up. 你需要累積租賃五輛汽車。

Scene 22　開車上路

Step 1　必備表達

停車位	parking space：parking「停車」；相關的還有 parking sign「停車標誌」。
停車場	parking lot：lot 指「（一小塊）土地」；停車的地方還有 parking area 停車區；ground parking 地面停車場。
單行道	one-way：單行道是指只允許一個方向行駛的車道。「單程的」也可以用這個詞表示，如：one-way ticket「單程票」。
禁止掉頭	No U-turn：U 表示調頭。
抛錨	break down：break down「抛錨」，此外還有「坍塌；中斷；情感崩潰」的意思。
爆胎	flat tire：這是非常道地的表達。除了「爆胎」之外，在美式口語中還有「枯燥無味的人」的意思。
路盡頭	dead end：blind ally 也可表示「死路，死胡同」。
剎車	brake：「剎車」可以用 apply the brake 來表示。
引擎	engine：start the engine 發動引擎。
匝道	ramp：匝道又稱引道，是立交橋和高架路上下兩條道路之間相連接的路段。ramp 的原意是「坡道」。

Step 2　句句精彩

① 這附近有停車場嗎？

A： Is there a parking lot nearby? 這附近有停車場嗎？

B： Yes, there is. Just behind the building. 有，這兒有。就在那棟樓後面。

Tips

■ Is there a parking lot near your home? 你們家附近有停車場嗎？

■ There is no place left in that parking area. 這個停車場已經沒有車位了。

■ Parking is not allowed here. 這裡不允許停車。

② 市區限速是多少？

A： What's the speed limit in the city area? 市區限速是多少？

B： The speed limit in the city area is 40 kilometers per hour. 市區限速每小時40公里。

Tips

■ Vehicles can seldom reach the speed limit of 40 kilometers per hour in the city. 市區內的車輛很少達到每小時 40 公里的限速。

■ There is a sign of speed in every cross road. 每個十字路口都設有速度標識。

■ Don't drive too fast, or you will surpass the speed limit. 不要開太快，要不然就要超過限速了。

③ 你確定我們沒走錯路？

A： Are you sure we're on the right route? 你確定我們沒走錯路？

B： I am sure. I just saw the road sign on the right side. 我確定。我剛剛看到右側的路標了。

Tips

■ Can we take any other route? 我們能走別的路嗎？

■ But this is the right one according to the map. 但地圖顯示這條路是對的。

■ This is the shortest one compared with others. 與其他的路相比，這條路最近。

④ 這車剎車不靈。

A： The brakes cannot hold well. 這車剎車不靈。

B： We have to take our car to a local garage for a check-up. 我們需要找一家當地的汽車修理廠來檢查一下我們的汽車。

Tips

■ We are on the expressway now. Can you try to park at the road side? 我們現在可是在高速公路上。你能試著停在路邊嗎？

■ Try as best as you can. I will call 119. 盡你最大的努力，我這就打 119。

■ You need to walk-through more carefully next time. 下次驗車時你需要更加謹慎。

⑤ 車爆胎了。

A： I've got a flat tire. 車爆胎了。

B： Don't worry. I remember we have a spare tire in the trunk. 別擔心。我記得後車箱裡有一個備胎。

Tips

spare tire 是「備胎」的意思，在換胎的時候我們還會需要 car jack「千斤頂」。

A tire blew out just now. 剛剛有一個輪胎爆了。

■ Let's jack the car and change the flat tire. 用千斤頂把車頂起來，然後換下爆了的輪胎。

⑥ 引擎出問題了。

A： Something is wrong with the engine. 引擎出問題了。

B： Terrible! We have to call a trailer to avoid causing road block. 真糟糕！我們需要叫拖車，以免堵塞道路。

Tips

The engine doesn't work well. 引擎出問題了。

We can ask help from the roadblock cleaning company of the expressway. 我們可以向高速公路的路障清理公司求助。

I'll call the garage man. 我打電話給汽車修理工。

⑦ 請派人來拖車好嗎？

A： Can you send somebody to tow it away? 請派人來把車拖走好嗎？

B： Sure. Please tell me your location right now. 好的。請告訴我你現在所在的位置。

Tips

tow away 拖走。

Can you dispatch somebody to tow it away? 請派人來把車拖走，好嗎？

Sure. 好的。

Step 3　情景模擬

① 詢問停車場

A： Is there a parking lot nearby? 這附近有停車場嗎？

B：Yes, there is. But it is very expensive. 是的，有停車場。但是那裡很貴。

A：Is there somewhere we can park for free? 有免費停車的地方嗎？

B：There is a public square in front of the bookstore. We can park there. 書店前面有一個公共廣場。我們可以把車停在那。

A：Can you show me how to get there? 能告訴我怎麼去那嗎？

B：Sure. Go across the road and you will see it. 好的。穿過馬路你就能看見它。

② 確定路線

A：Are you sure we're on the right route? 你確定我們沒走錯路？

B：I think so. I just saw the road sign on the right side. 我覺得沒有走錯路。我剛剛還看到了右側的路標。

A：Can you look at the map again? 你能再看一下地圖嗎？

B：I just looked and it showed that we have to drive across that hill. 我剛看了地圖，地圖顯示我們需要越過那座山坡。

A：OK. I am glad to hear that. 好的。很高興聽到這些。

B：We will be there soon. 我們就快到了。

③ 車輛爆胎

A：I've got a flat tire. 車胎爆了。

B：Have you got a spare tire in the trunk? 後車箱裡有備胎嗎？

A：Yes. Can you help me with jacking the car? I'm afraid I don't have enough strength. 有。你能幫我用千斤頂把車頂起來嗎？我怕我力氣不夠大。

B：Sure. But we have to park at the road side. 沒問題。但是我們需要先把車停在路邊。

A：OK. Thank you for help. 好的。謝謝幫忙。

B：Not a big deal. 小事一樁。

Scene 23　在加油站

Step 1　必備表達

加油站	gas station：gas「汽油」，還可以用 petrol 來表示。
油表	gas gauge：gauge 測量儀器，標準。
沒油了	run out of gas：run out of「用完，耗盡」，還可以用 use up 來代替。
加油機	petrol pump：pump 作名詞是「泵」的意思，作動詞可以表示「用泵輸出」。
油箱	gas / fuel tank：tank 油箱。
柴油	diesel：diesel engine 柴油機。
汽油	gasoline：美式英語中通常用這個詞表示「汽油」，gasoline consumption 即「汽油消耗量」。
機油	oil：還可以用 engine oil、machine oil 來表示這個意思。
公升	liter：相應的，decaliter 表示「十公升」，kiloliter 表示「千公升」。
自助式加油站	self-service gas station：self-service「自助的」，還可以用 self-help、self-serve 來表示這個意思。

Step 2　句句精彩

① 我們的車快沒油了，最近的加油站還有多遠？

A： We're running out of gas. How far is the nearest gas station? 我們的車快沒油了，離最近的加油站還有多遠？

B： The nearest gas station is 5 miles away next to a hospital. 離最近的加油站還有五英里遠，挨著一家醫院。

Tips

■ There isn't any gas in the tank. 油箱裡一點油都沒有了。

■ The gas station is 42 miles away from here. Do you have enough petrol to get there? 加油站離這兒 42 英里。你的汽油能支撐到那裡嗎？

■ There is no gas station around here. But there is a self-service station two miles away. 這附近沒有加油站。但是離這兩英里處有一個自助加油站。

② 請加滿。

A：How much do you want to fill? 你想加多少？

B：Fill it up, please. 請加滿。

Tips

■ Would you like to fill it up? 你想加滿油嗎？

■ Just fill half a tank. 加半箱油就行。

■ Please get the tank refueled. 請給油箱加油。

③ 您要加哪一種油？

A：What kind of gas would you like? 您要加哪一種油？

B：Regular, please. 普通汽油。

Tips

■ regular 在這裡表示「普通汽油」，unleaded petrol 則是「無鉛汽油」。

■ Diesel, please. 請加柴油。

■ No. 92 gasoline. 92 號汽油。

④ 請加 15 加侖的普通汽油。

A：Fifteen gallons of regular gas, please. 請加 15 加侖的普通汽油。

B：OK. 50 dollars in all, sir. 好的。總共 50 美元，先生。

Tips

■ Please fill ten gallons of regular gas. 請加 10 加侖的普通汽油。

■ Are 15 gallons OK? 15 加侖行嗎？

■ No problem. It will be filled up in two minutes. 沒問題。兩分鐘內加完。

⑤ 請幫我檢查一下胎壓。

A：Please check the tire pressure for me. 請幫我檢查一下胎壓。

B：Front tire 2.0 and back tire 2.4, sir. 先生，前輪 2.0，後輪 2.4。

Tips

■「胎壓」可以用 tire pressure 表示。

■ Please help me check the tire pressure. 請幫我檢查一下胎壓。

The front tire pressure is a little bit high. You need to release some air. 前輪胎壓有些高，你需要放些氣。

⑥ 可以告訴我怎麼給車加油嗎？

A： Could you show me how to fill up the car? 可以告訴我怎麼給車加油嗎？

B： You need to park your car next to the pipe so I can manage it. 你需要把車停在靠近輸送管的位置，剩下的我來解決。

Tips

How do I use the pump? 請問要怎麼加油？

First of all, you have to unscrew the fuel tank cap and then put the pipe into the tank. Press the button, done. 首先，你需要把油箱蓋擰下來，然後把輸送管插進油箱中。按下按鈕，完成。

⑦ 一升多少錢？

A： What is the price per liter? 一升多少錢？

B： The oil price rose yesterday. It is 8 yuan now. 昨天油價漲了。現在是八元一升。

Tips

gallon「加侖」，是美國常用的計量單位。

1.4 pounds for one liter. 1.4 英鎊每升。

Maybe I should wait for several days till it decreases. 也許我應該等一些日子，油價應該會降。

⑧ 先付款還是後付款？

A： Do I have to pay first or later? 先付款還是後付款？

B： You have to pay first, madam. 你需要先付款，女士。

Tips

Should I pay in advance? 我需要提前付款嗎？

You can pay it later. 你可以後付款。

Both are OK. 都可以。

Step 3　情景模擬

① 詢問加油站

A：We're running out of gas. How far is the nearest gas station? 我們的車快沒油了，最近的加油站還有多遠？

B：The nearest gas station is 75 miles away from here. 最近的加油站離這有 75 英里。

A：That is a long distance. I don't think my car can drive that far. 好長的一段路。我的車開不了那麼遠。

B：Well. I have stored some oil in the car. 好的，我已經在車裡備了一些汽油。

A：That's awesome! You are really considerate, thank you. 太好了！你考慮得真周到，謝謝你。

B：You are welcome. 不客氣。

② 加油

A：What kind of gas would you like? 請加油。

B：Fill it up, please. 您要加哪一種油？

A：Unleaded petrol, please. 請加無鉛汽油。

B：How much do you want? 你想加多少？

A：50 liters. How long should I wait for? 五十公升。我需要等多久？

B：It will be done soon. 一會兒就好。

③ 檢查胎壓

A：Please check the tire pressure for me. 請幫我檢查一下胎壓。

B：No problem. Have a seat, please. 沒問題。請坐。

A：Thank you. 謝謝。

B：The front tire pressure is a little bit high. 前輪胎壓有些高。

A：What should I do? 那我該怎麼辦？

B：Just release some air. 放些氣出來就好了。

Chapter

4

觀光娛樂

Scene 24　觀光旅遊

Step 1　必備表達

安排	schedule：pushing schedule 繁忙的日程；process schedule 進度時間表。
一日遊	one-day tour：one-day 一日的，一天的。
跟團遊	guided tour：guide 指導，導向；同義表達還有 package tour。
觀光勝地	tourist attraction：attraction 吸引，觀光勝地還可以用 scenic spots、sightseeing resort 來表示。
自由時間	free time：free 空閒的，自由的。
報名	sign up：也可以用 enroll、enter one's name 來表示。
遊覽車	tour bus：tour 旅行，觀光，還可用 sightseeing bus 來表示。
觀光指南	tourist brochure：brochure 小冊子，手冊。
必看之地	must-see：place of historic interest 名勝古蹟。
景點	scenic spots：scenic 風景，勝地。
包辦旅行	package tour：package 包價的。

Step 2　句句精彩

① 一日遊是怎麼安排的？

A：What's the schedule of the one-day tour? 一日遊是怎麼安排的？

B：We will go to the Great Wall in the morning and the Forbidden City in the afternoon. 我們上午去爬長城，下午去紫禁城。

Tips

■ What's the itinerary for tomorrow? 明天的安排是怎樣的？

■ We are going to the Summer Palace at 9:30 a.m. Afternoon is your free time. 上午九點半我們出發去頤和園。下午你們可以自由活動。

■ I will give you a time schedule later. 我稍後會給你一份時間安排表。

② 有哪些類型的旅遊方式？

A：What kind of tours are available? 你們有哪些類型的旅遊方式呢？

B：We have guided tour only. 我們只有跟團遊。

Tips

What tours can we choose from? 有哪些類型的旅遊方式可供選擇呢？

We have self-driving tour, DIY tour and guided tour. 我們有自駕遊、自助遊和跟團遊。

We will help you formulate a travelling plan. 我們會幫您制定一個旅遊方案。

③ 我想報名參加跟團遊。

A：I want to sign up for a guided tour. 我想報名參加跟團遊。

B：Please fill in this table and I will handle the procedures. 請填寫這張表格，我會為你辦手續。

Tips

I want to take part in a guided tour. 我想參加跟團遊。

Please show your ID card. I need a copy of it. 請出示你的身分證。我需要一張影本。

We have multiple choices. Which one do you prefer? 我們有幾個選擇項，你比較喜歡哪個？

④ 這個團參觀主要景點嗎？

A：Does the tour cover major tourist attractions? 這個團參觀主要景點嗎？

B：Yes, it covers four major tourist attractions. 是的，這個團參觀四個主要景點。

Tips

This tour goes to some beautiful natural scenes which seldom have tourists. 這個團會去一些風光秀美的自然景點，很少有遊客去那裡。

This tour just covers one major tourist attraction and the rest of time will be free time. 這個團只參觀一個主要景點，剩下的時間你們可以自由活動。

How many tourist attractions will this tour include? 這個團參觀多少個旅遊景點？

⑤ 這個團在每個景點停留多久？

A：How long does the tour spend at each spot? 這個團在每個景點停留多久？

B：About three hours at each spot. 每個景點大約停留三個小時。

Tips

It depends. The bigger the spots are, the more time we will spend on. 視情況而定。景點越大，停留的時間就越長。

■ The tour will spend one and half hours at each spot since we don't have much time. 由於時間不是很富裕，這個團在每個景點停留一個半小時。

■ I'm afraid I don't have enough time for free activity. 我擔心我沒有充足的自由活動時間。

⑥ 在頤和園，我們有自由活動時間嗎？

A：Do we have free time at the Summer Palace? 在頤和園，我們有自由活動時間嗎？

B：No, you don't, because we have only one hour there. 沒有，你沒有自由時間。因為我們在那只有一小時的時間。

Tips

■ Is the free time affluent at the Summer Palace? 我們在頤和園有富裕的時間嗎？

■ The first hour you have to follow the tour guide and the in the second hour you can look around and buy some souvenirs. 第一個小時你需要跟著導遊走。第二個小時你就可以到處逛逛，買些紀念品。

⑦ 你能給我介紹一些城裡有趣的觀光景點嗎？

A：Can you recommend some interesting places to visit in this town? 你能為我介紹一些城裡有趣的觀光景點嗎？

B：Yes, I can. We will go to some places downtown tomorrow and I will introduce them. 好的，可以。我們明天會去城裡的一些地方，到時候我介紹給你們。

Tips

■ There are some very traditional Chinese shops at Qianmen. 前門有很多中華特色的傳統店鋪。

■ If you want to go to bars, you can go to Houhai, which is very beautiful and lively at night. 如果你想去酒吧，可以去後海，那裡的夜景非常漂亮，也很熱鬧。

■ Another interesting place is the theme restaurant. You may have fun there. 另一個有趣的地方是主題餐廳，你會在那玩得很開心。

Step 3　情 景 模 擬

① 詢問遊覽安排

A：What's the schedule of the one-day tour? 一日遊是怎麼安排的？

B：We will go to the Summer Palace in the morning and the Forbidden City in the afternoon. 我們上午去頤和園，下午去紫禁城。

A： Where do we have lunch? 我們中午在哪用餐？

B： We will have lunch in a Chinese restaurant. 我們去一家中餐館吃午飯。

A：Really? Will we have traditional Chinese food? 真的嗎？我們會吃傳統的中餐嗎？

B： You can taste the famous Beijing roast duck there. 你們可以在那裡品嘗著名的北京烤鴨。

② 報名參加跟團遊

A： I want to sign up for a guided tour. 我想報名參加跟團遊。

B： We have multiple choices. Which one do you prefer? 我們有幾個團可供選擇，你想參加哪個？

A： I prefer this one-day Great Wall tour. 我想參加這個長城一日遊。

B： Please fill in this table and I will handle the procedures. 請填寫這張表格，我會為你辦手續。

A： OK. Thank you. 好的。謝謝。

B： And please show your ID card. I need a copy of it. 請出示你的身分證。我需要一張影本。

③ 停留時間

A： How long does the tour spend at each spot? 這個團在每個景點停留多久？

B： This tour spends about 2 hours at each spot. 這個團在每個景點大約停留兩個小時。

A： Do we have free time at the Summer Palace? 我們在頤和園有自由活動時間嗎？

B： Yes, you do. 是的，你有自由活動時間。

A： How long it will be? 多長時間？

B： Half an hour or so. I suppose. 我想大概有半個小時。

Scene 25　在博物館

博物館	museum：science museum 科技館。
展覽	exhibition：exhibition 表示「展覽」這個詞來自 exhibit「展覽品」，exhibit 也可以作動詞表示「陳列，展覽」。
展廳	exhibition hall：類似的 exhibition room 是「展覽室」的意思。
真跡	original：authentic work/genuine 也能表示這個意思。
公開展出	on show：public display 也有這個含義。
鑑定家	connoisseur：connoisseur of antique furniture 古家具鑑定家。
瓷器	porcelain ware：chinaware 也能表示「瓷器」。
珍寶	rare treasure：rare 稀有的，也能說 rare values「稀有珍寶」。
解說詞	commentary：comment 是「評論，解說」的意思，其名詞形式可以指博物館講解員的解說詞。
請勿拍照	No Photo：博物館裡通常禁止拍照，因為閃光燈會對展品造成損害。

Step 2　句句精彩

① 你能介紹一下博物館的展覽嗎？

A：Could you please introduce the exhibition in the Museum? 你能介紹一下博物館的展覽嗎？

B：Sure. This way please. Let's begin with a painting of Van Gogh. 好的，這邊請。我們從梵古的畫作開始。

Tips

■ Could you make comments of the exhibition in the Museum? 你能評論一下博物館的展覽嗎？

■ Wait for a moment. I will start introducing after everyone is inside the exhibition room. 請稍

等片刻。等所有人都進入展廳後，我再開始介紹。

■ You need to hire a commentator or rent an electronic interpreter. 你需要雇一個講解員或租一個電子講解器。

② 最近有什麼特別的展覽嗎？

A： Are there any special exhibitions these days? 最近有什麼特別的展覽嗎？

B： Yes, there is an exhibition of Leonardo da Vinci's paintings. 有的，有李奧納多•達文西的畫展。

Tips

Is there any special display these days? 最近有什麼特別的展覽嗎？

There is an ancient Chinese porcelain art exhibition on Monday and a Chinese ancient jade art Exhibition on Wednesday. 週一有中國古代瓷器藝術展。週三有中國古代玉器藝術展。

The museum is now closed for renovation so there is no exhibition at all. 博物館現在閉館整修，所以沒有任何展覽。

③ 請告訴我去展廳的路。

A： Please tell me the way to the exhibition hall. 請告訴我去展廳的路。

B： Go upstairs and turn left. You will see the exhibition hall. 上樓左轉你就能看到展廳了。

Tips

Can you tell me how to get to the exhibition hall? 能告訴我去展廳的路嗎？

Walk through the gate over there and you are supposed to show your tickets. 穿過那扇門，然後出示門票。

I am walking that way. Let me lead you the way. 我正朝那邊去。讓我給你帶路吧。

④ 三樓有青銅展。

A： There is an exhibition of bronze ware on the third floor. 三樓有青銅展。

B： I have a great interest in them. 我對它們有濃厚的興趣。

Tips

There is an exhibition of chinaware on the third floor. 三樓有瓷器展。

I have expected it for months! 我已經盼了好幾個月了！

I am a china fan. I especially love chinaware with glaze decoration. 我是一個瓷器迷。我尤其鍾愛釉飾瓷器。

⑤ 這場展覽到什麼時候結束？

A： When will this exhibition close? 這場展覽到什麼時候結束？

B： This exhibition is going to last for two weeks. 這場展覽將持續兩個星期。

Tips

■ This exhibition will be closed on 25th July. 這場展覽將於 7 月 25 日結束。

■ The exhibition will end next week. 展覽將於下個星期結束。

■ It will be closed tomorrow and half of the porcelain ware will be shipped back to the museum. 這個展覽明天結束，之後一半的瓷器展品會被運送回博物館。

⑥ 展覽品多久換一次？

A： How often do they change the exhibits? 展覽品多久換一次？

B： They change the exhibits every three months. 他們每三個月更換一次展品。

Tips

■ They do not change the exhibits. 他們不換展品。

■ All the exhibits are valuable, which won't be changed. 這些產品都很珍貴，不會被換掉。

■ They change one third of them every five months. 他們每五個月更換其中三分之一的展品。

⑦ 這些是僅供欣賞的裝飾品。

A： These are decorations, just for appreciation. 這些是僅供欣賞的裝飾品。

B： Wow, the emperor is really lavish. 哇，皇帝真是奢侈啊。

Tips

■ These vases are of great artistic value. 這些花瓶有很高的藝術價值。

■ Those bronze wares are pretty helpful to the study of Shang Dynasty culture. 那些青銅器對商代文化的研究有很大的幫助。

■ I bought a porcelain bowl at a very high price in auction. 我在拍賣會上以高價拍得了一個瓷碗。

Step 3　情 景 模 擬

① 近期展覽

A： Are there any special exhibitions these days? 最近有什麼特別的展覽嗎？

B： There is an ancient Chinese porcelain art exhibition. If you are interested in it, you can come to enjoy it. 有中國古代瓷器藝術展。

如果您對此感興趣，可以來看看。

A： Which dynasty did the porcelain wares come from? 這些瓷器是哪個朝代的？

B： Qing Dynasty. 清代。

A： Can I book a ticket for that ancient Chinese porcelain art exhibition now? 我現在能預訂中國古代瓷器藝術展的票嗎？

B： Of course. 當然可以。

② 詢問今日展覽

A： Excuse me. What exhibition do you have today? 打擾一下。今天有什麼展覽嗎？

B： There is an exhibition of bronze ware on the third floor. 三樓有青銅展。

A： Are there any other exhibitions? 還有其他的展覽嗎？

B： An exhibition of jade is on show on the second floor, too. 還有二樓的玉器展。

A： One ticket for the jade exhibition, please. 請給我一張玉器展的票。

B： OK. Here you are. 好的。給你。

③ 展覽期限

A： When will this exhibition be closed? 這場展覽到什麼時候結束？

B： The exhibition is going to be closed tomorrow. 這場展覽明天結束。

A： What a pity! One of my friends will come here from Japan the day after tomorrow and he is really a huge fan of jade. 真遺憾！我的一個朋友後天從日本過來。他是一個狂熱的玉器愛好者。

B： There will be another jade exhibition next month. Your friend can come if he is still here at that time. 我們下個月還會舉辦一個玉器展覽。如果那時你的朋友還在這裡的話，可以讓他來看看。

A： How long will that exhibition last? 那個玉器展覽會持續多久？

B： For one week. 一星期。

Scene 26 在美術館

Step 1 必備表達

美術館	gallery：National Art Gallery 國家藝術館。
流派	school：schools of literature 文藝流派；此外，還可以用 genre 來表示「流派」。
版畫	graphic：還可用作形容詞，表示「平面造型的」，如 graphic design「平面造型設計」。
油畫	oil paint：畫油畫時使用的「油畫顏料」就是 oil color。
水彩	water color：畫水彩畫的「畫筆」就是 water color paint brush。
素描	sketch：還可以表示為 pencil sketch。另外，sketch 還有「草圖」的意思。
雕刻	sculpture：還可以用 carve 和 grave 來代替。
古典派	classicism：對應的「現代主義」則是 modernism。
印象派	impressionism：post impressionism 後印象派。
抽象派	abstractionism：lyrical abstractionism 抒情抽象派。
畫風	brushwork：還可以表示為 painting style。

Step 2 句句精彩

① 這是什麼類型的美術館？

A：What kind of gallery is this? 這是什麼類型的美術館？

B：This is a gallery of sculpture. 這是雕塑藝術館。

Tips

■ What's the theme of this art exhibition? 這次藝術展的主題是什麼？

■ Our gallery features modern art. 我們的美術館以現代藝術為特色。

■ This art gallery shows international art. 這個藝術館展示國際藝術。

② 這家美術館的館藏規模有多大？

A： How big is the collection of this gallery? 這家美術館的館藏規模有多大？

B： This gallery collects the artwork of over 300 artists. 這家藝術館收藏了三百多位藝術家的作品。

Tips

Our gallery is very small with only a few dozen pieces of artwork. 我們這個美術館很小，只有為數不多的藏品。

Our gallery is the largest one in the country. 我們是全國最大的藝術館。

It's said that there is a Rodin sculpture in this art museum. 據說這家美術館收藏了羅丹的雕塑。

③ 那部分收藏品中最著名的畫作是什麼？

A： What is the most famous painting in that part of the collection? 那部分收藏品中最著名的畫作是什麼？

B： It is written on the plaque. 已經寫在標牌上了。

Tips

plaque 匾額。

■ I heard that this painting is drawn by a famous painter. 聽說這幅作品是一位非常有名的畫家畫的。

The title of this painting is Mona Lisa. 這幅畫的名稱是《蒙娜麗莎》。

④ 這座雕塑叫什麼名字？

A： Could you tell me the title of this sculpture? 這座雕塑叫什麼名字？

B： It is Piet. 是《哀悼基督》。

Tips

title 標題。此外，專輯的「主打歌曲」可以用 title song 來表示。

The sculptureis is called David. 這個雕塑是《大衛》。

⑤ 這是用什麼畫法畫的？

A： What kind of painting method was used on this? 這是用什麼畫法畫的？

B： This painting method was classicism. 這是古典主義畫法。

Tips

■ The method of this painting is impressionism. 這幅畫是印象派畫作。

■ It was abstractionism. 這是抽象主義畫法。

■ This is a painting of water color. 這是水彩畫。

⑥ 雕塑展廳怎麼走？

A：How can I go to the sculpture room? 雕塑展廳怎麼走？

B：Pass through the corridor and then turn left. 穿過走廊然後左轉。

Tips

■ corridor 走廊，廊道。

■ The sculpture room is on the second floor. 雕塑展廳在二樓。

■ You will find it on the first floor. 你在一樓可以找到它。

⑦ 這家畫廊裡收藏了從 1300 到 1800 年間的西歐畫作。

A：The gallery houses western European paintings from 1300 right up to 1800. 這家畫廊收藏了從 1300 到 1800 年間的西歐畫作。

B：Really? I can't wait to visit it. 真的嗎？我迫不及待去參觀它了。

Tips

■ house 在這裡作動詞，表示「把……儲藏在房內」。

■ I have collected more than 10 paintings of the famous painter from 1988 up until 2005. 我收藏了這位著名畫家從 1988 年至 2005 年的十餘幅作品。

■ This work of art is old. 這件藝術品年代久遠。

Step 3　情景模擬

① 期待參觀

A：What kind of gallery is this? 這是什麼類型的美術館？

B：The exhibits of this gallery are from the Renaissance. 這個藝術館的展品都是文藝復興時期的。

A：Does it include all key painters from the Renaissance? 包括文藝復興時期的所有主流畫家嗎？

B：Yes. They are all included. 是的。都包括。

A： I'm looking forward to visiting it. Is it open on Sunday? 我很期待去參觀。週日開門嗎？

B： Yeah! And you can get free admission on that day. 開門！而且那天你還能得到免費入場券。

② 美術館介紹

A： How big is the collection of this gallery? 這家美術館的館藏規模有多大？

B： Our gallery is the largest one in the country. 我們館是全國最大的藝術館。

A： Do you have paintings of Raphael? 你們有拉斐爾的作品嗎？

B： Yes, we have plenty of him. 有的，我們有很多他的作品。

A： When will this gallery hold a personal exhibition of him? 這個藝術館什麼時候會舉辦一次他的個人作品展？

B： I guess it will be next March. 我想應該是明年三月。

③ 雕塑作品

A： Could you tell me the title of this sculpture? 這座雕塑叫什麼名字？

B： Dying Slave. 《垂死的奴隸》。

A： Can you introduce more about it? 你能再詳細介紹一下嗎？

B： Yes. It was created by Michelangelo in 1513 for the Pope Julius II's tomb and the fettered arms and legs stood for the Oppression of the feudal society. 可以。這是米開朗基羅於 1513 年為教皇朱理二世的墓穴製作的，被束縛的四肢象徵著封建社會的壓迫。

A： It must be priceless. 這一定非常名貴。

Scene 27　在遊樂場

Step 1　必備表達

遊樂園	amusement park：amusement 娛樂。
雲霄飛車	roller coaster：roller 滾筒；coaster 環滑車道；「雲霄飛車」又名「雲霄飛車」。
摩天輪	Ferris wheel：Ferris 其實是個人名，它指的是美國人 George Washington Ferris。因為摩天輪是他在 1893 年為芝加哥的博覽會設計的，故以他的名字來命名。
旋轉木馬	merry-go-round：還可以用 whirling 來代替。
鬼屋	haunted house：haunted 鬧鬼的，而我們常說的「鬼魂」可以用 ghost 表示。
海盜船	pirate ship：pirate 海盜。
免費入場	admission free：admission 入場費；free 免費的；還可以用 free entry 來表示「免費入場」。
聯票	combination ticket：combination 組合。
學生票	student ticket：disabled ticket 殘疾人票；children ticket 兒童票。
售票亭	ticket booth：booth 指「貨攤」，如 telephone booth 就表示「電話亭」。另外，街邊的「報攤」就是 newsstand。

Step 2　句句精彩

① 我不敢玩雲霄飛車這類比較刺激的遊戲。

A：I can't take something exciting, like the roller coaster. 我不敢玩雲霄飛車這類比較刺激的遊戲。

B：OK. Let's take something else. 那好，我們玩玩別的。

Tips

I'm too young to ride the roller coaster. 我還太小，不能坐雲霄飛車。

The people whose heart condition is weak shouldn't ride a roller coaster. 心臟脆弱的人不應該玩雲霄飛車。

You cannot ride the pirate ship since you're shorter than 120 centimeters. 因為你身高低於 120 公分，所以你不能乘坐海盜船。

② 摩天輪的隊伍排得好長啊。

A： The lines for Ferris wheel are so long. 摩天輪的隊伍排得好長啊。

B： Yes, it may take us at least one hour. 是呀，估計至少得排一個小時的隊。

Tips

Is this the line for the Roller Coaster? 請問這是玩雲霄飛車的隊伍嗎？

Yes, I have been waiting for hours. 是的，我已經排了幾個小時的隊伍。

Don't cut in line. 別插隊！

③ 在耶誕節假期期間迪士尼樂園開放嗎？

A： Is Disneyland open during the Christmas holidays? 在耶誕節假期期間迪士尼樂園開放嗎？

B： Yes, it opens all day. 是的，全天開放。

Tips

Is Disneyland open on Christmas day? 在耶誕節那天迪士尼樂園開放嗎？

■ We have special operating hours — from 2 p.m. to 8 p.m. 我們有特殊的開放時間，從下午兩點至晚上八點。

Yes, normal business hours. 是的，按正常營業時間開放。

④ 我要兩張學生票。

A： I want two student tickets. 我要兩張學生票。

B： I need to see your valid student ID. 我需要看一下你的學生證。

Tips

I need to see the other person you are buying for. 我需要見一下你為其代買的人。

We do not offer student discounts. 我們不賣學生票。

I want one adult and two student tickets. 我想要一張全票、兩張學生票。

⑤ 這是通票嗎？

A： Does the admission include everything? 這是通票嗎？

B： Yes, it does. 是的，是通票。

Tips

- It only includes admission. You will still need to purchase tickets for the rides. 這只包括門票，其他專案你還需要另外買票。
- I'll take three all-inclusive tickets. 我要三張通票。
- Can I use this ticket for all the attractions? 用這張票可以參觀所有景點嗎？

⑥ 如果買遊樂園與動物園的聯票，會比較便宜嗎？

A： Is it cheaper to buy a combination ticket for the Amusement park and the Zoo? 如果買遊樂園與動物園的聯票，會比較便宜嗎？

B： Yes, it will save about 20% of the total price. 是的，會比總票價便宜 20%。

Tips

- It's almost the same. 幾乎是一樣的。
- It will save a little money. 能省一點錢。
- It's cheaper but we don't sell those here. You can only get those online. 會便宜。但是我們這不售聯票。你只能在網上買。

⑦ 售票亭前面人山人海。

A： There are too many people in front of the ticket booth. 售票亭前面人山人海。

B： That's because it's Saturday. 那是因為今天是星期六。

Tips

- We should have come on a weekday. 我們應該選在週一至週五的時間來。
- I hate to stay in long lines. 我討厭排隊。
- I've never seen so many people here before. 我以前從來沒見過這麼多人排隊。

Step 3　情景模擬

① 刺激項目

A： I can't take something exciting, like the roller coaster. 我不敢玩雲霄飛車這類比較刺激的遊戲。

B： But each one seems exciting. Have you ever tried? 但是每一項都看起來很刺激。你以前試過嗎？

A： Yes, I tried before so I do not want to try again. 是的，就因為以前試過，所以不想再試了。

B： Then let's go to play on the merrygo-round. 那咱們去玩旋轉木馬吧。

A： That would be great! 那個還不錯！

② 開放時間

A： Does Disneyland stay open on Christmas day? 在耶誕節假期期間迪士尼樂園開放嗎？

B： Yeah. But we have special operating hours — from 2 p.m. to 8 p.m. 開門，但是我們有特殊的開放時間，從下午兩點至晚上八點。

A： How about morning? 那早上開放嗎？

B： No, it does not open in the morning. 不，早上不開放。

A： Why not? 為什麼呢？

B： Because the staffs also need to enjoy the holiday. 因為工作人員也要享受假期。

③ 學生票

A： 我要兩張學生票。 I want two student tickets.

B： Please show me your student ID cards. 請出示你們的學生證。

A： Here you are. 給你。

B： I need to see the other person you're buying for. 我需要見一下你為其代買的人。

A： But she went to bathroom just now. 但是她剛剛去廁所了。

B： I am sorry then. I cannot sell her ticket without her presence. 那抱歉了，她若不在場，我無法售票。

Scene 28　體育館看比賽

Step 1　必備表達

場地票	ground pass：pass 在這裡用作名詞，表示「入場券」。
會員席	club seat：常提到的「會員身分」是 membership。
比分	score：score display 比分牌。
領先	lead：反義詞是 behind「落後」。
搶出風頭	steal the show：類似的表達還有 steal the limelight「吸引注意力；搶盡風頭」，show off「炫耀」。
犯規	foul：double foul 雙方犯規，這是籃球比賽中常用的說法。
加時賽	overtime：常被簡稱為 OT。
平局	draw：「打成平局」可以說成 play even。
啦啦隊	cheering squad：cheering 歡呼的，喝彩的；squad 小隊。
旗鼓相當的比賽	grudge match：表達「旗鼓相當」還可以用 horse and horse。

Step 2　句句精彩

① 請問在哪裡可以買到今天比賽的門票？

A：Where can I get tickets for today's match? 請問在哪裡可以買到今天比賽的門票？

B：You can't. They are all sold out. 你買不到了，已經賣光了。

Tips

■ match 比賽；be all sold out 票已售空

■ Excuse me, where is the ticket office? 請問，售票處在哪裡？

■ Tickets are right here. How many do you want? 就在這兒買。你要幾張？

② 我想要兩張靠近內場的票。

A：I want two tickets near the infield. 我想要兩張靠近內場的票。

B：OK, that'll be 50 dollars. 好的，50 美元。

Tips

■ infield 內場

We have two near the dugout, is that OK? 只有兩張靠近休息區的票，可以嗎？

For the home team or the visiting team? 主場還是客場？

(3) 請問可以在網上訂票嗎？

A： Can I book a ticket online? 請問可以在網上訂票嗎？

B： You can. Or you can buy one from me. 可以。你也可以在我這裡買。

Tips

They don't sell tickets online. 他們不在網上售票。

Yes, the website is www.ticketsonline.com. 可以，網址是 www.ticketsonline.com。

■ You will need a credit card to buy online. 在網上買票需要信用卡。

(4) 哪隊領先？

A： Which team is leading? 哪隊領先？

B： The visiting team is holding a safe lead. 客隊遙遙領先。

Tips

hold a safe lead 遙遙領先。

How about the score? 比分如何？

It looks like the home team is up by 10. 看起來好像是主場領先十分。

(5) 現在要打加時賽了。

A： The game goes into overtime now. 現在要打加時賽了。

B： It's getting more and more exciting. 比賽越來越激動人心了。

Tips

Maybe the Dodgers can still score another goal. 或許道奇隊還能再進一球。

It's a close game. 這是一場勢均力敵的比賽。

I haven't seen a game this close in years! 我已經很多年沒有看到過比分這樣接近的比賽了！

(6) 你支持哪個隊？

A： Which team do you support? 你支持哪個隊？

B： Home team, duh. 當然是主隊。

Tips

■ I'm with the visitors. 我支持客隊。

■ My son is playing for the home team. 我兒子是主隊的。

■ I don't support any of them. I just like the game. 我哪個隊也不支持，僅僅是喜歡比賽。

⑦ 他們長久以來都勢不兩立。

A：They have been long-term enemies. 他們長久以來都勢不兩立。

B：It looks like they might kill each other. 看起來他們已經開始準備廝殺了。

Tips

■ long-term 表示「長期的」，而與之相對應的「短期的」則是 short-term。

■ Look out for more fouls! 當心別再犯規！

Step 3　情景模擬

① 購買門票

A：Where can I get tickets for today's match? 請問在哪裡可以買到今天比賽的門票？

B：I'm sorry, the tickets today are all sold out. 很抱歉，今天的票已經售完。

A：Oh, no! I drove two hours here to watch this match. 哦，天哪！我開了兩個小時的車來這裡，就為了看這場比賽。

B：If you're lucky you might be able to buy one from someone outside the gate. 如果你運氣好的話，可以在大門外別人那裡買到票。

A：But it must be much higher than the original price. 但是票價一定比原來高很多。

B：Sure. It is up to you. 當然，那就看你自己了。

② 場內席位

A：I want two tickets near the infield. 我想要兩張靠近內場的票。

B：For the home team or the visitors? 主隊還是客隊？

A：For the home team. 主隊。

B：We don't have this kind of ticket available. 主隊沒有靠近內場的票了。

A：Any other tickets left? 還有其他的票嗎？

B：We have two near the dugout, is that OK? 還有兩張靠近休息區的票，可以嗎？

A：OK. Give me the two. 好的，就要這兩張吧。

③ 網上訂票

A：Can I book a ticket online? 請問可以在網上訂票嗎？

B：Yes. I often buy tickets online. 可以，我經常在網上買票。

A：Well, I prefer to buy tickets online too since it is more convenient. 嗯，我也更喜歡在網上買票，那樣更便捷。

B：Okay, the website is www.ticketsonline. com. 好的。網址是 www.ticketsonline. com。

A：Thank you for telling me. 謝謝你告訴我。

B：No problem. And you will need a credit card to fulfill the payment. 沒事。還有，在網上買票你需要用信用卡支付。

Scene 29　照相

Step 1　必備表達

閃光	flash：相機上的「閃光燈」就是 flashlight。
三腳架	tripod：tripod leg 三腳架腳。
焦距	focal length：focal 焦點上的；focal distance length 焦距長度。
一卷膠捲	a roll of film：roll 一卷；photographic film 膠片，底片。
按快門	press the shutter：shutter button 快門按鈕。
沖洗膠捲	develop film：black-and-white film 黑白相片。
電池	battery：storage battery 蓄電池；「充電」則要用 charge 來表示。
笑一笑	say cheese：cheese「乳酪」的發音嘴型同中文中的「茄子」相似，都是微笑的樣子。
背景	background：「景色」則可以用 landscape 來表示。
不在畫面內	out of the frame：inside the frame 在畫面內。
快照	snap：take a snap 拍快照。

Step 2　句句精彩

1 我可以在此拍照嗎？

A：Am I allowed to take a picture here? 我可以在此拍照嗎？

B：Yes. You may as long as the flashlight is off. 可以，但是要關掉閃光燈。

Tips

■ No Photos. 禁止照相。

■ No photography or recording is allowed here. 這裡不准照相，也不准錄影。

■ No cameras are allowed here. 這裡不准拍照。

2 我可以和你一起拍張照片嗎？

A：Would you mind if I take a picture with you? 我可以和你一起拍張照片嗎？

B： I would't mind at all. 當然可以。

Tips

句型「Would you mind...?」常用來詢問對方的意見，意思是「你介意......嗎？」，實際上就是「我可以......嗎？」的意思。

I wouldn't mind at all. 根本不介意。

Only if I can take one with you later. 除非你稍後也跟我照一張。

③ 你能幫我們在這兒拍張照嗎？

A： Could you help us take a picture here? 你能幫我們在這兒拍張照嗎？

B： OK, how does this camera work? 可以。這個相機怎麼用？

Tips

Now smile and say「cheese」. 笑一笑，說「茄子」。

Sorry, I'm in a hurry. 不好意思，我趕時間。

Why don't you try to stand over there? 你們站在那邊怎麼樣？

④ 以我們對焦，然後按快門就可以了。

A： Just focus on us and press the button. 以我們對焦，然後按快門就可以了。

B： OK. Say cheese. 好的，說「茄子」。

Tips

Which button did you say? 你說按哪個鍵？

Stay closer. 靠近點。

Don't move! 別動！

⑤ 在哪裡可以沖洗這些膠捲？

A： Where can I develop the films? 在哪裡可以沖洗這些膠捲？

B： You can go to that supermarket. 你可以去那家超市。

Tips

What kind of film is it? 什麼樣的膠捲？

Why don't you use a digital camera? 你怎麼不用數位相機呢？

I remember there is a store at the corner of the street. 我記得街角有一家商店。

What size of prints would you like to have? 你想洗哪種尺寸的？

⑥ 你可以換一下相機的電池。

A： You can replace the batteries of this camera. 你可以換一下相機的電池。

B： I did not carry them with me. Where can I buy? 我沒隨身帶著電池。哪裡有賣電池？

Tips

■ replace 代替，更換。

■ I don't know how to replace them. Can you help me? 我不知道怎麼換電池，你能幫我嗎？

■ You can find these pretty much anywhere. 你幾乎在哪都可以買到電池。

⑦ 這裡不允許用閃光燈拍照。

A： Flash photograph is not permitted here. 這裡不允許用閃光燈拍照。

B： OK, sorry. I didn't know. 好的，對不起，我不知道。

Tips

■ Is it OK without the flashlight? 把閃光燈關了行嗎？

■ Can you help me figure out how to turn the flashlight off? 你能不能幫我看看怎樣關閃光燈？

■ I can't turn the flashlight off. 我關不掉閃光燈。

Step 3　情 景 模 擬

① 與人合照

A： Would you mind if I take a picture with you? 我可以和你一起拍張照片嗎？

B： I'm terribly shy. 我特別害羞。

A： Don't worry. Just look at the camera and smile. 別擔心，只要看著鏡頭，然後微笑即可。

B： Well, OK. 嗯，那好吧。

A： Say 「cheese」! 笑一個，說「起司」！

B： Cheese! 起司！

② 幫人拍照

A： Could you help us take a picture here? 你能幫我們在這兒拍張照嗎？

B： OK, can you show me how to use this camera? 好的。你能告訴我這個相機怎麼用嗎？

A： Just focus on us and press the button. 以我們對焦，然後按快門就可以了。

B： Which button did you say? 你剛才說哪個按鈕？

A： Shutter button. 快門鍵。

B： OK. Now smile and say「cheese」. 好的。現在笑一笑，然後說「起司」。

③ 沖洗膠捲

A： Where can I develop the films? 在哪裡可以沖洗這些膠捲？

B： You can go to ABC photo shop to develop them. 你可以去 ABC 照相館沖洗膠捲。

A： Are there any on this street? 這條街上有嗎？

B： Yes, you can see one next to the post office. 有的。郵局旁邊有一家。

A： On this side or the opposite? 在街這邊還是街對面？

B： This side. 這邊。

Scene 30　音樂會和歌劇

Step 1　必備表達

音樂會	musical performance：還可以用 concert 來表示「音樂會」,「去聽音樂會」就是 go to a concert。
包廂席	balcony seat：balcony 包廂；box seat 包廂座位。
座位平面圖	seating chart：seating 就座；chart 示意圖。
日場（音樂會）	matinee：midnight matinee 子夜場。
節目	program：TV program 電視節目。
舞台燈光效果	stage-lighting effect：stage decoration light 舞台裝飾燈。
音響效果	sound effect：sound effects processing 音效處理。
中場休息	interval：in the intervals 不一會兒,不久。
歌劇	opera：Peking Opera 京劇。
站立席	standing seat：front-row seating 前排坐席。

Step 2　句句精彩

① 現在最火的表演是什麼？

A：Which show is the most popular now? 現在最火的表演是什麼？

B：It depends. Do you like musicals? 這個得看你喜好。你喜歡音樂劇嗎？

Tips

■ What's hot now? 現在什麼最火？

■ I think this is a great show and the singer is really world-class. 我認為這演出很棒,這個歌手可是世界級的。

■ Is there an opera that I shouldn't miss? 有哪一部歌劇是我不能錯過的嗎？

② 請問有哪幾種票價？

A：What are the prices? 請問有哪幾種票價？

B： There are three different prices — $80, $100 and $150. 有 80 美元、100 美元和
150 美元三種價位。

Tips

What is the ticket price range? 請問有哪些票價？

The only seats left are the $100 ones. 目前只剩下 100 美元的座位了。

Everything is sold out except the $100 seats. 目前只剩下 100 美元的座位了。

③ 這是有史以來最棒的音樂會。

A： It was the best musical performance ever. 這是有史以來最棒的音樂會。

B： I think I'll come again before I leave. 我想在我離開之前，我會再來看一次。

Tips

The performance is wonderful! 演出真是太精彩了！

The lighting and sound effects are first-class. 舞台燈光和音響效果都是一流的。

It wasn't as good as the performance of the Blue Man Group I saw last week. 沒有我上週看
的藍人樂團的表演好。

④ 請問還有包廂席嗎？

A： Do you have a balcony seat left? 請問還有包廂席嗎？

B： Yes, we do. How many tickets would you like? 有的，我們還有包廂席。請問你
要幾張？

Tips

Do you have any box seats of this show? 這場演出還有包廂席位嗎？

How much is it for seats in the front row? 最前排的座位多少錢？

The only seats left are standing seats. 只剩站位了。

⑤ 你可以看看座位圖。

A： You can look up the seating chart. 你可以看看座位圖。

B：I think the best view is going to be rows from 3 to 6. 我認為 3 至 6 排的視角最好。

Tips

These seats are too far from the stage. 這些座位離舞台太遠了。

Do you still have a seat available in the upper circle? 樓上還有空位嗎？

I'd like to have three seats next to each other. 我要三張連著的座位。

⑥ 從哪裡可以拿到最近的演出表？

A：Where can I get a list of the current play? 從哪裡可以拿到最近的演出表？

B：Our shows and show times are posted over there. 我們的演出表和時間都張貼在那邊。

Tips

■ Could you please tell me where I can get the information about what's currently playing? 能告訴我在哪裡可以找到正在上演的節目資訊？

■ We're in the middle of changing the performance information, so you'll have to check later. 我們正在更新演出資訊，請您稍後查看。

■ What's on at the ABC Theater tomorrow night? 請問 ABC 劇院明天晚上有什麼表演？

⑦ 請問有中場休息時間嗎？

A：Is there any break in between? 請問有中場休息時間嗎？

B：There's a 15 minutes' intermission after the second act. 第二幕之後有十五分鐘的中場休息。

Tips

■ There are no breaks during this show. 這個節目中間沒有中場休息。

■ How long is the performance? 演出持續多長時間？

■ The performance runs for one hour and 30 minutes, including an interval. 這場表演持續 1 小時 30 分鐘，包括中場休息。

Step 3　情景模擬

① 談論表演

A：Which show is popular now? 現在流行的表演是什麼？

B：I think it must be Cats. 我想一定是《貓》。

A：Oh, I love it! 是呀，我非常喜歡！

B：I think this is a great show. The team is really world-class. 我認為這個演出非常棒，這個表演團隊可是世界級的。

A：Where can I buy tickets? 我在哪裡能買到票？

B：You'd better buy tickets online. 你最好上網買。

② 談論音樂會

A： It was the best musical performance ever. 這是有史以來最棒的音樂會。

B： I can't believe that John didn't like this. 真不敢相信約翰居然不喜歡。

A： He just wants to show off his knowledge. 他只是想炫耀自己的學識而已。

B： I'm going to tell all my friends about it. 我會把它介紹給我所有的朋友。

A： Me too. Do you think we can go backstage? 我也是。你覺得我們能去後台嗎？

B： I'm afraid not. 恐怕不能。

③ 選擇座位

A： How many seats are left now? 還剩下多少座位？

B： You can look up the seating chart. 你可以看看座位圖。

A： I can't tell which seats are occupied or not. 我分不清哪些座位已賣完。

B： The blue ones are available and the red ones are taken. 藍色是沒有人的，紅色是已經預訂的。

A： OK. I'd like these two. 好的，我要這兩張。

B：Here are your tickets. Your seats are in the sixth row of the dress circle. 這是您的票。您的座位在特等包廂第六排。

Scene 31　看電影

Step 1　必備表達

電影	movie：還可以用 film 來表示，「看電影」就是 go to the movies。
放映	show：如「放映電影」就是 show a film。
良好口碑	public's praise：full of praise 讚不絕口。
恐怖片	horror movie：「動作片」是 action movie；「科幻片」是 Sci-Fi movie；「愛情片」是 Romance movie。
零食	snack：late snack 宵夜。
銀幕	screen：也可以用 projection screen 來表示。
女主角	leading actress：還可以用 main actress 來表示，此外，「男主角」是 leading actor，而「配角」則是 supporting role。
感動	touch：be touched to tears 就是「感動地落淚」。此外，move 也有「感動」的意思。
無聊的	boring：與其意思相反的就是 interesting「有趣的」。
爆米花	popcorn：popcorn corner 爆米花店。
(電影院)小吃攤	concession stand：concession 在這裡不是表示「讓步」而是指「租地營業小吃部　商攤」的意思；stand 表示「售貨台·售貨處」(電影院)。
3D	3-dimensional: dimensional ……維的。

Step 2　句句精彩

① 這部電影好糟糕啊。

A：The movie sucked. 這部電影好糟糕啊。

B：It might be the worst movie ever. 它可能是有史以來最糟糕的一部電影了。

Tips

suck 糟糕，差勁。

This movie is boring. 這部電影很沒勁。

The leading character of the movie didn't act well with the rest of the cast. 電影的主角和其他角色配合得不好。

② 這是一部口碑很好的電影。

A： This is a critically acclaimed film. 這是一部口碑很好的電影。

B： Yeah, it's really worth watching. 嗯，真的很值得一看。

Tips

critically 善於評論的，有判斷力的；acclaimed 受到讚揚的

It's a real blockbuster. 確實是一部震撼大片。

The actor who played the main role did well. 男主角的演得不錯。

③ 現在正在上映什麼片子？

A： Wha's playing now? 現在正在上映什麼片子？

B： Let's check online. 咱們上網查查。

Tips

What are showing now? 現在上映什麼片子？

Can you recommend any good movies? 你能給我推薦一部好看的電影嗎？

What's the title of the box office's top movie? 票房最好的電影片名是什麼？

④ 還有好位子嗎？

A： Are there any good seats left? 還有好位子嗎？

B： There's a seat in the middle. 有一個中間的座位。

Tips

Let's grab seats in the middle. 我們隨便挑中間的座位吧。

The only seats available are in the front row. 只剩下前排的位子了。

Let's buy the tickets online so we don't have to wait in line. 咱們上網訂票吧，這樣就不用排隊了。

⑤ 你想要靠近走道還是中間的座位？

A： Do you want a seat by the aisle or in the middle? 你想要靠近走道還是中間的座

位？

B： Middle is always the best. 當然是中間的座位好。

Tips

- aisle 走道
- Doesn't matter to me. 無所謂。
- I'll take anything I can get. 只要有票哪兒都行。

⑥ 不要打擾周圍的人。

A： Don't annoy people around us. 不要打擾周圍的人。

B： Sorry, I just can't help laughing. 對不起，我只是忍不住想笑。

Tips

- Tell the person next to you to be quiet. 請你旁邊的人安靜一點。
- Please turn off your cell phone before the movie starts. 電影開場前請關掉手機。
- It was really annoying that somebody was talking on the phone during the movie. 有人在電影放映時打電話，真的很煩人。

⑦ 我想去買點零食，你想吃什麼？

A： I'm going to buy some snacks. What do you want to have? 我想去買點零食，你想吃麼？

B： I'm fine, thanks. 不用，謝謝。

Tips

- I'll have some popcorn, extra butter. 我想來點爆米花，多加些奶油。
- It's too expensive here. 這裡的東西太貴了。
- Coke, please. 一瓶可樂。

Step 3 情 景 模 擬

① 評價電影

A： What do you think of this movie? 你覺得這部電影怎麼樣？

B： This is a critically acclaimed film. But I think it's a little violent. 這是一部口碑很好的電影。但是我覺得有一些暴力。

A： Yeah, it is. And it's not suitable for children to watch. 是的，的確是這樣。這部電

影不適合孩子看。

B： Can you recommend a good movie? 你能推薦一部好看的電影嗎？

A： I think The Croods is very interesting and touching. 我覺得《瘋狂原始人》很有意思，也很感人。

B： OK. I'll go to watch it this Friday. 好的，我這週五去看。

② 正在上映

A： What is showing now? 現在正在上映什麼片子？

B： Let's check online. 我們上網查查。

A： Okay. 好的。

B： There are some new movies this week. 這週又上映了一些新電影。

A： Which one do you want to watch? 你想看哪部？

B： Let me see. This action movie looks interesting. 讓我看看。這部動作片看起來很有趣。

③ 買電影票

A： Two tickets, please. 兩張票。

B：Do you want seats by the aisle or in the middle? 你想要靠近走道還是中間的座位？

A：I have to go to the bathroom a lot, so aisle seat is better for me. 我上廁所比較頻繁，所以還是靠近走道的座位比較適合我。

B： OK. $20 in total. 好的，一共 20 美元。

A： I have membership card. Can I get a discount? 我有會員卡，可以打折嗎？

B： Yeah, then it's $16. 可以，那樣的話就是 16 美元。

Scene 32　節日和運動

Step 1　必備表達

萬聖節	Halloween：萬聖節必備的裝飾品就是 pumpkin lamp「南瓜燈」。
感恩節	Thanksgiving day：在感恩節通常都會吃 turkey「火雞」。
復活節	Easter Day：Easter eggs 復活節彩蛋。
潑水節	Water-Sprinkling Festival：sprinkle 灑。
露營	camping：camping site 露營地。
遠足	hiking：go hiking 去遠足。
戶外的	outdoor：outdoor recreation 戶外運動。
極限運動	extreme sports：extreme 極度的。
愛好者	enthusiast：enthusiastic 熱情的，狂熱的。
笨豬跳	bungee jumping：bungee 原指笨豬跳用的「橡皮繩」，引申為「笨豬跳」的意思。
潛水	dive：sky dive 跳傘。
衝浪	surf：surf the internet 上網。

Step 2　句句精彩

① 我很高興我們能在西雅圖過萬聖節。

A：I'm so glad we are here in Seattle for Halloween. 我很高興我們能在西雅圖過萬聖節。

B：Did you ever see the movie Sleepless in Seattle? 你看過《西雅圖未眠夜》那部電影嗎？

Tips

■ What are you dressing up as for Halloween? 你萬聖節要裝扮成什麼樣？

■ I was thinking about dressing up as a vampire. 我想打扮成一個吸血鬼。

■ Trick or treat! 不給糖就搗亂！

② 你們通常怎麼慶祝感恩節？

A： How do you usually celebrate Thanksgiving Day? 你們通常怎麼慶祝感恩節？

B： My family come from all over the world for Thanksgiving. 我的家人會從世界各地趕回來，慶祝感恩節。

Tips

■ Just cook a turkey and watch the football game. 烤一隻火雞，然後看足球比賽。

■ I'll invite some friends and family over. 我會邀請一些朋友以及家人過來。

■ I will go back home for the holidays. 我會回家慶祝節日。

③ 耶誕節對西方人來說是最重要的節日。

A： Christmas is the most important holiday for Western people. 耶誕節對西方人來說是最重要的節日。

B： It's a time for gift giving and being with family. 那是一個互贈禮物、與親人團聚的時刻。

Tips

■ Do you celebrate Christmas? 你們慶祝耶誕節嗎？

■ Just like Spring Festival to Chinese people. 就像春節一樣。

■ I heard that every family has a Christmas tree and hangs gifts on it. 我聽說每家都有一棵聖誕樹，然後會把禮物掛在上面。

④ 願你有個最棒的耶誕節。

A： I hope you have the best Christmas ever. 願你有個最棒的耶誕節。

B： The same to you. 你也是。

Tips

■ May you have the best Christmas ever. 願你有個最棒的耶誕節。

■ Merry Christmas! 耶誕節快樂！

■ May the joy of Christmas be with you through the whole year. 願耶誕節的快樂一年四季與你同在。

⑤ 露營是一項令人激動的戶外活動。

A： Camping is an exciting outdoor activity. 露營是一項令人激動的戶外活動。

B： Camping in September is the best. 九月是露營的最好時節。

Tips

- Camping can bring us closer to nature. 露營可以讓我們更接近大自然。
- We can use the campfire to cook when go camping. 去露營的時候可以用營火來做飯。
- Stretch the tent, please. 請拉緊帳篷。

⑥ 我是極限運動愛好者。

A： I'm an enthusiast of extreme sports. 我是極限運動愛好者。

B： They are too dangerous! 那太危險啦！

Tips

- I'm a real fan of extreme sports. 我是極限運動愛好者。
- I want to try extreme sports too. But I dare not. 我也想嘗試極限運動，但是我不敢。
- I always want to try bungee jumping. 我一直都想試試笨豬跳。

⑦ 攀岩是我最喜歡的戶外運動。

A： Rock climbing is my favorite outdoor sports. 攀岩是我最喜歡的戶外運動。

B： Have you ever climbed Mt. Vernon? 你攀登過弗農山嗎？

Tips

- rock climbing 攀岩。
- What mountains have you climbed? 你都爬過哪些山？

Step 3　情 景 模 擬

① 萬聖節

A： I'm so glad we are here in Seattle for Halloween. 我很高興我們能在西雅圖過萬聖節。

B： Yes, me too! 是啊，我也是很開心！

A： Look at those pumpkin lamps! They are so scary! 看那些南瓜燈！它們好嚇人！

B： This is their tradition to celebrate Halloween. 這是他們慶祝萬聖節的傳統。

A： Let's dress up and take part in the party. 我們裝扮一下去參加派對吧。

B： Let's go! 一起走！

② 慶祝感恩節

A： How do you usually celebrate Thanksgiving Day? 你通常怎麼慶祝感恩節？

B： I always spend Thanksgiving with my family. 感恩節我通常是和家人一起過。

A： Do you cook some special food to celebrate it? 你們會做什麼特別的食物來慶祝節日嗎？

B： We usually eat turkey or ham for Thanksgiving. 感恩節時，我們通常會吃火雞或火腿。

A： Does every family cook turkey? 每個家庭都會做火雞嗎？

B： Most of the families do. 大部分會。

③ 露營

A： Do you like to go camping? 你喜歡露營嗎？

B： Yeah. Camping is an exciting outdoor activity. 喜歡。露營是一項令人激動的戶外活動。

A： That would be great! We are planning to go camping this weekend. Would you like to join us? 太好了！我們計畫這週末去露營，你願意加入嗎？

B： Sure. Have you prepared all we need for camping? 當然。要露營的東西都準備好了嗎？

A： No, not yet. We have to prepare sleeping bags, folding tables, food, tents and so on. 沒有，還沒準備好。我們得準備睡袋、折疊椅、食物、帳篷等等。

B： OK. Then I'll prepare food and tents. 好的，那我來準備食物和帳篷吧。

Scene 33   其他娛樂

Step 1   必備表達

水族館	aquarium：dream aquarium 夢幻水族館。
水箱	water tank：tank 表示「水槽」。
物種	species：常說的「瀕危物種」就是 endangered species。
海底世界	underwater world：還可以表示為 sea world。
海洋生物	aquatic creature：aquatic 表示「水生的；水棲」，如 aquatic product「水產品」；aquatic environment「水生環境」；aquatic plant「水生植物」。
賭場	casino：「賭博」用英語表達就是 gamble。
賭注	bet：關於 bet 的常用片語有：bet amounts 下注金額；make a bet 打賭。
中獎	hit the jackpot：jackpot 頭獎，大筆收入。
夜總會	nightclub：nightclub bar 酒吧夜店。
迪斯可	disco：disco dancing 跳迪斯可。
卡拉 OK	Karaoke bar：KTV(Karaoke TV) 歌廳。

Step 2   句句精彩

① 這個水族館最激動人心的地方在哪裡？

A： What's the most exciting area of this aquarium? 這個水族館最激動人心的地方在哪裡？

B： You can watch the dolphin show. 你可以觀看海豚表演。

Tips

■ Which part attracts you most in this aquarium? 這個水族館最吸引你的是哪個部分？

■ There are「professional mermaids」dancing in the pool. 水池中「職業美人魚」正在表演。

■ There is a sea dog show in the pool. 游泳池那邊有海獅表演。

② 遊客們可以近距離觀賞危險動物而無須害怕。

A： What's the most characteristic part of this aquarium? 這個水族館最具特色的地方是什麼？

B： Visitors can watch dangerous creatures up close without fear. 遊客們可以近距離觀賞危險動物而無須害怕。

Tips

I've never seen a shark up close. 我從來沒這麼近距離地看過一條鯊魚。

■ We can see the boa constrictor dancing with the trainer from a layer of glass. 我們就在一層玻璃之外觀看蟒蛇和訓練師一起跳舞。

Can you imagine being in the water with one of those predators? 你能想像在水中和那些掠食者親密接觸嗎？

③ 我們可以看到許多海洋生物，還可以觀看有關海底世界的影片。

A： We can see many sea creatures and watch a movie about underwater life. 我們可以看到許多海洋生物，還可以觀看有關海底世界的影片。

B： I can't wait to go there. 我都迫不及待要去了。

Tips

■ There will be documentary movies about the sea animals. 這裡會播放關於海洋動物的紀錄片。

The movies are surprisingly interesting, which show the mysterical world of sea. 電影真是有趣極了，將神奇的海洋世界展現了出來。

This is a 4D movie, which makes you feel at sea. 這是 4D 電影，會讓你彷彿置身於海洋中。

④ 您推薦我去哪個賭場？

A： Which casino would you suggest me going? 您推薦我去哪個賭場？

B： There's only one in this area near Twin Peaks. 這附近只有一個賭場，在雙子峰附近。

Tips

You should check out the casinos on the west side of Vegas. 你應該查查拉斯維加斯州西部地區的賭場。

I would suggest you saving your money and not wasting it on gambling. 我建議你把錢省下來，別浪費在賭博上。

The Las Vegas is the must-place for those who are fond of gambling. 拉斯維加斯對於那些

喜歡賭博的人來說是必去之地。

⑤ 最少要下注多少？

A： What's the minimum bet? 最少要下注多少？

B： Minimum wager is 5 dollars. 最少五美元。

Tips

■ minimum 最小的，最少的；它的反義詞是 maximum「最多的，最大的」。

■ It's an open table (means any bet). 這是一張開放桌（意思是任意賭注都行）。

■ You can bet what you like here. 隨便下注。

⑥ 有爵士樂俱樂部嗎？

A： Are there any Jazz clubs? 有爵士樂俱樂部嗎？

B： Yes, you will find it on the second floor. 有，在二樓。

Tips

■ There's one down the block by the liquor store. 街區那頭的酒莊旁有一個。

■ Sorry, I don't know. But there is a disco bar which is very popular. 抱歉，我不知道。但是有一家迪斯可酒吧非常火。

■ Sorry, there isn't any of this kind. 對不起，這裡沒有這種風格的俱樂部。

⑦ 年齡限制是多少？

A： What's the age limit? 年齡限制是多少？

B： You have to be at least 21 to get into the casino. 你必須要滿二十一歲才能進賭場。

Tips

■ Is there a minimum age? 有沒有規定要多少歲才能進去？

■ How old do you have to be to get in? 多大才能進去？

■ We don't have a limit. 我們這沒有年齡限制。

Step 3　情景模擬

① 水族館表演

A： What's the most exciting thing of this aquarium? 這個水族館最激動人心的地方在哪裡？

B：There are a lot of dolphins and kids all like them. 這裡有很多海豚，很多孩子都喜歡。

A：Is there a dolphin show? 那有海豚表演嗎？

B：Yes. The show is on every two hours. 有的。每兩個小時就有一場表演。

A：Do we need to buy another tickets? 我們需要另外買票嗎？

B：Yes. 是的。

② 水下世界

A：What are these uniforms used for? 這些制服是做什麼的？

B：Visitors can watch dangerous creatures up close without fear. 遊客們可以近距離觀賞危險動物而無須害怕。

A：What kind of dangerous creatures? 什麼樣的危險動物？

B：You can see it on this brochure. 你可以在這個宣傳冊上看到。

A：Wow, we can see sharks! That's terrific! 哇，我們可以看鯊魚！這太棒了！

B：And there are plenty of others. 還有很多其他的呢。

③ 觀看海底影片

A：Where are we now? 我們這是在哪？

B：We are in a video room. We can see many sea creatures and watch a movie about underwater life. 我們在視聽室。我們可以看到許多海洋生物，還可以觀看有關海底世界的影片。

A：What is the style of this movie? 這是什麼類型的電影呢？

B：This is a 4D movie, which makes you feel at the sea. 這是 4D 電影，會讓你感覺彷彿置身於海洋。

A：The movies are surprisingly interesting. 這個電影真是太有趣了。

B：Glad you like it. 很高興你喜歡。

Chapter

5

購物

Scene 34　詢問訊息

Step 1　必備表達

百貨商店	department store：department 還有「部門」，「科」的意思。
營業時間	business hours：closing time 結束營業的時間。
紀念品	souvenir：tourist souvenir 旅遊紀念品。
營業部	sales department：sales 是「銷售的，有關銷售的」意思。
櫃檯	counter：service counter 服務台。
購物中心	mall：pedestrian mall 步行街。
電器用品	electric appliance：home appliance 家用電器；electric 表示「電的」，注意區分它與 electrical「跟電有關的」。
跳蚤市場	flea market：又叫「廉價市場」，在這裡可以買到便宜的東西。
二手貨	second-hand goods：second-hand 表示「二手的」，比如：second-hand smoke 二手菸；second-hand house 二手房；second-hand information 二手訊息。
購物中心	shopping center：還可以用 mall 或 plaza 來代替。

Step 2　句句精彩

① 這附近有沒有百貨商店？

A：Is there a department store nearby? 這附近有沒有百貨商店？

B：Yes. There's one two blocks away from here. 有。兩個街區外有一家。

Tips

■ Is there a shopping center around here? 這附近有購物中心嗎？

■ No, there is not. You have to go to downtown. 沒有。你需要去市中心。

② 賣外套的區域在哪裡？

A：Where is the outerwear section? 賣外套的區域在哪裡？

B： It is on the second floor. 在二樓。

Tips

outerwear 外套。

Where's the shoe department? 賣鞋子的地方在哪？

The men's shoes counter is on the fourth floor. 男鞋的櫃檯在四樓。

(3) 商店幾點開門？

A： What time does the store open? 商店幾點開門？

B： The store opens at 9 a.m. 商店上午九點開門。

Tips

When is the business hour of the store? 商店的營業時間有多久？

How late are you open? 你們最晚開到幾點？

Do you know any other store that's open today? 你知道今天有其他商店開門嗎？

(4) 你知道在哪裡可以買紀念品嗎？

A： Do you know where I can buy souvenirs? 你知道在哪裡可以買紀念品嗎？

B： There is a souvenir shop in the corner of the street. 街角有一家紀念品商店。

Tips

Are there any good stores to buy souvenirs? 有什麼好的商店賣紀念品嗎？

What kind of souvenir do you want? 你想要什麼樣的紀念品？

There are no souvenirs sold here, as far as I know. 據我所知，這裡沒有賣紀念品的。

(5) 這裡有賣當地特色產品嗎？

A： Can I find some local specialty here? 這裡有賣當地特產嗎？

B： Go downstairs and turn left, then you will see specialty goods section there. 下樓左轉，你就能看見土產區域。

Tips

local specialty 當地特產。

I'm looking for something special made in this country. 我想買本地特有的商品。

What do you recommend as a souvenir from this country? 你可以推薦一些讓我帶回去的紀念品嗎？

⑥ 請問電梯在哪裡？

A： Where can I find the elevator? 請問電梯在哪裡？

B： Can you see the food counter over there? The elevator is behind it. 你能看到那邊的食品櫃檯嗎？電梯就在它後面。

Tips

■ elevator 和 lift 是「升降電梯」；escalator 是「扶梯」。

■ The elevator is under repair, and you have to take the stairs. 電梯正在維修，你只能走樓梯了。

■ You can follow the signs and you will find it. 你可以順著指示牌走，然後你就能看到了。

Step 3　情景模擬

① 百貨商店

A： Is there a department store nearby? 這附近有沒有百貨商店？

B： Yes, there is one near the subway station. 有的，地鐵站附近有一個百貨商場。

A： Where is the subway station? 地鐵站在哪裡？

B： Turn right at the traffic light and you won't miss it. 紅綠燈右轉，你不會錯過的。

A： Got it. Thank you very much. 知道了，非常感謝。

B： It's my pleasure. 不用謝。

② 詢問櫃檯

A： Where is the outerwear section? 賣外套的區域在哪裡？

B： The outerwear section is on the 5th floor. 賣外套的區域在五樓。

A： How can I get there? 我怎麼才能上去呢？

B： By elevator. 坐電梯。

A： Where can I find the elevator? 請問電梯在哪裡？

B： You can follow the signs and you will find it. 你可以順著指示牌走，然後你就能看到了。

③ 營業時間

A： What time does the store open? 商店幾點開門？

B： The store opens at 10 a.m. 上午十點開門。

A： When is the business hour of the store? 營業時間是什麼時候？

B： It's from 10 a.m to 9 p.m. 上午十點到晚上九點。

A： Will the store open on Christmas day? 商店耶誕節開業嗎？

B： No. The store will be closed on that day. 不開，那天休息。

Scene 35　挑 選 商 品

Step 1　必 備 表 達

厚／薄衣服	heavy/light clothes：還可以用 weight clothes 表示「厚衣服」。
新款到店	new arrival：arrival 是「到達」的意思。通常新款衣服上都會掛有 New Arrival 的標識。
高跟鞋	high-heel shoes：對應的「平跟鞋」就是 flat heeled。
棉質的衣服	cotton clothing：cotton 表示「棉質的」。
適合	suit：in suit with 表示「與……協調一致」；還可以用 a suit of 表示「一套」。
淺顏色	light color：dark color 深顏色。
最新產品	latest product：latest style 最新款。
流行	fashion：come into fashion 開始流行；out of fashion 過時。
材料	material：raw material 原材料。
款式	style：in style 流行的。

Step 2　句 句 精 彩

① 我想買一件秋天穿的毛衣，不要太厚也不要太薄。

A： I want to buy a sweater for the autumn, neither too heavy nor too light. 我想買一件秋天穿的毛衣，不要太厚也不要太薄。

B： Here, try this one. 這件，來試試吧。

Tips

■ Neither...nor... 既不……也不……

■ We have several designs that you might like. 我們這有幾款你可能會喜歡的款式。

■ We have many styles and shades for you to choose from. 我們的商品種類很多，花色齊全，供您隨意挑選。

② 我想找棉質的衣服。

A： I'm looking for some cotton clothing. 我想找棉質的衣服。

B： We have an extensive collection in cotton. 我們有許多的棉質衣服。

Tips

> Most of our T-shirts are cotton. 我們大部分的 T 袖衫都是棉質的。
>
> What about a cotton polyester blend? 棉和滌綸混紡的怎麼樣？
>
> I am looking for a woollen sweater. 我想買一件羊毛衫。

③ 請問你們有沒有正式的服裝？

A： Do you have any formal clothes? 請問你們有沒有正式的服裝？

B： We have lots of suits and formal dresses for you to choose from. 我們有很多套裝和正式的裙子，可供您選擇。

Tips

> formal clothes 表示「正裝」，常說的 「休閒裝」 則是 casual clothes。
>
> Do you mean formal for going out at night or business attire? 你是指參加晚宴還是商務會談的正裝？
>
> For business or business casual? 是商務裝還是商務休閒裝？

④ 這件衣服作為冬裝，感覺顏色過淺。

A： It's too light in color for the winter. 這件衣服作為冬裝，感覺顏色過淺。

B： Then how about this one in a darker shade? 那這件顏色深點的怎麼樣？

Tips

> OK, we have this style in a dark color over here. 好的，這款也有深顏色的。
>
> Actually it's the new fashion for winter. 其實這件是冬季最新款。
>
> You can look at some others in darker color. 你還可以看看顏色深點的其他款。

⑤ 這件還有別的顏色嗎？

A： Do you have this in different colors? 這件還有別的顏色嗎？

B： What you see is what you get. 這款的幾種顏色都在這了。

Tips

> I think this color suits you better. 我認為這個顏色更適合你。
>
> Is this the only color? 這是唯一的顏色嗎？
>
> I'm sorry, but this color is out of stock. 很抱歉，這個顏色的衣服缺貨。

⑥ 這件不是我的風格，我想找件適合自己的。

A： This is not my style and I want to find one that suits me. 這件不是我的風格，我想找件適合自己的。

B： Can you tell me what kind of style you have in mind? 你能告訴我你想要什麼風格的嗎？

Tips

■ I don't like this lady style; I prefer a more punk one. 我不喜歡淑女風，我更喜歡朋克風。

■ I strongly recommend you to try this one, because it's just your syle. 我強烈建議你試試這一件，因為這件就是你的風格。

■ Why don't you try to change for a new style? 你為什麼不嘗試換個新風格呢？

⑦ 這些都是新款。

A： These are new arrivals. 這些都是新款。

B： They look great. 看起來真不錯。

Tips

■ This one is newly recommended. 這件是新推薦款。

■ This collection just came from Paris. 這款衣服剛剛從巴黎運過來。

■ Is this the latest fashion? 這是最新款嗎？

Step 3　情景模擬

① 挑選毛衣

A： I want to buy a sweater for the autumn, neither too heavy nor too light. 我想買一件秋天穿的毛衣，不要太厚也不要太薄。

B： What kind of material are you thinking about? 你想要什麼料子的？

A： I am thinking about woolen ones. 我想要羊毛的。

B： We have several designs that you might like. 我們這有幾款你可能會喜歡的款式。

A： Do you have light colors? 有淺顏色的嗎？

B： Yeah, try it. 有，試一下吧。

② 正式服裝

A： Do you have formal clothes? 請問你們有沒有正式的服裝？

B： Do you mean formal for attending parties or business attire? 你是指參加晚宴還是商務會談的正裝？

A： Business attire. 參加商務會談的正裝。

B： Then you can see these clothes. These are new arrivals. 那你就可以看看這些衣服。這些都是新款。

A： They look not bad. I want to try this on. 看起來都不錯。我想試試這件。

B： Can you tell me about your size? 您要什麼尺寸的？

A： The one in 8 is OK. 8 碼就行。

③ 挑選顏色

A： You look great in this. 你穿這件很好看。

B： It's too light in color for the winter. 這件衣服作為冬裝，感覺顏色有點淺。

A： But it looks really good with your skin tone. 但是這件衣服與你的膚色真的很配。

B： Do you have darker ones? 有深顏色的嗎？

A： Yes, we have this in a darker color over here. 有的，那兒有這款，是深色的。

B： Then I will try this darker one. 那我試下這件深色的。

Scene 36　尺碼與試穿

Step 1　必備表達

試穿	try on：try on hat 試戴帽子；try on new dress 試穿新衣服。
尺碼	size：size label 尺碼標籤。
特小號	XS/extra small：extra small size 特小號。
中號	M/medium：medium scale 中等規模。
特大號	XL/extra large：XXL/extra extra large 超特大號。
腰圍	waist circumference：chest circumference 胸圍；hip size 臀圍。
試衣間	fitting room：dressing mirror 穿衣鏡。
測量	measure：made to measure 定做的（鞋子、衣服）。
女性三圍	dimensions：overall dimensions 外形尺寸。
緊	tight：衣服穿著顯小或者緊都可以用這個詞來表示。
鬆	loose：除了表示「衣服大了」，還有「布料稀疏、不緊湊」的意思。

Step 2　句句精彩

① 我能試穿這雙鞋嗎？

A：May I try on this pair of shoes? 我能試穿這雙鞋嗎？

B：Sure, what size do you need? 當然。你穿多大碼？

Tips

■ What's your size? 你多少碼？

■ Can I try this dress on? 我能試穿一下這件裙子嗎？

■ Yes. There is a mirror over there. 可以。那兒有鏡子。

② 這個有 41 碼的嗎？

A：Do you have this in size 41? 這個有 41 碼的嗎？

B： We don't have that size in stock. 這個碼的鞋子沒有現貨了。

Tips

Do you know what size is that in US? 你知道換算成美國尺碼是多少碼？

This style is a little bit small. I recommend you to try the 42 if you wear 41 as usal. 這個款有點小，如果你平時穿 41 碼，我建議你這款試穿 42 碼。

I'm sorry, we're out of stock on that size. 不好意思，庫存中沒有那個尺碼了。

③ 有尺碼在一些的嗎？

A： Do you have any bigger size? 有尺碼大一些的嗎？

B： Yes, we do. Let me get that for you. 有，我們有大一碼的。這就幫你拿來。

Tips

I think you might want to go two sizes bigger. 我覺得你應該需要大兩碼的號。

Actually you should wear these a little tight. They will get more comfortable as you wear them. 實際上你需要穿稍微緊一點的，穿一穿就合適了。

■ I think it's a little bit small. 我覺得這件有點小。

④ 試衣間在哪？

A： Where is the fitting room? 試衣間在哪？

B： It's on the 2nd floor. 在二樓。

Tips

Can you see the very long queue? It is right there. 你能看見那個長隊伍嗎？就在那。

You can bring a maximum of five pieces. 您最多可以帶五件進去試穿。

Sorry, all the rooms are occupied. 抱歉，所有的試衣間都有人。

⑤ 這個有我穿的尺碼嗎？

A： Do you have this in my size? 這個有我穿的尺碼嗎？

B： I'll have to check the tag. 我需要看一下標籤。

Tips

All we have is on the rack here. 所有尺碼都在這個架子上。

If we don't have it, I can check with one of our other stores. 如果我們店沒有，我可以查看其他店鋪是否有貨。

I will bring it for you, please wait a minute. 我幫你拿過來，請等一下。

⑥ 你能幫我量一下嗎？

A：Could you please measure me? 你能幫我量一下嗎？

B：You're a 38 in the waist. 您的腰圍是 38。

Tips

■ Are we measuring for suits or what? 你是量西服尺寸還是別的？

■ Would you like me to take your measurements? 需要我幫您量尺寸嗎？

■ Do you know your waist circumference? 您知道您的腰圍是多少嗎？

⑦ 這個尺碼我剛好可以穿。

A：The size is just right for me. 這個尺碼我剛好可以穿。

B：It looks like a perfect fit. 看上去簡直就是量身定做的。

Tips

■ I think it might be tight in the back. 我覺得後邊有點緊。

■ It was made for you. 這件衣服就是為你而做的。

■ I think you will be more perfect with this pair of shoes. 我覺得再配上這雙鞋就更完美了。

Step 3　情 景 模 擬

① 詢問尺碼

A：Do you have this in size 41? 這個有 41 碼的嗎？

B：We don't have that size in stock. 我們沒有那個尺碼了。

A：What a pity. I really like this pair of shoes. 真可惜。我真的很喜歡這雙鞋。

B：In fact, you can try this pair in 42, because this style is a little small. 事實上，你可以試試 42 碼的，因為這個款式偏小。

A：Well, then bring the size in 42. 好，那就給我試試 42 碼吧。

B：OK. Just wait for a moment. 好的，請稍等。

② 合適尺碼

A：Do you have this one size bigger? 這件有大一碼的嗎？

B：Yes, we do. Let me get that for you. 有的。我這就給你拿來。

A：Thank you. But they seem a little bit tight too. 謝謝。但是好像還是有點緊。

B：I think you might need one size bigger. 我覺得你應該穿大一碼的。

A： Oh, boy! I gained almost 20kg in one month. I never tried this size. 哦，天哪！我一個月之內幾乎胖了 20 公斤。我從來沒有穿過那個尺碼。

B： It's OK. 沒關係。

③ 試衣間

A： Where is the fitting room? 試衣間在哪？

B： It's around the corner behind the suit rack. 就在西裝貨架後面的轉彎處。

A： This one is a little loose. Can you get me a bigger one? 這件有點鬆了，你能拿件大的嗎？

B： OK, please wait fot a moment. 好的，請稍等。

A： Can my friend go inside with me too? 我朋友能和我一起進去嗎？

B： Sure. 當然可以。

Scene 37　化妝品和首飾

混合型皮膚	combination skin：combination 混合；skin 皮膚；此外，我們常說的「T 字部位」則可以表示為 T-zone。
油性（皮膚）	oil skin：oily 油的，油質的。
乾性（皮膚）	dry skin：乾性皮膚則需要滋潤型的產品，「滋潤」的英文就是 nourish。
敏感性（皮膚）	sensitive skin：highly sensitive 高度敏感的。
保濕霜	moisturizer：night moisturizer 夜間乳液；「保濕精華」則是 hydratation active moisture boost。
睫毛膏	mascara：mascara brush 睫毛刷。
防曬霜	sun block：sun block cream 防曬乳液。
項鍊	necklace：pearl necklace 珍珠項鍊。
耳環	earring：diamond earring 鑽石耳環。
手鐲	bracelet：jade bracelet 玉鐲。
翡翠	emerald：oriental emerald 東方祖母綠。
水晶	crystal：除了作名詞，還可以作形容詞，表示「水晶的，透明的」。
珍珠	pearl：pearl powder 珍珠粉。

① 我是混合型肌膚，我的 T 區很油。

A：I have combination skin and my T-zone is oily. 我是混合型肌膚，我的 T 區很油。

B：Look at our products over here. 來這邊看看我們的產品。

Tips

■ T-zone 所指的是「面部的前額和鼻子區域」。

■ We do have some facial cleanser that will help you with oily skin. 我們這有一些洗面乳可

以改善油性皮膚。

■ I recommend the moisture lotion. It's pretty good. 我推薦這款保濕乳液，很好用。

② 我不用睫毛膏，因為我不知道如何卸掉它。

A： I don't use mascara, because I don't know how to remove it. 我不用睫毛膏，因為我不知道如何卸掉它。

B： This brand is very easy to remove with water. 這個牌子的睫毛膏容易用水洗掉。

Tips

remove 在這裡可以用來表示「卸妝」，而「卸妝乳」就是 remover。

The mascara will make your eyes look so good. I really think you should try. 睫毛膏會讓你的眼睛看上去非常漂亮。我真的認為你應該試試。

Applying mascara can make eyelashes long and thick. 使用睫毛膏會使眼睫毛顯得又長又密。

③ 它能遮住雀斑和痘痘嗎？

A： Does it cover the freckles and pimples? 它能遮住雀斑和痘痘嗎？

B： It will definitely cover the blemishes. 它能非常好地遮住瑕疵。

Tips

freckle 雀斑；pimple 痘痘；blemish 瑕疵。

You wouldn't need to apply much there. 只需輕輕塗抹即可。

This concealer can effectively cover the freckles. 這款遮瑕膏能夠有效地遮住你的雀斑。

④ 我想要買一款有防曬功效的粉底。

A： I want to buy a foundation with sun protection. 我想要買一款有防曬功效的粉底。

B： This new arrival has the function. 這款新品有這個功能。

Tips

This foundation has the function of sun protection. 這款粉底有防曬效果。

We recommend you this new arrival which can protect you from sun. 我們建議你試試這個新款，可以防曬。

⑤ 這珍珠是真的嗎？

A： Is this pearl genuine? 這珍珠是真的嗎？

B： All of our jewelry is certified. 我們所有的首飾都是經過鑑定的。

Tips

■ genuine 真的，真實的。

■ Yes. You can tell a real pearl from a fake one by the imperfections in the pearl. 是真的。你可以透過珍珠中的瑕疵來辨別真偽。

■ This pearl is highly artificialed. 這是高仿的。

6 這是幾 K 金的？

A： How many karats is the gold? 這是幾 K 金的？

B： This is 18k. 這是 18K 金的。

Tips

■ How many Karats is this diomand ring? 這款鉑金戒指是多少 K 的？

■ This is 100% 24k pure gold, the very best you can have. 這是 24K 足金，是最好的。

Step 3　情景模擬

1 混合型皮膚

A： I have combination skin and my T-zone is oily. 我是混合型肌膚，我的 T 區很油。

B： Then you can look at our products over here. I strongly recommend this facial cleanser which will help you with oily skin. 那您可以來這邊看看我們的產品。我強烈建議你使用這款洗面乳，可以改善油性皮膚的。

A： Really? Does it work well? 真的嗎？這個很管用嗎？

B： Yes. And you'd better change your diet if you want to get rid of oil completely. Fried foods can cause oily skin. 是的。如果你真的想徹底除油，你最好是改變飲食習慣。油炸食物會導致皮膚變油。

A： Thank you for your advice. How much is this facial cleanser? I will take this one. 謝謝你的建議。這款洗面乳多少錢？我就拿這一款了。

B： It's 10 dollars. 10 美元。

2 睫毛膏

A： I don't use mascara, because I don't know how to remove it. 我不用睫毛膏，因為我不知道如何卸掉它。

B： It has a lot to do with how you put it on and what brand you're using. 這和你怎樣刷睫毛膏和使用什麼牌子的睫毛膏都有關係。

A： Can you be specific? 你能說詳細點嗎？

B： This brand is very easy to remove with water. Let me show you how to remove it. 這個牌子的睫毛膏容易用水卸掉。讓我示範給你看怎麼卸掉它。

A： It looks very easy. 看上去很簡單。

B： Yes. And it makes your eyes look brighter. I really think you should try it. 是的。這款睫毛膏還會讓你的眼睛看上去更加有神采。我真的認為你應該試試。

③ 婚禮首飾

A： Could you recommend some wedding jewelry to me? 你能給我推薦一些婚禮戴的首飾嗎？

B： What kind of jewelry are you looking for? 你想要什麼樣的首飾？

A： Something elegant and decent. 典雅端莊的。

B： Then how about this set of jewelry? 這一套首飾怎麼樣？

A： Oh, it's too complicated and showy. 哦，太複雜，太豔麗了。

B： Maybe you should look at this. It's new arrival.
或許您應該看看這個，這個是新款。

Scene 38　電子和數位產品

Step 1　必備表達

數位相機	digital camera：panoramic camera 全景攝影機；stereo camera 立體攝影機。
鏡頭	lens：「廣角鏡頭」的英文是 wide angle lens，「變焦鏡頭」則是 zoom lens。
圖元	pixel：mega pixel 百萬圖元。
智慧型手機	smartphone：smart card 智慧卡。
筆記型電腦	laptop：desktop 桌上型電腦。
平板電腦	tablet：該詞還含有「藥片」的意思。
懷錶	pocket watch：wrist watch 腕錶。
防水的	waterproof：-proof 是表示「防……的」尾碼，比如，fireproof 防火的。
機械錶	mechanical：相對應的「電子錶」就是 electric watch。
內置的	built-in：external 外置的。

Step 2　句句精彩

① 這是一隻有報時功能的夜光錶。

A：It's a luminous watch with time-reminder function. 這是一隻有報時功能的夜光錶。

B： It looks like a great watch. 這隻錶看起來真不錯。

Tips

■ luminous 自發光的；time-reminder 報時

■ You mean it can be read in the dark? 你的意思是在晚上也能看清楚？

■ What's a time-reminder function? 什麼是報時功能？

② 這隻手錶防震嗎？

A： Is this watch anti-shock? 這隻手錶防震嗎？

B： Yes, it has this function. 是的，它可以防震。

Tips

anti-shock 防震，還可以用 shockproof 來表示。

Do you mean it is shock resistant? 你是說它能抵抗震盪嗎？

Apart from being anti-shock, it's also water-proof. 除了防震，還可以防水。

③ 你們賣情侶錶嗎？

A： Do you sale pair watches? 你們賣情侶錶嗎？

B： You mean his and hers? Yes, we do. 你是說男女同款的嗎？是的，我們這有。

Tips

pair watches 情侶錶。

We don't have any in stock right now. 現在庫房裡沒有貨。

No, but our online store has several in stock that you can choose from. 沒有，但是我們的網店裡有。你可以在網上挑選。

④ 我想要買筆記型電腦。

A： I'm looking for a laptop. 我想要買筆記型電腦。

B： Come over here. We have a big selection. 到這邊來，我們有很多選擇。

Tips

What kind of price range are you thinking of? 你想要什麼價格的？

Is there anything you can recommend? 有沒有推薦的機型？

This model is the slimmest. 這款機型是最薄的。

⑤ 你有沒有推薦的數位相機？

A： Do you have any digital cameras to recommend? 你有沒有推薦的數位相機？

B： This is a newly-released compact digital camera. 這是新推出的輕巧型數位相機。

Tips

I'm going to recommend Sony RX18; it takes the best pictures. 我推薦索尼 RX18 機型。它拍出來的照片效果最好。

What kind of price range are you thinking of? 你考慮哪些價格範圍？

⑥ 它有什麼特別的功能？

A： What special function does it have? 它有什麼特別的功能？

B： It has face and smile recognition function. 它有臉部和微笑識別功能。

Tips

- ■ This one has standard features, but also comes with powerful photo editing software. 這款具有標準功能，但同時也帶有強大的照片編輯軟體。
- ■ This camera offers a soft skin mode. 這部相機有美化膚質的模式。
- ■ This camera features an 8x optical zoom lens. 這部相機以八倍光學變焦鏡頭為主要特色。

⑦ 我想買個平板電腦，但我沒有太多預算。

A： I want to buy a tablet but I only have a low budget. 我想買個平板電腦，但我沒有太多預算。

B： You should check out these Asus tablets. 你可以看看華碩的平板電腦。

Tips

- ■ What kind of budget do you have? 你的預算是多少呢？
- ■ Have you thought about a netbook instead? 你有沒有想過買一個小筆電？
- ■ You'll get a discount when buying extra memory cards. 同時加購記憶卡，你可以享受折扣。

Step 3　情 景 模 擬

① 多功能手錶

A： Can I have a look at this watch? It looks cool. 我可以看看你的新錶嗎？看起來不錯啊。

B： Of course. It's a luminous watch with timereminder function. 當然。這是一隻有報時功能的夜光錶。

A： You mean it can be read in the dark? 你的意思是說在晚上也能看清楚？

B： Yes, you are right. And it can also remind me of the time. 是的，你說的對。並且它還能報時。

A： Sounds great. 聽起來不錯啊！

B： Apart from that, it's water proof. 此外，它還防水。

②　購買筆記本

A： What can I do for you? 我能為你做點什麼？

B： I'm looking for a laptop. 我想要買筆記型電腦。

A： Are you thinking of Mac or PC? 你想要多用途電腦還是個人電腦？

B： PC please. 個人電腦。

A： Come over here. We have a big selection. 到這邊來，我們有很多供您選擇。

B： It seems that I come to the right place. 看來我來對地方了。

③　數位相機

A： Do you have any digital cameras to recommend? 你有沒有推薦的數位相機？

B： It depends on your use. We have cameras for casual use and for professionals. 這得看你的用途是什麼了。我們有休閒款和專業款。

A： Just for casual use. 休閒款就可以。

B： Can you tell me what you're going to do with the camera? 你能告訴我你都用相機做什麼嗎？

A： Taking pictures of my families and friends. 幫家人和朋友照相。

B： Then I'm going to recommend Sony RX18; it takes the best pictures. 那麼，我推薦索尼 RX18 機型。它拍出來的照片最好。

Scene 39 在超市

Step 1 必備表達

購物車	shopping cart：cart 推車，還可以用 shopping trolley 來表示「購物車」。
廣告商品	advertised item：「廣告商品」通常也是 discounted product「打折商品」。
農副產品	agricultural products：類似的還有 dairy product 乳製品。
嬰兒用品	baby accessories：accessory 表示「附件」。
保固期	expiration date：「生產日期」則是 date of manufacture。
水果區	fruit section：section 可以表示超市里的不同區域，如：vegetable section 蔬菜區。
環保袋	reusable bag：類似的還有 canvas bag 帆布袋。
買一送一	two for one：buy one and get one free 也有相同的意思。
只收現金結帳通道	Cash Only Lane：Credit Card Only Lane 信用卡通道。
條碼	barcode：scan the barcode 掃描條碼。

Step 2 句句精彩

① 快看那些牙膏！買一送一。

A： Look at the toothpaste! Buy one and get one free. 快看那些牙膏！買一送一。

B： Aw, I just bought some the other day. 啊，我前幾天剛買了一些。

Tips

■ toothpaste 牙膏，相應的還有 tooth brush「牙刷」。

■ The toothpaste needs to be bought with tooth brush. 這個牙膏必須和牙刷一起買。

■ You'd better stock up while there is a sale. 你最好在促銷的時候多買些。

② 我排隊，你快去拿衛生紙。

A： I wait in line and you can run to get the paper towels. 我排隊，你快去拿衛生紙。

B： Thanks for holding my place. 謝謝你幫我占位。

Tips

paper towels 衛生紙

Go ahead and pay for yours first. 往前走，你先付款吧。

Grab me a roll of toilet paper, too. 幫我也拿一捲衛生紙。

③ 這些熱帶水果在這個國家賣得太貴了。

A： These tropical fruits are so expensive in this country. 這些熱帶水果在這個國家賣得太貴了。

B： That's because they're all imported. 因為它們都是進口的。

Tips

tropical fruit 熱帶水果。

We can wait until they go on sale. 我們可以等到打折的時候再買。

④ 這是快速結帳通道嗎？

A： Is this an express lane? 這是快速結帳通道嗎？

B： No, it's not. The express lane is over there. 不是。快速結帳通道在那邊。

Tips

express lane 快速結帳通道。

You should use the self-checkout. 你應該使用自助結帳通道。

You can queue in express lane as long as you have less than 10 items. 只要少於十件商品，你就可以在快速通道結帳。

⑤ 我要寄放包包。

A： I need to check this bag. 我要寄放包包。

B： You don't need to check bags here. Just go in. 這裡不用寄放包包，直接進去就可以。

Tips

check bag 寄放包包。

Take a ticket over there and you can store your stuff there. 去那邊領一下票據，你就可以把

包包寄放在這了。

■ It's OK. You don't have to check it. 沒關係，可以不用寄放。

⑥ 請問這裡賣有機蔬菜嗎？

A： Do you sell organic vegetables here? 請問這裡賣有機蔬菜嗎？

B： Yes, it's in the vegetables section. 有的。在蔬菜區。

Tips

■ organic 有機的，我們常說的「有機食品」就是 organic food。

■ If it's organic, it will have a sticker on it. 有機蔬菜上會貼有標籤。

■ If you want organic food, you should go to a larger supermarket. 如果你想買有機食品，你應該去更大的超市。

⑦ 恐怕您不能用信用卡支付，因為您在只收現金結帳通道上。

A： I'm afraid you can't pay by credit card, because you are on the Cash Only Lane. 恐怕您不能用信用卡支付，因為您在只收現金結帳通道上。

B： Where can I pay by card? 我在哪能用信用卡支付呢？

Tips

■ Only cash is acceptable. 只接受現金。

■ Do you accept debit card? 用借記卡支付可以嗎？

Step 3　情景模擬

① 買一贈一

A： Look at the toothpaste! Buy one and get one free. 快看那些牙膏！買一送一。

B： We'd better stock up some. 我們最好多買些。

A： Aw, it's a real bargain. 啊，這真的很划算。

B： It's good that they have specials all the time. 他們一直都有特價商品，真好。

A： Yes. So I come to this supermarket frequently. 是的。所以我經常來這家超市。

B： Me, too. 我也是。

② 排隊結帳

A： I wait in line and you can run to get the paper towels. 我排隊，你快去拿紙巾。

B： Thanks for holding my place. 謝謝你幫我占位。

A： It's nothing. 不用謝。

B： OK. Do you need me to get something for you? 好的，需要我幫你拿點什麼嗎？

A： No. Just be quick. 不用。快點回來。

B： I'll be right back. 我馬上就回來。

③ 談論價格

A： These tropical fruits are so expensive in this country. 這些熱帶水果在這個國家賣得太貴了。

B： These fruits are delivered from tropical zone. 這些水果都是從熱帶地區運送過來的。

A： No wonder they are so expensive. I don't think we can afford them. 難怪這麼貴。我覺得我們負擔不起。

B： We can wait until they are on sale. 我們可以等到特價的時候再買。

A： But the fruits won't be fresh then. 但水果到那時就不新鮮了。

B： You are right. Maybe we can buy less today. 你說的對，也許我們今天可以少買一點。

Scene 40 討價還價

打折	discount：discount price 折扣價格。
促銷	promotion：promotion 即可以表示「升職」，也可以表示「推廣，促銷」，如：product promotion 產品推廣。
最後價格	final price：這個片語指最終敲定的價格，final 是「最終的」意思。
討價還價	bargain：bargain 作動詞表示「討價還價」，作名詞則可以指「便宜的商品」，便宜貨，如：real bargain 划算的商品。
標價	marked price: mark 有「做標記」的意思，因此 marked 就表示「標示的」。
降價	lower the price：對應的 rise the price 是「漲價」。
殺價	beat down：cut down 也有同樣的意思。
還價	haggle：haggle over price 討價還價。
半價	half price：half price ticket 半價票。
成本	costing：這個詞來自 cost。

① 這個多少錢？

A： How much will this cost? 這個多少錢？

B： 43 dollars in total. 一共 43 美元。

Tips

■ That is $29.99 plus tax. 29.99 美元，含稅。

■ Let me check the price for you. 讓我看一下價錢。

■ Make me an offer. 你先出個價吧。

② 這真的很划算。

A： It's a real bargain. 這真的很划算。

B： The price won't stay long. 這個價格不會持續很久。

Tips

> You'd be a fool to pass on this deal. 過了這村就沒這店了。
>
> It is a great deal. 這真的很划算。
>
> How long will the special go on? 這個價格會持續多久？

③ 能不能便宜一點？

A： Can you make it cheaper? 能不能便宜一點？

B： It's already the best price I can offer. 這是我能給的最優惠的價格了。

Tips

> If you buy more, I can offer you some discount. 如果你多買一些，我可以給你優惠點。
>
> What price do you think is fair? 你覺得多少錢合適？
>
> Take it or leave it. 不買就算了。

④ 買多一點有折扣嗎？

A： Can I get a discount if I buy more? 買多一點有折扣嗎？

B： We don't offer discounts for quantity. 多買沒有折扣。

Tips

> ■ It depends on how many you buy. 那要看你買多少。
>
> I can offer a 5% discount if you're buying more than one. 購買一個以上可以得到 5% 的折扣。
>
> It is already the bottom price and I cannot offer a better one. 這個價錢已經是最低的了，沒法再降了。

⑤ 最低價是多少？

A： What would be the final price? 最低價是多少？

B： With tax, it would be 103.56 yuan. 含稅總共 103.56 元。

Tips

> ■ The final price is the price as marked. 標價就是最低價了。
>
> With installation and setup fee, it'll be 268 dollars. 算上安裝和設置費用，一共 268 美元。
>
> Just offer the bottom price. 直接報最低價吧。

6 耶誕節有什麼促銷活動嗎？

A： Do you have any Christmas promotions going on? 耶誕節有什麼促銷活動嗎？

B： We are always running promotions. 我們一直都有促銷活動。

Tips

■ Check out our print ads this Friday. 你可以週五查看我們的印刷廣告。

■ Our Christmas promotions are outrageous. 我們的耶誕節促銷是大手筆的。

■ There will be a big promotion during the Christmas holiday. 聖誕假期時會有大促銷。

7 不買就算了。

A： Take it or leave it. 不買就算了。

B： Come on, surely you can give me a more reasonable price. 拜託，你可以給我一個更合理的價格。

Tips

■ Is this really the best offer? 真的不能再便宜了？

■ Don't be so rigid. 別這麼死板。

■ Won't you think twice about it? 您不再考慮一下嗎？

Step 3　情景模擬

1 價錢划算

A： It's a real bargain. 這真的很划算。

B： You'd be a fool to pass on this deal. 過了這村就沒這店了。

A： How long is the sale going on? 這個促銷會持續多久？

B： It won't last for a long time. 不會持續很久。

A： OK. I'll take two. 好，我要兩個。

B： Here you are. 給你。

2 討價還價

A： Can you make it any cheaper? 能不能便宜一點？

B： I really can't. It's already the best price I can offer. 真的不行。這是我能給的最優惠的價格了。

A： Can I get a discount if I buy more? 多買一點有折扣嗎？

B： I can offer you a 5% discount if you buy more than five. 購買五件以上可以減 5%。

A： How about 7% discount? 減 7% 怎麼樣？

B： If you buy 10 pieces, yes. 如果你買十件，就可以。

③ 詢問最低價

A： What would be the final price? 最低價是多少？

B： The final price is the price as marked. 標價就是最低價了。

A： Come on, surely you can do better. How about offering me a wholesale price? 拜託，你還能再便宜點。你給我個批發價怎麼樣？

B： With tax, it would be $110. Is that OK? 含稅一共 110 美元。這樣行嗎？

A： I will take it if it is 100. 100 美元我就買。

B： Deal. 成交。

Scene 41　清潔與保存

Step 1　必 備 表 達

機洗	machine-wash：這是一個合成詞，反過來則是 washing machine 「洗衣機」。
手洗	hand-wash：有時在衣服的標籤上可以看到這個詞，表示只能手洗，不能機洗。
乾洗	dry-clean：dry-clean washer 乾洗機。
掉色	fade：fade away 逐漸消失。
縮水	shrink：shrink-proof 不縮水的。
鞋油	shoe polish：polish 作動詞是「擦」的意思，作名詞則可以表示「上光劑」。
避光	keep out of the sun：keep in dark place 也可以表示同樣的含義。
冷藏	refrigerate：名詞 refrigeration 可以表示「製冷」，而生活中常見的「冰箱」則是 refrigerator，也可以簡寫為 fridge。
儲存	store：這個詞表示「商店」的意思很常見，但它也有「儲存，倉庫」的意思。
通風	ventilate：ventilate the room 可以表示「讓房間通風」，此外，ventilator 是 ventilate 的派生詞，表示「通風機，換氣扇」。

Step 2　句 句 精 彩

① 請問它可以用洗衣機洗嗎？

A：Is it machine-washable? 請問它可以用洗衣機洗嗎？

B：No, dry clean only. 不可以，只能乾洗。

Tips

■ Yes, but you have to use cold water. 可以，但是只能用冷水。

Yes, it cleans very easy. 可以，它很容易清洗。

I wouldn't recommend using a machine. You'd better hand-wash it. 我不建議用洗衣機洗。你最好手洗。

② 它需要乾洗嗎？

A： Do I need to dry-clean it? 它需要乾洗嗎？

B： If you don't dry clean, it will be ruined. 如果不乾洗的話，衣服會被洗壞。

Tips

Both dry clean and machine wash are OK. 乾洗和機洗都可以。

You absolutely must dry clean it. 你必須得乾洗。

It was written on the mark. 標籤上寫著呢。

③ 這需要手洗，不要放入洗衣機。

A： It needs to be hand-washed and don't put it into the washing machine. 這需要手洗，不要放入洗衣機。

B： Thank you for your reminding. 謝謝你的提醒。

Tips

It is hand-wash only. 這個必須手洗。

Does it need to be dry-cleaned? 這需要乾洗嗎？

You must hand wash it although it is troublesome. 雖然會很麻煩，但你必須手洗。

④ 這件襯衫會縮水嗎？

A： Will the shirt shrink? 這件襯衫會縮水嗎？

B： This material won't shrink when being washed. 這種材料洗後不會縮水。

Tips

It will shrink if you wash it by hot water. 如果用熱水洗就會縮水。

You can stretch it before hanging it to dry. 你可以在晾衣服之前伸展一下它。

It is shrink-proof. 這個是不會縮水的。

⑤ 我要怎麼保存這雙鞋子？

A： How do I store this pair of shoes? 我要怎麼保存這雙鞋子？

B： I suggest you putting them in a box. 我建議你把它們放入盒子。

Tips

- Just buy a shoe rack. 買個鞋架就好。
- Here are some shoe bags, you can put them in. 這有一些鞋袋，你可以把鞋放在裡面。
- You can buy some empty shoe boxes. 你可以買一些空鞋盒。

6 可以用濕布擦拭鞋子。

A： You can wipe the shoes with wet cloth. 可以用濕布擦拭鞋子。

B： Won't the leather be ruined? 這樣皮子不會被毀了嗎？

Tips

- wipe 擦拭。
- Do I need to use shoe polish? 不用鞋油嗎？
- How can I get rid of the dirt on the shoes? 我該怎樣除去鞋子上的灰塵？

7 把衣服放平，不要掛在衣架上。

A： Put it somewhere flat and don't use a hanger. 把衣服放平，不要掛在衣架上。

B： It is better to fold them and put them into the wardrobe. 把它們疊起來放在衣櫃裡比較好。

Tips

- hanger 衣架。
- Do I need to lay something on the top of it to flatten it? 需不需要在上面放點東西來把它們壓平？
- Putting your clothes in a compressing bag can save room. 把衣服放在壓縮袋裡可以節省空間。

Step 3　情 景 模 擬

1 洗滌方法

A： Is it machine-washable? 請問它可以用洗衣機洗嗎？

B： It needs to be hand-washed. Don't put it into the washing machine. 這需要手洗，不要放入洗衣機。

A： Or it would be ruined, right? 否則就洗壞了，對嗎？

B： Yes, because it is 100% silk. 是的，因為這是 100% 真絲的。

A：But it is troublesome to wash it by hand every time. 可是每次都用手洗太麻煩了。

B：You have to hand-wash it if you really like it. 如果你真的喜歡這件衣服就必須手洗。

② 防止縮水

A：Will the shirt shrink? 這件襯衫會縮水嗎？

B：It will if you use hot water. 如果用熱水洗就會縮水。

A：So it isn't made of water-proof materials? 所以這不是用防縮水材料製作的？

B：To be frank, woolen is easy to shrink. 說實話，羊毛很容易縮水。

A：OK, I'll take it. 好吧，我就買這件。

B：It'll be OK as long as you are careful enough. 只要你足夠小心，就沒問題。

③ 清潔鞋子

A：How to polish this pair of shoes? 怎麼擦拭這雙鞋？

B：You can wipe the shoes with wet cloth. 可以用濕布擦拭鞋子。

A：Is it OK to put them under running water? 把它們放在水龍頭底下沖洗可以嗎？

B：Since it is made of rubber, it would be OK. 因為是橡膠製作的，所以沒問題。

A：Do you have a brush? I want to get rid of the mud. 你有刷子嗎？我要把這些泥弄掉。

B：Yes, here it is. 有，給你。

Scene 42　購買結帳

Step 1　必備表達

分期付款	installment：pay by installment 採取分期付款的方式。
收銀台	cashier desk：也可以用 checkout counter 來代替。
收銀機	cash register：結帳時收銀員操作的「收銀機」也可以用 cash machine 表示。
簽名	signature：結帳時如果刷卡，需要在單據上簽名。而「簽名」的動作可以用 sign one's name 表示。
現金	cash：「以現金結帳」要用固定搭配 in cash 表示。
POS 機	POS machine：POS 就是 point-of-sale「銷售點」的縮寫。
收據	receipt：return receipt 回執。
發票	invoice：make out an invoice 開發票。
密碼	password：password protection 密碼保護。
優惠券	coupon：gift coupon 贈券，獎券；也可以用 voucher 表示「禮券」。
把（售貨金額）	ring up：ring up the sale on… 將銷售記錄錄入到……中錄入機器。

Step 2　句句精彩

① 您怎麼付帳？

A：How will you pay for this? 您怎麼付帳？

B：I'll pay in cash. 我用現金付款。

Tips

■ Cash, credit card or charge? 現金，刷卡還是記帳？

■ Do you accept credit card? 能刷信用卡嗎？

■ How about traveler's checks? 旅行支票可以嗎？

② 我要按三個月分期付款。

A： I'll pay on a three-month installment plan. 我要按三個月分期付款。

B： That's subject to credit approval. 那需要信貸審批。

Tips

Do you have credit card of the following banks? 你有下面這些銀行的信用卡嗎？

You can't pay by installment here. 這裡不支持分期付款。

③ 我可以刷卡嗎？

A： Do you accept credit cards? 我可以刷卡嗎？

B： We accept Visa and MasterCard. 我們接受 Visa 信用卡和 Master 信用卡。

Tips

We accept all kinds of credit cards. 我們接受各種信用卡。

I'm not sure whether we can accept this card. 我不確定我們能否接受這種卡。

We only take debit cards. 我們只接受金融卡。

④ 你找的錢不對。

A： You haven't given me the right change. 你找的錢不對。

B： Oh, I'm sorry about that. 哦，不好意思。

Tips

Check it again, please. 請您再核對一遍。

■ There is a mistake on the receipt. 收據上有個錯誤。

You can keep the change. 不用找錢了。

⑤ 請給我一張收據好嗎？

A： May I have a receipt? 請給我一張收據，好嗎？

B： The receipt is in the bag. 收據已經在袋子裡了。

Tips

Please give me an invoice. 請給我一張發票。

I have to change the tape on my register. Please wait a minute. 我需要換一下收銀機上的紙帶，請稍等一分鐘。

Here is the receipt. 給你收據。

6 紙袋還是塑膠袋？

A： Paper or plastic bag? 紙袋還是塑膠袋？

B： Paper bag, please. 請給我紙袋。

Tips

■ I've brought a shop bag myself. 我自己帶購物袋了。

■ I have an environment-friendly bag. 我有一個環保袋。

■ Please give me a reusable bag. 請給我一個可以重複利用的袋子。

7 請輸入您的密碼。

A： Input your pin number, please. 請輸入您的密碼。

B： The card has no pin number. 這張卡沒有密碼。

Tips

■ pin 是 personal identification number 的意思，即「個人識別碼」。

■ Which button should I press next? 我接下來該按什麼鍵？

■ I can't remember my passport. 我不記得密碼了。

Step 3　情 景 模 擬

1 付款方式

A： How will you pay for this? 您怎麼付帳？

B： Can I pay by installments? 我可以分期付款嗎？

A： No, it is not acceptable. 不行，我們不接受分期付款。

B： Do you accept credit card? 能刷信用卡嗎？

A： Yes, sir. Please show me your card. 可以，先生。請出示你的卡。

B： Here you are. 給你。

2 分期付款

A： I'll pay on a three-month installment plan. 我要按三個月分期付款。

B： Do you have a credit card of these banks? 您有這些銀行的信用卡嗎？

A： Yeah, I have a visa card. 有，我有 visa 卡。

B： OK. The products are 90 dollars in total, and you need to pay 30 dollars monthly.

好的。商品是 90 美元，您每個月需要付 30 美元。

A： Do I need to pay any extra fees? 我需要付額外費用嗎？

B： No. This price is already a little higher than the regular one. 不需要。這個價錢已經比普通的價格高一些了。

③ 請開收據

A： May I have a receipt? 請給我一張收據好嗎？

B： Sure. No problem. 好的，沒問題。

B： I have to change the tape on my register first. Please wait a moment. 我需要換一下收銀機上的紙帶，請等一會兒。

A： What should I do if I also need an invoice? 如果我還需要發票，該怎麼辦？

B： You can bring the receipt to the service counter, and they will make out the invoice for you. Here is the receipt. 你可以把收據帶到服務台，他們會給您開發票。 給你收據。

Scene 43　缺貨與訂貨

Step 1　必備表達

有貨	in stock：stock 庫存，存貨。
缺貨	out of stock：out of 缺少；out of stock 是 in stock 的反義詞。
分店	sub branch：branch 分支。
訂貨	order goods：order 訂購；place an order「下單」。
存貨	inventory：inventory level 庫存量。
運費	freight charge：freight 運費；「免運費」可以用 free shipping 來表達，注意包含 ship 的 shipping 並不是專指海運，而包含 car 的 cargo 卻是指「海運貨船」。
訂單	order form：purchase order 也表示「訂單」。
交貨	delivery：delivery service 送貨服務。
訂金	deposit：作名詞可以指「保證金 押金」，作動詞表示「預付定金，交押金」。
預付	payment in advance：類似的 cash on delivery 表示「貨到付款」。

Step 2　句句精彩

① 恐怕這種鞋子已經賣完了。

A：I'm afraid this kind of shoes is out of stock. 恐怕這種鞋子已經賣完了。

B：What a pity. I really love this kind of shoes. 真可惜。我真的很喜歡這種鞋子。

Tips

■ We are out of this shirt in this color. 這種顏色的這款襯衫都賣完了。

■ Do you have anything like these? 有類似款式的嗎？

■ When will it be in stock again? 什麼時候能再有貨？

② 你們還會再進貨嗎？

A： Will you get any more in? 你們還會再進貨嗎？

B： We will have a batch of new products this Friday. 週五會有一批新貨送到。

Tips

I'm afraid that we won't because these were clearance items. 恐怕不會了，因為那些是清倉商品。

Let me check in the storeroom. 我來查看一下庫房是否還有貨。

These are limited edition. 它們是限量款。

③ 我會打電話給另一家分店，看那裡是否有貨。

A： Do you have a bigger one? This one is too tight. 你們有大一號的嗎？這個太緊了。

B： We don't have. I will call another sub branch to see if it's available there. 我們沒有了。我會打電話給另一家分店，看那裡是否有貨。

Tips

Can you check the other branches? 你能查一下其他分店嗎？

We can have it shipped here or you can pick it up there. 他們可以郵寄過來，或者你可以去那邊取。

■ They're sold out everywhere. 所有店鋪都沒貨了。

④ 我想要下單訂購。

A： I want to place an order. 我想要下單訂購。

B： OK, we will inform you when the product you want is here. 好的，等您要的產品送來時，我們會通知您。

Tips

place an order 訂購，下單。

What should I do if you want to order this one? 我該如何訂購這個？

Please leave your personal information if you want to order this. 如果想訂購這個商品，請留下您的個人資訊。

⑤ 這些書還有存貨嗎？

A： Do you have books in stock? 這些書還有存貨嗎？

B： Yes. But it may not be adequate since it is not a popular book. 有。但由於這不是一本暢銷書，我們的存貨可能並不充足。

Tips

■ We still have some on the shelves near the aisle. 靠近走道的書架上還有一些存貨。

■ We still have one in the storeroom. 在庫房裡還有一些。

6 包含運費一共是 100 美元。

A：With shipping charge, your total will be 100 dollars. 包含運費一共是 100 美元。

B：The shipment fee is too high. 運費太高了。

Tips

■ shipping charge 相當於 freight charge，即「運費」。

■ How long will it take to arrive in my country? 要多久才能到我的國家？

■ Will you offer free shipping? 你能包郵嗎？

7 我該付多少錢的訂金？

A：How much deposit should I pay for? 我該付多少錢的訂金？

B：It will be $5. 5 美元。

Tips

■ It's a nonrefundable $500 deposit. 押金 500 美元而且不能退還。

■ I can hold it for a few days for you without deposit. 我可以為你保留幾天，不需要押金。

■ Do I need to deposit it? 我需要為其付押金嗎？

Step 3　情景模擬

1 商品售完

A：I'm afraid this kind of shoes is out of stock. 這種鞋子恐怕已經賣完了。

B：I really want them though. 但是我真的很想要。

A：Yeah, they are very popular. 是啊，這種鞋非常受歡迎。

B：Will you get any more in? 你們還會再進貨嗎？

A：The goods we ordered would be here this Friday. You can come and have a look then. 我們訂的貨會在週五送到。你到時候可以過來看看。

B：Good. I will come again on Friday. 好的。我週五會再來。

② 訂購商品

A： This shirt is really cute. Can I try it on? 這件襯衫真好看。我能試穿一下嗎？

B： I am sorry. It is for presale. 不好意思，這是預售的。

A： I want to place an order.Could you send it to Canada? 我想要下單訂購。你們能把它寄到加拿大嗎？

B： OK. What size do you want? 可以。你想要什麼尺碼？

A： Size M. M 號。

B： Please write your detailed information here. 請把您的詳細資訊寫在這裡。

③ 運費

A： How much is it altogether? 一共多少錢？

B： 包含運費一共是 100 美元。 With shipping charge, your total will be 100 dollars.

A： Wow, I don't know the shipment fee is so high. 哇，我沒想到郵費這麼高。

B： A little bit. But the item is quite heavy. 是有點貴。但這個物品確實很重。

A： Yeah. And could you please wrap it up carefully since it is fragile? 是啊。那你們能把它仔細包裹起來嗎？這很容易碎。

B： No problem. 沒問題。

Scene 44　換貨退貨

Step 1　必備表達

退貨	return of goods：return 返回，歸還。
瑕疵	defective：defective goods 瑕疵品，不合格品。
打折商品	on sale item：類似的 fire sale 可以指「大拍賣」。
賠償費	damages：claim damages 要求賠償。
保修期	warranty period：quality guarantee period 保固期。
顧客服務部	customer service department：after-sale service department 售後服務部。
退貨期限	return period：in period 在週期內。
換貨	exchange goods：exchange 交換，兌換。
全額退款	get a full refund：refund 退款，退還。
提出投訴	make a complaint：如果對產品品質不滿，可以投訴。complaint 可以表示「投訴」，其動詞形式是 complain。

Step 2　句句精彩

① 我想退掉這個。

A：I'd like to return this. 我想退掉這個。

B：Is there any problem with it? 這個有什麼問題嗎？

Tips

■ Sorry. It is not refundable. 對不起，這個不能退。

■ Did you cut off the label? 你剪標籤了嗎？

■ Did you keep the receipt? 你保留收據了嗎？

② 我買的裙子太小了，可以換大一點的嗎？

A：The skirt I bought is too small for me; can I change for a larger one? 我買的裙子

太小了，可以換大一點的嗎？

B： Yes, you can. Did you bring it here? 可以，你可以換。裙子帶來了嗎？

Tips

　This is the largest size we have. 這是我們的最大號了。

　We already sold out this skirt. 這款裙子已經售光了。

　We don't have larger ones in stock. 大一碼的沒貨了。

③ 我想要退款。

A： I would like to get a refund. 我想要退款。

B： May I know the reason? 我能知道原因嗎？

Tips

　I want to get my money back. 我想要退款。

　You can apply for refund on Internet first. 你可以先在網上申請退款。

　Sure. Can you give me your invoice? 好的。能把發票給我嗎？

④ 減價商品不退不換。

A： Things on sale are not allowed to be refunded or changed. 減價商品不退不換。

B： But you did not inform me in advance. 但是你們之前沒有說過。

Tips

　This is a defective product. 這個是瑕疵品。

　What if it is not suitable? 如果不合適怎麼辦？

⑤ 如果你把它弄壞了就需要付賠償金。

A： You will have to be charged for the damage if you break it. 如果你把它弄壞了，就需要付賠償金。

B： But I'm not intentional. 可我不是故意的。

Tips

　I didn't even touch it. 我都沒有碰它。

　I broke it accidentally. 我是不小心弄壞的。

⑥ 這次可以例外嗎？

A： Can you make an exception? 這次可以例外嗎？

B： Sorry, the rules are the rules. 對不起，規定就是規定。

Tips

■ make an exception 破例，例外。

■ OK, but this time only. 好吧，但僅此一次。

■ I can't violate the regulations. 我不能違反規定。

⑦ 如果它有問題可以退貨。

A： It can be refundable if there is something wrong with it. 如果它有問題，就可以退貨。

B： Within how many days can I return it? 幾天之內可以退貨？

Tips

■ refundable 可退還的，可退款的。

■ Should I bring the receipt with me if I want to return it? 如果我想退貨，需要帶收據來嗎？

■ Can I mail it to you if there is any problem since I am leaving tomorrow? 如果有問題，我能寄給你嗎？因為我明天就要離開這裡了。

Step 3　情 景 模 擬

① 退貨

A： I'd like to return this. 我想退掉這個。

B： Is there anything wrong with it? 這個有什麼問題嗎？

A： I bought it for my father but I'm afraid he doesn't like it. 這個是給我父親買的，但我怕他不喜歡。

B： We do have it in different colors. You can change to another one if you want. 我們還有別的顏色的。如果你願意可以更換。

A： No. Thanks. 不用了，謝謝。

B： OK. Please give me the shirt. 好的，請把襯衫給我吧。

② 換尺碼

A： The skirt I bought is too small for me; can I change for a larger one? 我買的裙子尺碼太小了，可以換大一點的嗎？

B： We don't have larger ones in stock. 尺碼大一些的沒貨了。

A： Can you check the other stores? 你能查一下其他店嗎？

B：Sure. Wow, there is one in another store. We can ask them to mail it to us. 好的。喔，另一家店有一件。可以讓他們幫我們寄過來。

A： When will it arrive at here? 什麼時候能到你們店呢？

B： Tomorrow afternoon. 明天下午。

③ 例外情況

A：Can I return this mug? My friend bought me a same one. 我能退掉這個馬克杯嗎？我朋友給我買了一個一模一樣的。

B： Sorry, it is not refundable. 抱歉，這個是不能退的。

A： Can you make an exception? 這次可以例外嗎？

B： I'm sorry, I'm afraid not. 抱歉，恐怕不能。

A： Well, can I change for a different one? 嗯，那我能換個不一樣的嗎？

B： OK, but this time only. 好吧，但僅此一次啊。

Scene 45　退税免税

Step 1　必備表達

退税	tax rebate：也可以用 refund 代替 rebate。
免税商品	duty-free item：duty-free 是「免税」的意思，常見搭配還有：dutyfree shop 免税店。
划算	cost-effective：effective 有效地，實際的。
免税限額	tax-free limit：如果你購買的免税品超過了限額，則需要繳納關税。
退税單	tax refund form：退税單是退税的憑證。如果沒有填寫退税單，則無法退税。
退還	reimbursement：apply for reimbursement 申請報銷。
申請退税	claim for tax refund：claim for 申請。
税務部門	department of taxation：相關的「税務局」是 tax bureau。
合乎退税標準	qualified for a refund：qualified 合格的，有資格的。
管道	channel：marketing channel 銷售管道。

Step 2　句句精彩

① 在免税店買東西真划算。

A：It's a great deal to make a purchase in the duty-free shop. 在免税店買東西真划算。

B：Yes. It is much cheaper than other places. 是的，比別的地方便宜很多。

Tips

■ a great deal 划算

■ It is half of what you pay. 價錢便宜一半。

■ But your total expenditure cannot be over 300 dollars. 但是你的總消費不能超過 300 美元。

■ It is sure that all the commodities in the duty-free shop are genuine. 可以確定免税店裡的化妝品都是正品。

194

② 請問我購買免稅酒的限額是多少？

A： What's my duty-free wine allowance? 請問我購買免稅酒的限額是多少？

B： They cannot be over 4500ml. 不能超過 4500 毫升。

Tips

allowance 允許，限額。

And the limit cigarettes are 400. 香菸限量 400 支。

③ 我要買多少才能退稅？

A： How much do I have to spend to get the tax refund? 我要買多少才能退稅？

B： You have to spend at least 150 euros to get it. 你至少要消費 150 歐元才能退稅。

Tips

各個國家對退稅金額有不同的規定。若達到了各國退稅標準所規定的最低消費金額，方可退稅。

As long as you spend 90 euros here, you can get tax refund. 只要滿 90 歐元就可以辦理退稅。

How much refund will I get? 請問能拿到多少退稅款？

④ 請問我該如何辦理退稅？

A： What can I do to get the tax refund? 我該如何辦理退稅？

B： Fill out this form, and you can get the refund at the customs. 填好這張表格，這樣你可以到海關領取退稅。

Tips

You have to fill in this form first with your specific address and your passport number. 你需要先在這張表格上填寫詳細位址和護照號碼。

All the goods you bought have to be listed on the tax refund form. 你購買的所有商品必須列在退稅單上。

When you leave the country, you have to show the tax refund invoice to the customs and get a stamp on it. 當你離開該國時，你需要把退稅發票出示給海關查看並蓋章。

⑤ 您想以何種方式得到這筆錢？

A： How would you like to receive the money? 您想以何種方式得到這筆錢？

B： I would like to receive it in cash. 我想要現金。

Tips

■ Will you pay for the money into my credit card account? 你們會把錢打到我的信用卡帳戶上嗎？

■ How would you like to receive this, by check or into your bank account? 您需要我們寄支票還是轉帳給您？

⑥ 我還沒有收到退稅款。

A：I have not yet received the tax refund. 我還沒有收到退稅款。

B：May I have your name and passport number? 能告訴我你的名字和護照號碼嗎？

Tips

■ Which way did you choose to get the tax refund? 你是選擇哪種方式退稅的？

■ Have you checked your account? 你查過你的帳戶嗎？

■ We are still in process, so please wait for another few days. 我們仍在走程式 請再稍等幾天。

⑦ 只要您合乎退稅標準，我們會馬上退錢給您。

A：How long do I have to wait for the refund? 我要多久才能收到退款？

B：We will return your money at once if you are eligible for refund. 只要您合乎退稅標準，我們會馬上退錢給您。

Tips

■ eligible 合格者，適任者。

■ What should I offer to get the refund? 要得到退稅款，我需要提供什麼？

Step 3　情景模擬

① 免稅限額

A：What's my duty-free wine allowance? 請問我購買免稅酒的限額是多少？

B：You can buy at most 4,500ml. 最多可以買 4500 毫升。

A：What if I buy more than 4,500ml? 如果我買了超過 4500 毫升的酒呢？

B：You have to pay the tax at the customs. 你需要在海關交稅。

A：How can I buy more? 我怎麼才能多買些？

B：You can ask your friends to buy for you. 你可以讓你的朋友幫你購買。

② 詢問如何退稅

A： What can I do to get the tax refund? 請問我該如何辦理退稅？

B： You have to fill in this form first. 你需要先填寫這張表格。

A： Should I list everything I bought here? 我需要把在這兒買的東西都寫上嗎？

B： Yes. All the goods you bought have to be listed on the tax refund form. 是的。你購買的所有商品必須記錄在退稅單上。

A： OK, I finished. 好的，我填完了。

B： When you leave the country, you have to show the tax refund invoice to the customs. 當你離開本國時，要把退稅發票出示給海關。

③ 退稅方式

A： How would you like to receive the money? 您想以何種方式得到退稅款？

B： How about paying for them into my credit card account? 把錢打到我的信用卡帳戶上怎麼樣？

A： No problem. Please write down your credit card number. 沒問題。請寫下你的信用卡卡號。

B： And how long can I receive the money? 還有，錢多久能到帳？

A： Within 3 months. 三個月內。

B： OK. Thank you. 好的，謝謝你。

Chapter

6

餐飲

Scene 46　選擇與預定餐位

Step 1　必備表達

兩人桌位	table for two：table cloth 桌布；table knife 餐刀；table salt 食用鹽。
保留桌位	hold the table：hold 持有，保留；cancel the table 取消桌位。
電話預訂	telephone reservation：reservation 預定。
客滿	no vacancy：vacancy 空缺；vacant 空閒的。
靠角落的桌位	corner table：corner 角落。
靠窗的桌位	table by the window：window blind 百葉窗。
非吸菸區桌位	non-smoking table：smoking table 吸菸區桌位。
取消預定	cancellation：cancel 取消。
最低消費	minimum charge：charge 費用；charge account 記帳。
包廂	booth：sidewalk snack booth 大排檔；private room 私人包廂。

Step 2　句句精彩

① 我想預訂張 3 人桌。

A：Hello, this is the Bata Restaurant. May I help you? 您好，Bata 餐廳。可以為您服務嗎？

B：Yes. I'd like to reserve a table for three. 是的。我想訂張三人桌。

Tips

■ I'd like to make a reservation for eight. 我想訂張八個人的桌子。

■ I want to make a reservation for eight. 我想訂張八個人的桌子。

■ I'd like to reserve a table for a group of eight. 我想訂張八個人的桌子。

② 我們可以坐靠窗的那張小桌子嗎？

A：What can I do for you? 我能為您做點什麼？

B：Can we take the small table by the window? 我們可以坐靠窗的那張小桌子嗎？

Tips

■ Could we have a table close to the band? 我們能不能要個靠近樂隊的桌位？

Could we get a table near the band? 我們能不能要個離樂隊近一點兒的桌位？

Could we have a table near the performers? 我們能不能要個離演出人員近些的桌位？

③ 這裡有便宜一點的飯店嗎？

A： I haven't been in this area before. Do you know any cheaper restaurant here? 我以前沒來過這個地方。這裡有便宜一點的飯店嗎？

B： Yes. It's just down the road. 有。就在這條街上。

Tips

Which restaurant do you suggest? 你推薦哪家餐館？

Which restaurant do you recommend? 你推薦哪家餐館？

④ 很抱歉，恐怕那個時段都訂滿了。

A： There are just three of us. Surely you must have a small table for us. 我們只有三個人。所以你得給我們找個小桌子。

B： I'm sorry. I'm afraid we don't have any tables available at that time. 很抱歉，恐怕那個時段都訂滿了。

Tips

We're all booked up tonight. 今天晚上都訂滿了。

I'm sorry. We're full tonight. 對不起，今天晚上都訂滿了。

⑤ 可以打電話預訂嗎？

A： Is it possible to make a reservation on the phone? 可以打電話預訂嗎？

B： Sure. Here is the number. 當然可以。這是電話號碼。

Tips

make a reservation 預訂；place an order 下訂單。

I'd like to book a table. 我想預定一個桌位。

I'd like to reserve a table. 我想預定一個桌位。

⑥ 這個位子你們能為我保留多久？

A： How long can you hold the table for me? 這個位子你們能為我保留多久？

B： We can only hold the table for 10 minutes. 只能保留十分鐘。

Tips

■ Will you hold our table if we are late? 如果我們遲到了，你能幫我們留桌麼？

■ Will you keep our table if we are tardy? 如果我們遲到了，你能幫我們留桌麼？

⑦ 我能取消今晚的預訂嗎？

A：I'm sorry. Can I cancel my reservation tonight? 對不起。我能取消今晚的預訂嗎？

B： That's OK, sir. What name is the reservation under? 沒關係，先生。您訂餐時用的什麼名字？

Tips

■ cancel one's reservation 取消預訂。

■ under... name 以......的名義。

■ I'm sorry, but I have to cancel my reservation. 對不起，我想取消預訂。

Step 3　情景模擬

① 預定位子

A： I'll be coming later tonight with three friends. I'd like to reserve a table for three. 今晚我要和三個朋友一起過來。我想訂張三個人的桌子。

B： Sure. When would you like to have dinner? 當然可以。您想幾點用餐？

A： About 6 o'clock. 大約六點鐘。

B： OK. 好的。

A： I know it's last minute, but I was hoping that we could get a private room. 我知道時間有點晚，但是我希望我們能訂到包間。

B： All right. There is one left. 好吧。正好還有一個。

② 預定已滿

A： Can I help you? 能為您做點什麼？

B： I'd like to book a booth for 5 people. 我想訂一個五人包間。

A： For which day, sir? 哪一天，先生？

B： Tomorrow evening, about 7 o'clock. 明天晚上，大約七點鐘。

A： I'm afraid we don't have any tables available at that time.
很抱歉，那個時段都訂滿了。

B： What time can we reserve for? 可以預定幾點的？

A： We can only fit you in at either 5:30 p.m or 8:00 p.m. 我們只能為您安排在下午五點半或者八點。

B： All right. 8 o'clock. 好吧。八點吧。

③ 推薦餐廳

A： I have to have dinner alone. Do you know any cheaper restaurant here? 我得一個人吃飯了。這裡有便宜一點的餐館嗎？

B： Yes. There is one where I usually have dinner. 是的。有一個我經常去。

A： Where is the restaurant located? 在什麼地方？

B： It's at the corner of Ontario Street and 4th Avenue.
在安大略街和第四大道的轉角處。

A： How do I get there? 我怎麼去那兒呢？

B： You can walk there. It'll take you ten minutes. 你可以步行。十分鐘就能到。

A： Thank you. 謝謝。

Scene 47 進入餐廳

Step 1 必備表達

菜單	menu：an English menu 英文菜單；menu in Japanese 日語菜單。
點餐	order：ordered 安排好的；take an order 接受訂單。
特色菜	specialty：special 特殊的。
開胃菜	appetizer：appetite 食欲。
主菜	main dish：main 主要的；main menu 主菜單。
配菜	side dish：side 次要的。
素菜	vegetarian dish：vegetarian 素食的；素食者。
甜點	dessert：dessert plate 點心碟；dessert spoon 甜點匙。
套餐	set meal：set 一套；Western buffet 西式自助餐。
挑食	be picky about food：picky 好挑剔的。

Step 2 句句精彩

① 這裡沒人坐吧？

A：Is this place vacant? 這裡沒人坐吧？

B：No. What can I do for you? 沒有。您要點什麼？

Tips

- Is this place available? 這裡有人嗎？
- I have a reservation. 我預訂了位子。
- I made a booking. 我預訂了位子。

② 請給我菜單。

A：Hello, how can I help you? 你好，來點什麼呢？

B：Could I have a menu, please? 請給我菜單。

Tips

■ May I have a look at the menu, please? 能給我看看菜單嗎？

Could I have a peek at the menu, please? 把功能表給我看一下好嗎？

Do you have a menu in Japanese? 有日語的菜單嗎？

③ 您要點菜嗎？

A： Hello and welcome to Taco Time. May I take your order? 您好，歡迎光臨 Taco Time。您要點菜嗎？

B： Yes, I'd like two beef burritos and a Sprite, please. 是的，請來兩份牛肉玉米煎餅和一杯雪碧。

Tips

take one's order 點菜。

Have you decided what you want? 決定要什麼了嗎？

What can I get for you? 您要點菜嗎？

④ 你可以準備清淡一點的菜嗎？

A： Could you fix something light? 你可以準備清淡一點的菜嗎？

B： I'll ask the chef, ma'am. Wait for a minute. 我去問問廚師，夫人。稍等一下。

Tips

light 在這裡表示「清淡的」，相當於 less spicy。

Can you make it less spicy? 能做清淡一些嗎？

This has a strong / weak flavor. 味很重／淡。

⑤ 你可以告訴我這些菜的特色嗎？

A： Can you tell me the different features of these dishes? 你可以告訴我這些菜的特色嗎？

B： Sure. 當然可以。

Tips

What's your best dish? 你們的招牌菜是什麼？

What's the house recommendation? 本店的招牌菜是什麼？

Do you have any local specialties? 您這兒有什麼地方特色菜嗎？

6 您要再點些配菜嗎？

A： Would you like some more side dishes? 您要再點些配菜嗎？

B： Nope. That's it. 不要了。就這些吧。

Tips

■ Will that be all? 就要這些嗎？

■ Anything else you want? 別的還要嗎？

■ That's all. 夠了。

7 牛排的配菜是什麼？

A： What else can I do for you? 還需要其他的嗎？

B： What comes with the steak? 牛排的配菜是什麼？

Tips

■ How would you like it cooked/grilled/done? 要幾成熟的？

■ Well-done, please. 全熟的。

■ Rare. 三成熟。

■ Medium. 五成熟。

Step 3　情景模擬

1 進入飯店

A： Is this place vacant? 這裡沒人吧？

B： Yes. What can I do for you? 是的。您有什麼需要？

A： We have a reservation under the name of John Miller. 我們以 John Miller 的名字訂了位子。

B： Let me check. Yes. This way, please. Here's your table. Will it do? 讓我看看。是的。請走這邊。這是您的桌子。行嗎？

A： Actually, I'd prefer one in the corner if you don't mind. Can I sit there? 事實上，如果你不介意的話，我更喜歡角落裡的位子。我能坐在那兒麼？

B： All right. 好的。

A： Thank you. 謝謝。

② 準備點菜

A： Are you ready to order? 可以點菜了嗎？

B： I haven't figured out what I want yet. We need a couple of minutes to decide. 我還沒想好點什麼菜呢。我們要等一會兒再點。

(A moment later) （片刻過後）

B： Waiter, we are ready to order now. 服務員，我們準備點菜了。

A： Yes. 好的。

B： Could I have a menu, please? 請給我菜單。

A： Sure. Just to let you know, our potato soup is on sale today. 當然。我想告訴您，今天我們的馬鈴薯湯優惠。

B： Great. Give me one. 太好了。點一個。

③ 介紹特色

A： May I tell you our specialties? Here are all the special dishes. 我能為您推薦我們的特色菜嗎？這是所有的特色菜。

B： Can you tell me the different features of these dishes? 你可以告訴我這些菜的特色嗎？

A： The lamb chops are excellent. It's very special. You can taste it. 羊排很好吃。味道很特別。您可以嘗嘗。

B： Anything else? 還有其他的嗎？

A： Today we are serving stuffed turkey on Italian wheat bread with a side of Caesar. 今天我們特供填製的火雞，配搭凱薩醬的義大利小麥麵包。

Scene 48　用餐中

Step 1　必備表達

餐具	tableware：disinfected tableware 消毒餐具；ceramic tableware 陶瓷餐具。
弄灑了酒	spill wine：spill out 灑出，溢出；spill over 溢出。
變壞	spoil：spoiled 變質的。
生的	raw：raw material 原料；raw sugar 粗糖。
肉老的	tough：相反，「肉嫩的」則是 tender。
沒味道	tasteless：taste 味道；biting taste 辛辣味；harsh taste 澀味；taste sensation 味覺；taster 品嘗員；tasty 美味的；tastily 美味地。
餐巾紙	napkin：napkin paper 餐巾紙；napkin tissues 餐巾薄紙。
趕時間	pressed for time：在形容「匆忙，著急」時，還可以用 in a hurry。
美味的	yummy：還可以表示為 delicious。
道歉	apologize：在表示「因為……道歉」時，可以用 apologize for...。

Step 2　句句精彩

① 我點的菜還沒來。

A：My order hasn't come yet. We are pressed for time. Please hurry. 我點的菜還沒來。我們趕時間，請快點。

B：OK. I will ask them to be quicker. 好的。我讓他們快點。

Tips

■ I'm still waiting for my food. 我點的菜還沒上。

■ Where are our dishes? 我們的菜怎麼還沒來啊？

② 這個肉還是生的。

A： Waiter, this meat is still raw. 服務員，這個肉還是生的。

B： Oh, I apologize for that. We'll give you a 50% discount. 哦，真對不起。我們給您打五折。

> **Tips**
>
> discount 折扣；20 percent discount 八折優惠。
>
> This dish is too greasy. 這道菜太油了。
>
> ■ This meat is tough. 這肉太老。

③ 我們可以把酒換成熱茶嗎？

A： Could I have hot tea instead of wine? I get drunk easily. 我們可以把葡萄酒換成熱茶嗎？我酒量小。

B： Sure. 當然可以。

> **Tips**
>
> get drunk 喝醉；tipsy 喝醉的；intoxicated 喝醉的。
>
> I can't handle alcohol very well. 我酒量小。
>
> I'd like another cup of coffee. 再要一杯咖啡。

④ 非常不好意思，我把牛奶打翻了，弄得整張桌子都是。

A： I'm terribly sorry. I spilled milk all over the table. 非常不好意思，我把牛奶打翻了，弄得整張桌子都是。

B： It doesn't matter. We'll deal with it. 沒關係。我們來處理。

> **Tips**
>
> ■ spill 打翻。
>
> This tastes strange. 味道很怪。
>
> Please clean up our table. 請幫我們清理桌子。

⑤ 能再給我張餐巾紙嗎？

A： Can you get me another napkin? 能再給我張餐巾紙嗎？

B： Sure. Here you are. 當然可以。給您。

> **Tips**
>
> Just get me a napkin. My mouth's watering! 給我拿張紙巾吧，我的口水都要流出來了。

■ Get me a napkin. This food looks delicious! 給我張紙巾吧，這食物看起來真好吃。

■ Get me a napkin. I'm drooling! 給我張紙巾吧，我都流口水了。

⑥ 這個十分美味！

A：Here's your veal chops. 這是您要的小牛排。

B：It's quite yummy! 這個十分美味！

Tips

■ This looks great! 看上去真好吃！

■ They all look so delicious. 它們看上去都好吃。

■ All the dishes look yummy. 所有的菜看上去都好吃。

⑦ 能把胡椒遞給我嗎？

A：Could you pass me the pepper? 能把胡椒遞給我嗎？

B：Here you are. 給您。

Tips

■ Hand me the pepper, please. 請把胡椒遞給我。

■ Please pass me the salt. 請把鹽遞給我。

■ Could I have the salt, please? 請把鹽遞給我，好嗎？

Step 3　情 景 模 擬

① 上菜太慢

A：Can I get you something, ma'am? 夫人，我能為您提供什麼幫助？

B：My order hasn't come yet. I'm extremely hungry. 我點的菜還沒來。我都快餓死了。

A：I'm sorry; I'll ask them to be quick. 很抱歉，我會讓他們快點的。

B：OK. We're really hungry. 好的，我們真的很餓。

A：The restaurant is really busy right now. We'll do our best. 現在餐館裡很忙。我們會盡力。

B：Thank you. 謝謝。

② 菜品問題

A： What's the problem? 怎麼了？

B： This meat is still raw. 這個肉還是生的。

A： Sorry. I will change one for you. 對不起。我給您換一份。

B： By the way, could I have hot tea instead of wine? I can't handle alcohol very well.
   順便問一句，我們可以把葡萄酒換成熱茶嗎？我酒量小。

A： No problem. 沒問題。

B： Thank you. 謝謝。

③ 美味佳餚

A： Shall I give you some of this dish? 我幫你夾點菜好嗎？

B： Oh, that would be very kind of you. 噢，你真是太好了。

A： Do you ever eat sweet and sour spareribs? 你有沒有吃過糖醋排骨？

B： Never. 沒有。

A： I know you can't eat spicy food. Is this flavor suitable for you? 我知道你不能吃辣
   的。這道菜合你的胃口嗎？

B： It's quite yummy! 這個十分美味！

Scene 49　用餐後

Step 1　必備表達

打包	pack：bulk pack 散裝；pack up 把……打包。
打烊	close：be close to 接近……；bring to a close 結束；close down 關閉；close the door on 拒之門外。
打嗝	burp：還可以用 belch、eruct、bubble 等來代替。
分開付帳	separate check：separate 分開；separation 分開；隔開；treat 請客。
服務費	service charge：service 服務；give good service 服務周到。
小費	gratuity：還可以用 tip 來代替。
吃飽	be stuffed: stuff 填塞，填滿；stuff with 用……塞滿；eat one's fill, be full 也可表達「吃飽」。
用餐愉快	enjoy the meal：也可用 have a good time 來代替。
滿意的	satisfied：satisfy 使滿意，be satisfied with 對……感到滿意。
打包袋	doggie bag：doggie 小狗，美國俗語裡「打包袋」的直譯就是「狗袋」。因為美國人以前外出吃飯，不好意思說要把剩下的食物帶回家吃，就說帶回去給家裡的狗。

Step 2　句句精彩

① 請給我一個打包袋，行嗎？

A：Could you give me a doggie bag, please? 請給我一個打包袋，行嗎？

B：OK. Here you are. 好的。給您。

Tips

■ Could you pack this up, please? 請將這個打包，行嗎？

■ Could you doggy bag this? 請將這個打包，行嗎？

■ I'd like to take the leftovers home. 我想把剩下的菜打包帶走。

② 總共多少錢？

A： Check, please. How much is it in total? 結帳。總共多少錢？

B： Fifty dollars. 五十美元。

Tips

Bill, please. 結帳。

I'd like to check please. 結帳。

I'll pay for drinks. 我來付飲料的錢。

③ 這次我來付。

A： You pay all the time and I feel bad. Let me pay this time. 總是你付錢，我覺得不好意思。這次我來付。

B： OK. It's very nice of you. 好的，你真好。

Tips

■ Let's divide the cost. 我們分開付款。

Could we have separate checks? 我們可以分開付款嗎？

Could we have our own checks? 我們可以各付各的嗎？

④ 恐怕你多收錢了。

A： I'm afraid you have overcharged me. 恐怕你多收了錢。

B： Oh, let me double check the bill. 哦，我再算一下。

Tips

overcharge 對……索價過高

I'm afraid this isn't correct. 恐怕這兒算錯了。

I'm afraid there is a mistake here. 恐怕得這兒算錯了。

⑤ 我不明白帳單上這五美元是什麼費用。

A： I don't understand what this extra $5 is for. 我不明白帳單上這五美元是什麼費用。

B： It's the charge for paper tissue. 這是餐巾紙的錢。

Tips

The price is not reasonable. 價格不合理。

The price is unfair. 價格不公道。

The price is unmerited. 價格不合適。

213

⑥ 包括服務費了嗎？

A： Is the service charge included? 包括服務費了嗎？

B： Yes. All the charge is included. 是的。所有的費用都包括在內了。

Tips

■ Is tax included in the price? 這個價格含稅嗎？

■ Does the bill include the tip? 帳單包含小費嗎？

Step 3 情景模擬

① 打包服務

A： That was tasty. Could you give me a doggie bag, please? I want to wrap this up. 那個很好吃。請給我一個打包袋，行嗎？我想打包。

B： OK, I'll pack it up for you and bring you the bill. 好的，我去給你裝起來，然後把帳單拿來。

A： Thank you. 謝謝。

B： Did you have a good time here? 您用餐愉快嗎？

A： Yes. The special dishes are very delicious. 是的。特色菜很好吃。

B： We hope that you can come next time. 期待您下次光臨。

② 辦理結帳

A： Would you like any dessert? 要甜點嗎？

B： No dessert. Just a check, please. How much is it in total? 不要甜點了，請結帳。總共多少錢？

A： That's $42.24. 一共 42.24 美元。

B： Here's $45. Keep the change. 這是 45 美元。不用找錢了。

A： Thank you. 謝謝。

B： And may I have an invoice, please? 請開張發票。

③ 請客

A： How much is the bill? 多少錢？

B： Oh, don't worry. It's on me. 噢，不要擔心。我請客。

A：You always pay all the money. Let me pay this time. 總是你付錢。這次我來付吧。

B： Thank you. It's very nice of you. 謝謝，你真好。

A： Err... I don't have enough cash on me. Do you accept personal checks? 呃……我現金不夠。你們接受個人支票嗎？

C： I'm sorry, we don't. We accept debit and credit cards. 對不起，我們不接受。我們接受簽帳金融卡和信用卡。

A： OK. Here is the credit card. 好的。給您信用卡。

Scene 50 速食店

Step 1 必備表達

雞塊	chicken nuggets：nugget 塊；a nugget of food 一小塊食物。
炸薯條	French fries：chip 薯片。
在店內就餐	dine in：dine-in only 僅限店內就餐；dine 用餐；dine and wine 吃喝；dine together 聚餐。
帶走	take out：takeout 外帶。
番茄醬	ketchup：tomato ketchup 番茄醬；prawns with ketchup 茄汁蝦。
三明治	sandwich：cheese sandwich 乳酪三明治；chicken sandwich 雞肉三明治；ham sandwich 火腿三明治；omelet sandwich 炒蛋三明治；sandwich biscuit 夾心餅乾。
奶昔	milk shake：sundae 聖代。
洋蔥圈	onion rings：onion 洋蔥；onion green 青蔥；onion soup 洋蔥湯；donut 炸麵圈，甜甜圈。
續杯	refill：fill 裝滿；fill up 裝滿。
套餐	combo：也可用 combo meals 代替。

Step 2 句句精彩

① 我要一個牛肉漢堡。

A：What can I get for you today? 今天您要什麼？

B：I'd like a beef-burger, please. 我要一個牛肉漢堡。

Tips

■ Can I have two hotdogs, please? 請給我兩個熱狗。

■ May I have two wieners, please? 請給我兩根小香腸。

■ I'd like a hamburger and an iced tea. 我要一個漢堡和一杯冰茶。

② 一杯奶昔帶走。

A： So, what can I get for you? 那麼，您需要什麼？

B： A milk shake to go, please. 一杯奶昔帶走。

Tips

...to go 外帶；其他還有 take out, carryout, take away 等。

Um, I'd like a cup of coffee to go, please. 呃，一杯外帶咖啡。

③ 在這吃還是帶走？

A： Will that be for here or to go? 在這吃還是帶走？

B： I'd like it to go please. 我要帶走。

Tips

Will you be dining in or taking it away? 在這兒吃還是帶走？

How long do we need to wait for the carryout? 外帶要等多久？

I'd like to place an order for takeout. Is it possible to pick it up in half an hour? 我要點外帶，半小時後去拿可以嗎？

④ 你們的送餐服務怎麼收費？

A： How much do you charge for your delivery service? 你們的送餐服務怎麼收費？

B： 5 dollars once. 一次五美元。

Tips

■ Do you offer delivery service? 你們提供送餐服務嗎？

Can I have a second helping? 請再給我一份行嗎？

⑤ 我要外帶一大包薯條和一大杯可樂。

A： What would you like? 您要點什麼？

B： One large French fries and one Coke to go, please. 我要外帶一大包薯條和一大杯可樂。

Tips

I want a burger with an iced tea. 我想要一個漢堡和一杯冰茶。

Give me a burger with an iced tea. 給我來一個漢堡和一杯冰茶。

⑥ 我想要一份兒童套餐，帶走。

A：What do you want, sir? 先生，您要點什麼？

B：I want to have a kid's meal to go, please. 我想要一份兒童套餐，帶走。

Tips

■ kid's meal 兒童餐；family meal 全家桶。

■ I'd like to have dinner for less than thirty dollars including drinks. 我要一份 30 美元以內帶飲料的晚餐。

⑦ 這裡最受歡迎的套餐是什麼呢？

A：What's the most popular set meal here? 這裡最受歡迎的套餐是什麼呢？

B：kid's meal. 兒童套餐。

Tips

■ 通常看著圖片就知道幾號是什麼套餐，因此點套餐時只要說 Combo number one，或是 number one 就好了。有時店員會問 Do you want to go large? 如果你需要，他會給你大份薯條和可樂。

■ Is coffee included in this meal? 套餐裡包括咖啡嗎？

■ Would you like to order a meal or à la carte? 您要點套餐還是單點？

Step 3　情景模擬

① 點餐

A：What can I get for you today? 今天要吃點什麼？

B：I'd like a beef-burger, please. 我要一個牛肉漢堡。

A：Would you like fries to go with that? 要不要薯條？

B：Yes, and one Sprite. 要，再要一杯雪碧。

A：Do you want to go large? 加大嗎？

B：Yes, please. Thank you. 是的。謝謝。

② 外帶

A：Here is your order. Is that all? 這是您點的餐。就這些嗎？

B：Yes. That's it. 是的。就這些吧。

A： Will that be for here or to go? 在這吃還是帶走？

B： How much do you charge for your delivery service? 你們的送餐服務怎麼收費？

A： Ten dollars. 十美元。

B： I'd like to place an order for takeout. 我想點外帶。

③ 兒童套餐

A： What would you like to order? 您想點什麼？

B： I want to have a kid's meal to go, please. With ketchup and mustard, please. 我想要一份兒童套餐，帶走。 請加番茄醬和芥末。

A： OK. Will that be for here or to go? 好的。在這兒吃還是帶走？

B： To go, please. 帶走。

A： Fifty five dollars. 五十五美元。

B： Here is the money. Keep the change. 給您錢。不用找錢了。

Scene 51　酒吧、咖啡廳

Step 1　必備表達

酒單	wine list：wine 葡萄酒；aging wine 陳釀葡萄酒；appetizer wine 開胃酒；barley wine 大麥酒。
特價酒	special wine：special price 特價；special discount 特別折扣。
雞尾酒	cocktail：cocktail party 雞尾酒會；cocktail set 雞尾酒具。
釀酒	brew：brewery 啤酒廠，釀酒廠；brew tea 泡茶。
不含酒精	non-alcoholic：alcoholic 含酒精的；alcoholic beverage 酒精飲料。
低咖啡因	decaf：相當於 decaffeinated coffee，decaffeinated 不含咖啡因的。
糖包	sugar pack：brown sugar 紅糖；crystal sugar 冰糖；cube sugar 方糖；fruit sugar 果糖；milk sugar 乳糖。
攪拌棒	stir stick: stir 攪拌。
生啤酒	draft beer: 也可以用 draught beer 來代替。
酒保	bartender: 即調酒師。通常在高檔飯店或酒吧裡都有調酒師，主要從事配製酒水、銷售酒水的工作。

Step 2　句句精彩

① 乾杯！

A： Bottoms up! 乾杯！

B： Cheers. 乾杯！

Tips

■ Let's make a toast! 乾杯。

■ Why don't we make a toast? 我們開一杯吧！

■ Here's to your health! 為您的健康（乾杯）！

② 你想要什麼牌子的酒？

A： What brand do you want? 你想要什麼牌子的酒？

B： I want Yanjing. 我想要燕京牌的。

Tips

What kind of beer do you have? 你們有哪種啤酒？

Do you have any foreign beers? 你們這裡有進口啤酒嗎？

③ 我想要無酒精的雞尾酒。

A： What do you want to drink? 您想要喝點什麼？

B： I want non-alcoholic cocktail. 我想要不含酒精的雞尾酒。

Tips

I'll have a diet Coke. 我喝健怡可樂。

I'll have a decaf. 我要一杯不含咖啡因的咖啡。

A cup of decaf, please. 我要一杯不含咖啡因的咖啡。

④ 您的意思是這杯飲料是免費的嗎？

A： Do you mean that this drink is on the house? 您的意思是這杯飲料是免費的嗎？

B： Yes. It's free. 是的。這是免費的。

Tips

on the house 免費，相當於 for free。

It's on me. 我來埋單。

I'm paying. 我來埋單。

⑤ 我要兩杯加冰的威士忌。

A： What would you like to drink? 您想喝點什麼？

B： I'll have a double whiskey on the rocks. 我要兩杯加冰的威士忌。

Tips

Make it a cold one. 我要冰鎮的。

I'd like it on the rocks. 我想要加冰塊的。

I'll have it on ice. 我想要加冰塊的。

⑥ 我的咖啡可以續杯嗎？

A： Can I have a refill of coffee, please? 我的咖啡可以續杯嗎？

221

B： Yes. Here you are. 可以。給您。

Tips

■ Do you charge for refills? 飲料續杯要收費嗎？

■ I'd like a large cappuccino, low-fat and decaffeinated. 我要一個大杯卡布其諾，低脂、不含咖啡因。

⑦ 我可以看一下下午茶的功能表嗎？

A： What can I do for you? 您要點什麼？

B： May I have a look at the afternoon tea menu? 我可以看一下下午茶的功能表嗎？

Tips

■ afternoon tea 下午茶；high tea 下午茶。

■ Have some snacks, please. 吃點小吃吧。

Step 3　情 景 模 擬

① 酒的品牌

A： What do you feel like doing? 你想做什麼？

B： Let's go and get a drink. 我們去喝一杯吧。

C： What would you like to drink? 你想喝點什麼？

B： I'd like to drink some beer. 我想喝點啤酒。

C： What brand do you want? 你想要什麼牌子的酒？

B： Do you have any imported beer? 你們這裡有進口啤酒嗎？

C： Yeah, we have Corona. 有，我們有可樂娜啤酒。

B： Two bottles, please. 來兩瓶。

② 飲品要求

A： Is this seat taken? 這個座位有人嗎？

B： No, go ahead. What would you like to order? 沒有，請坐。你想點什麼？

A： May I have a look at the afternoon tea menu? 我可以看一下下午茶的功能表嗎？

B： Here you go. 給您。

A： I'll have a cup of coffee, please. 我要一杯咖啡。

B： How do you like your coffee? 您想喝什麼咖啡？

A： With cream and sugar, please. 加奶和糖的。

B： OK. 好的。

③ 飲品價格

A： Here is your juice. 這是您的果汁。

B： Sorry. We didn't order this. 對不起。我們沒點這個。

A： It's free. 這是免費的。

B： Do you mean that this drink is on the house? 您的意思是這杯飲料是免費的嗎？

A： Yes. Help yourself, please. 是的。請慢用。

B： Thank you. 謝謝。

Chapter

7

突發狀況與
其他場景

Scene 52　迷路問路

Step 1　必備表達

迷路	lose one's way：lose 遺失，使迷路；還可以用 get lost 表示。
地標	landmark：mark 是「標誌，符號」，因此 landmark 這個合成詞可以表示「地標」。
方向	direction：這個詞來自 direct 徑直的，直接的。除了「方向」，direction 還有「指導」的意思。
紅綠燈	traffic lights：traffic signal 也可以表示「交通燈」。
街區	block：這個單字還有「障礙物，阻塞」的意思。
在轉角	at the corner：類似的 around the corner 也表示「在轉角處」，但還有「即將發生」的意思。
穿越馬路	cross the street：cross 在這裡是動詞，表示「橫過」的意思，派生詞 crossing 則可以表示「十字路口」。
公共廁所	public restroom：還可以用 toilet、lavatory、bathroom 表達「洗手間」這個意思。
直走	go straight on：類似的 go straight along 意為「沿著……一直往前走」。
在左／右手邊	on the left / right：類似的 turn left / right 表示「向左／右轉」。

Step 2　句句精彩

① 很抱歉打擾你，但是我覺得我迷路了。

A： Excuse me, but I've got a feeling that I'm lost. 很抱歉打擾你，但是我覺得我迷路了。

B： Don't worry. Let me help you. 別擔心。我來幫助你。

Tips

I'm sorry, but I'm lost. 對不起。我迷路了。

Can you help me? I think I'm lost. 你能幫我嗎？我覺得我迷路了。

I can't find my way. 我找不到路了。

② 不好意思，請問 ABC 飯店怎麼走？

A： Could you tell me the way to the ABC Hotel? 不好意思，請問 ABC 飯店怎麼走？

B： Sure, it's at the corner of 6th Street and Madison Street. 當然。在第六街和麥迪遜大道的轉角處。

Tips

I don't know how to get to the train station. 我不知道怎麼去火車站。

Excuse me, can I ask you where we are? 勞駕，你能告訴我現在是在哪兒嗎？

③ 你可以在地圖上指給我看嗎？

A： Could you show me on the map? 你可以在地圖上指給我看嗎？

B： Sure, let me show you. 當然，我指給你看。

Tips

Where am I on this map? 我在地圖上的什麼地方？

Could you mark it here? 你幫我標明一下好嗎？

④ 沿著這條街的左手邊走。

A： Where is the restroom? 哪裡有洗手間？

B： Just go down the street on the left. 沿著這條街的左手邊走。

Tips

Take the second road on the left and go straight on. 從左邊第二條馬路一直往前走。

It's two blocks straight ahead. You can't miss it. 過了前面兩條街，你就可以看到了。

Well, let me see. Oh, yes, it's just around the corner. 嗯，我想想看。喔，對了，就在轉角的地方。

⑤ 沿著這條街往回走大約五分鐘，就可以看到動物園。

A： Excuse me. Can you tell me the way to the zoo? 打擾一下。能告訴我去動物園怎麼走嗎？

B： Go straight back down this street for about five minutes and you'll find yourself at the zoo. 沿著這條街往回走大約五分鐘，就可以看到動物園。

Tips

■ Go that way for three blocks, then turn right. 往那裡走經過三個街區，然後向右轉。

■ Just go down this street, you won't miss it. 直接沿著這條路走，你肯定能看到。

⑥ 一直走到路的盡頭。

A： Excuse me. Can you tell me the way to the nearest supermarket? 打擾一下。您能告訴我去最近的超市怎麼走嗎？

B： Keep going until you come to the end. 一直走到路的盡頭。

Tips

■ Cross the street, and you will find the school. 穿過馬路，你就會看見學校。

■ Just go down this street, and you'll find the hotel. 沿這條路往前走，你就可以找到那家旅館。

■ Please go to the end of this road. 請走到這條馬路的盡頭。

⑦ 對不起，我對這裡也很陌生。

A： Can you tell me where the mall is? 你能告訴我購物中心在哪兒嗎？

B： Sorry, I'm a stranger here myself. 對不起，我對這裡也很陌生。

Tips

■ Sorry, I've never been here before. 對不起，我之前也沒來過這兒。

■ I'm sorry. This is my first time here. 對不起，我也是第一次來。

■ I'm afraid I don't know. 恐怕我也不知道。

Step 3 情景模擬

① 迷路

A： Excuse me, but I've got a feeling that I'm lost. 很抱歉打擾你，但是我覺得我迷路了。

B： Where are you going? 你要去哪兒？

A： I want to go to the hotel which is called ABC. 我要去一家叫做 ABC 的飯店。

B： I see. Well, do you know any landmarks near the hotel? 這樣啊。那你知道飯店附近有什麼地標嗎？

A： Oh, yes, my friend told me that it is near the Central Railway Station. 哦，有的，我朋友說是在中央火車站附近。

B： Then you'll have to take a bus and get off at the Central Railway Station. 那麼你就坐公車到中央火車站下車。

A： Can you show me where the Central Railway Station is on this map? 可不可以請你指給我看，中央火車站在地圖上的什麼地方呢？

B： OK. It's here. 可以啊。在這兒呢。

② 問路

A： Excuse me, could you tell me the way to the ABC Hotel? 不好意思，請問 ABC 飯店怎麼走？

B： Go down the main road. You can't miss it. 沿著大路往前走就可以找到。

A： How long will it take me to get there? 到那裡大概要多久？

B： It's only a five-minute walk. 只要走五分鐘。

A： Thank you very much. 非常感謝。

B： You're welcome. 不用客氣。

③ 確認路線

A： Excuse me, I want to go to the zoo. But I can't find it. Can you tell me the way? 打擾一下。我想去動物園。但是我找不到。您能告訴我怎麼嗎？

B： Go straight back down this street for about five minutes and you'll find yourself at the zoo. 沿著這條路往回走大約五分鐘，就可以找到動物園。

A： Is this the correct direction? 這個方向對嗎？

B： Yes. I'm also going that way. I'll show you. 是的。我正好要去那裡。我帶您去吧。

A： Thank you so much. You are so nice. 非常感謝。您太好了。

B： It's nothing. Is this the first time that you come to Taipei? 不客氣。這是您第一次來臺北嗎？

A： Yes. I haven't been here before. 是的。我以前沒來過這裡。

Scene 53　物 品 遺 失

Step 1　必 備 表 達

派出所	police station：station 除了表示車站，還有「站、局、所」的意思。
失物招領處	Lost and Found：lost 和 found 這兩個單字分別是 lose 和 find 的過去式和過去分詞，用 and 連接在一起可以表示「失物招領處」。
報警	call the police：在美國一定得記住 911 這個電話號碼。無論遇到什麼困難都可以打這個電話，員警會立即過來幫你解決。
扒手	pickpocke：thief 也可以指「小偷」。
失物登記表	lost property report：property 財產。
被搶	be mugged：mug 對⋯⋯行兇搶劫。
闖入	break into：break 打破，類似片語搭配還有 break in 闖入，強行進入。
保安人員	security officer：secure 安全的。
掛失	report the loss of：report 此處作動詞，表示「報告」。
補辦登記	post-register：register 登記，註冊。

Step 2　句 句 精 彩

① 我遇上扒手了。

A：Where's your wallet? 你的錢包呢？

B：I had my pocket picked. 我遇上扒手了。

Tips

■ Something is stolen. 我丟東西了。

■ I was robbed by a pickpocket. 我遇上小偷了。

② 失物招領處在哪裡？

A：Where is the Lost and Found? 失物招領處在哪裡？

B： Right here. 就在這兒。

Tips

Can you tell me where the Lost and Found is? 你能告訴我失物招領處在哪裡嗎？

How could the lost be found? 怎麼找到丟的東西？

Maybe I should go to the Lost and Found to try my fortune. 或許我應該去失物招領處碰碰運氣。

③ 我想知道是否有人撿到錢包交到這裡了。

A： I was wondering if anyone has turned in a wallet. 我想知道是否有人撿到錢包交到這裡了。

B： Let me check. 我查一下。

Tips

turn in 上交，歸還。

I think you dropped this. 我想這是你丟的吧！

Doesn't this belong to you? 這是你的吧？

④ 我不在的時候有人闖入了我的房間。

A： You look pale. What's wrong with you? 你看起來臉色不太好。發生什麼事了？

B： Someone broke into my room when I was out. 我不在的時候有人闖入了我的房間。

Tips

look pale 看起來臉色蒼白。

My friend has been robbed. 我的朋友被搶了。

They knocked him down and robbed him of his briefcase. 他們把他打倒在地，搶走了他的公事包。

⑤ 我能補辦護照嗎？

A： Can I have my passport reissued? 我能補辦護照嗎？

B： Sure. But you have to wait for 15 days, you can't get it today. 當然。但是你得等十五天，今天拿不走。

Tips

reissue 補發。

I've lost my passport. Do you know where the foreign affairs office is? 我的護照掉了，你知

道外交辦事處在哪裡嗎？

■ I need a copy of the missing item report. 請開一張失竊證明給我。

⑥ 我在火車上被偷了錢包。

A：You seem to be in trouble. What can I do for you? 您似乎遇到麻煩了。我能為您做點什麼？

B：My purse was stolen when I was on the train. 我在火車上被偷了錢包。

Tips

■ in trouble 有麻煩，有困難。

■ I had my bag stolen. 我的包被偷了。

■ Please freeze my account. 請凍結我的帳戶。

⑦ 我不知道把手機丟在哪了。

A：I've called you the whole morning. Why didn't you answer the phone? 我給你打了一個早上的電話。你怎麼不接電話呢？

B：I have no idea where my phone is. 我不知道把手機丟在哪了。

Tips

■ I seem to have left my purse in the lobby of the hotel. 我的錢包好像掉在旅館大廳了。

■ He lost his credit card. 他丟了信用卡。

■ I've been forgetful these days. 最近我總是丟三落四的。

Step 3　情 景 模 擬

① 遇上扒手

A：Oh, my god. I had my pocket picked. Who should I report it to? 哦，天啊。我遇上扒手了。我該告訴誰？

B：We'd better call the police. 我們最好報警。

A：My phone is out of battery, and there is no police station nearby. What should I do? 我手機沒電了，而且這周圍也沒有派出所。我該怎麼辦？

B：You can use mine. 你用我的手機吧。

A：Thank you very much. 非常感謝。

B： You are welcome. 不客氣。

② 失物招領

A： Where is the Lost and Found? 失物招領處在哪裡？

B： It's here. How can I help you? 就在這。有什麼需要幫忙的？

A： I need to report something stolen. My wallet was stolen on the bus. 我要報失竊。我的錢包在公車上被偷了。

B： How much money inside? 裡面有多少錢？

A： About 300 dollars. 大約 300 美金吧。

B： OK, can you fill out this form? I need a report on this theft and we'll call you if we find it. 好的，你能填一下這張表嗎？請你寫一下被盜經過，我們找到後會跟你聯繫的。

③ 補辦護照

A： Excuse me, sir. I've been in a big trouble. 打擾一下，先生。我遇到大麻煩了。

B： Don't worry. Can you give me some detailed information? 別擔心。您能說說詳細情況嗎？

A： I lost my passport when I was on the train. But I have to finish my traveling plan. Can I have my passport reissued? 我乘火車的時候把護照弄丟了。但是我得完成旅行計畫。我能補辦護照嗎？

B： I think so. But it takes some time. 可以。但是這需要點時間。

A： Never mind. I can wait. 沒關係。我可以等。

B： OK, just fill out this form. 好的。請填一下這張表格。

Scene 54　打　電　話

Step 1　必 備 表 達

電話亭	telephone booth：booth 公用電話亭。
公用電話	public phone：手機則是 cellphone。
發簡訊	send message：留言則是 leave a message。
斷線	disconnect：connect 連接，相關片語有 connect to 與……通電話。
總機	switchboard：switch 轉換。
占線	busy line：line 指「電話線」，offline 即「斷線」。
國際電話首碼	international prefix：prefix 首碼。
接線員	operator：來自 operate 運轉，操作。
對方付費電話	collect call：collect 作形容詞表示「由對方付費的」。
分機號碼	extension number：extension 電話分機。
電話區號	area code：code 編碼。

Step 2　句 句 精 彩

① 我想打對方付費電話到紐約。

A： What can I do for you? 能為您做些什麼？

B： I would like to make a collect call to New York. 我想打由對方付費的電話到紐約。

Tips

■ I want to make a call to Macao, China. 我要打一通電話到澳門。

■ Do you think I could use your phone? 我能借用一下電話嗎？

② 請問哪裡有公共電話？

A： Do you know where can I find a public phone? 請問哪裡有公共電話？

B： Just around the corner. 就在轉角處。

around the corner 還可以表示「即將來臨」。

I want to make a call with the pay phone. 我想用公共電話打個電話。

I need some coins to use the public phone. 我需要一些硬幣來使用公用電話。

③ 那個公共電話可以打國際長途嗎？

A： Can I make an international call from that pay phone? 那個公共電話可以打國際長途嗎？

B： No, local calls only. 不能，只能打本地電話。

Tips
Can I make a long distance call with this phone? 我能用這個電話打長途嗎？

How can I make a call with this phone? 怎麼用這個電話機打電話？

④ 如果要打電話到香港，哪種電話卡的話費最低？

A： Which card has the cheapest rate if I want to make a call to Hong Kong? 如果要打電話到香港，哪種電話卡的話費最低？

B： This one. It's very popular. 這個。這個很受歡迎。

Tips
Do you sell international phone cards? 這裡有賣國際電話卡的嗎？

Here's the phone bill. 這是電話費通知單。

How much should I pay if I make a call to Hong Kong? 打電話到香港多少錢？

⑤ 我一定是打錯電話了。對不起打擾您了。

A： I must have the wrong number. Sorry for bothering you. 我一定是打錯電話了。對不起打擾您了。

B： It doesn't matter. 沒關係。

Tips
bother 打擾。

Sorry, I dialed wrong. 對不起，我打錯了。

Sorry, I made a mistake. 對不起，我打錯了。

⑥ 你能告訴我加拿大的國際電話首碼嗎？

A： Can you tell me the international prefix of Canada? 你能告訴我加拿大的國際電

話首碼嗎？

B： Please wait for a moment. I'll have a check. 請稍等。我查一下。

Tips

■ What's Chicago's area code? 芝加哥的區號是多少？

■ I'm looking for the number of the electric company. 我想查一下電力公司的電話。

■ I am trying to reach John Smith. Do you have his number? 我想給約翰‧史密斯打電話。您有他的電話嗎？

⑦ 您能幫我轉接到銷售部嗎？分機號是 2467。

A： Can you put me through the Sales Department? The extension number is 2467. 您能幫我轉接到銷售部嗎？分機號是 2467。

B： Sure. Please wait for a moment. 當然。請稍等。

Tips

■ put through 接通。

■ Please connect me to the HR Department. 請給我轉到人力資源部。

■ Extension 522, please. 請轉接 522。

Step 3　情景模擬

① 打電話

A： Can I help you? 我能幫你嗎？

B： Well, Can I make an international call from that pay phone? 是的。那個公共電話可以打國際長途電話嗎？

A： Sure. Here is the phone. 當然。給您電話。

B： Could you tell me how to make an international call? 您能告訴我怎麼打國際長途電話嗎？

A： You should dial the area code first. 你需要先撥區號。

B： OK, I got it. 好的，我知道了。

② 打錯電話

A： Hi, is that Kara speaking? This is Steven. 喂，是卡拉嗎？我是史蒂文。

B： No. Sorry, there is no one named Kara. 不是，對不起，這兒沒有人叫卡拉。

A： I must have the wrong number. Sorry for bothering you. 我一定是打錯電話了。
     對不起打擾您了。

B： Never mind. 沒關係。

A： I'll check the number. Good bye. 我再確認一下。再見。

B： Bye. 再見。

③ 查號碼

A： Can you tell me the international prefix of Canada? 你能告訴我加拿大的國際電
     話首碼嗎？

B： One moment please. It's 001. 請稍等。區號是 001。

A： Can you help me dial this number? I can't get through. 你能幫我撥一下這個號碼
     嗎？這個號碼我打不通。

B： Certainly. One moment, please. 當然可以。請稍等。

A： Thank you. 謝謝。

B： Well, I'm afraid you have the wrong number. 嗯，恐怕你的號碼是錯了。

Scene 55　尋 求 幫 助

Step 1　必 備 表 達

交流障礙	communication barrier：communication 交流，barrier 障礙。
再說一遍	beg one's pardon：beg 請求。這句話的語氣不同，含義也不同。如果用疑問語氣，則是請對方再說一遍；如果是陳述語氣，則是請求對方的原諒。
譯者	translator：translate 翻譯，更偏重於「筆譯」，interpret 則是「口譯」，interpreter 是「口譯工作者」。
被困	get trapped：trap 困住。
大使館	embassy：diplomatic 外交上的，diplomat 外交官。
與……走散	get separated from：separate 分開，常用搭配為 separate from 從……分開。
幫某人一個忙	give sb. a hand：這個意思還可以用片語 lend a hand、do a favor 來表達。
交通事故	traffic accident：與 traffic 相關的搭配還有：traffic control 交通管制，traffic jam 交通堵塞，traffic signal 交通信號。
故障	stoppage：還可以用單字 breakdown，bug 來表達相同的意思。
鎮定	calm down：calm 使平靜。

Step 2　句 句 精 彩

① 別人聽不懂我說話。

A：I can't make myself understood. 別人聽不懂我說話。

B：Do you have a French-English dictionary? Maybe that would help.
你有法英詞典嗎？或許那會有用。

Tips

dictionary 字典。

He doesn't understand me. 他聽不懂我說話。

Can you follow me? 你懂我的意思嗎？

② 我不知道用法文怎麼說。

A： Ask this guy if they are selling hamburgers here. 問問那個小夥子是不是在這裡賣漢堡。

B： I don't know how to say it in French. 我不知道用法文怎麼說。

Tips

hamburger 漢堡。

I can't speak French. 我不說法語。

My English is not good enough. 我的英語不夠好。

③ I didn't quite get it. 我沒太聽懂你在說什麼。

A： Can you speak a little slower? I didn't quite get it. 你能慢點說嗎？我沒太聽懂你在說什麼。

B： Sure. I'm asking, where are you from? 當然。我是說，你來自哪裡？

Tips

I didn't quite catch that. 我沒太聽懂你在說什麼。

I'm not totally sure what you mean. 我沒完全聽懂你在說什麼。

④ 我和朋友走散了。

A： Why are you crying? 你怎麼哭了？

B： I got separated from my friend and can't find her. 我和朋友走散了。

Tips

Everybody gets together. 大家靠在一起，不要走散了。

Follow me. 跟著我。

⑤ 我們的車子拋錨了。可以幫我嗎？

A： Our car has broken down. Could you please do me a favor? 我們的車子拋錨了。可以幫我嗎？

B： Of course. Let me see. 當然。我看看。

Tips

■ break down 拋錨。

■ It might be the engine. 可能是引擎出問題。

■ Can you send somebody to tow it away? 請派人來把車拖走好嗎？

⑥ 來人啊！有人被困在電梯裡了。

A： Somebody！Someone is trapped in the elevator. 來人啊！有人被困在電梯裡了。

B： Hold on! I'll get someone to get you out of there. 等著！我叫人救你出來。

Tips

■ I'm stuck in the elevator and the doors won't open. 我被關在電梯裡，門打不開。

■ I can't get out of the lift. 我在電梯裡出不去了。

⑦ 請幫忙叫輛救護車，有人受傷了。

A： What can I do to help? 我能幫上什麼忙嗎？

B： Please call for an ambulance. Someone is injured. 請幫忙叫輛救護車，有人受傷了。

Tips

■ ambulance 救護車。

■ Please call a doctor! 請叫大夫！

■ Someone is having a heart attack. Please call for an ambulance. 有人心臟病發作了，快叫救護車。

Step 3　情 景 模 擬

① 語言不通

A： I think we are lost. We should ask someone for directions. 我覺得我們迷路了。我們應該找人問問路。

B： I don't know how to say it in Spanish. I can't make myself understood. 我不知道用西班牙語怎麼說。別人聽不懂我說話。

A： I think we need somebody who can speak English. 我想我們需要找一位會說英語的人。

B： Maybe that would help. 或許那會有幫助。

A： Or we can call the police and get some help. 或許我們可以打電話找員警幫忙。

B： That's a good idea. 好主意。

② 汽車拋錨

A： What's wrong? 怎麼了？

B： Our car has broken down. Could you please do me a favor? 我們的車子拋錨了。可以幫我嗎？

A： What's the matter with it? 出了什麼毛病？

B： The car isn't running smoothly. I'd like to have a look at it. 車子開起來不大對勁，我想檢查一下。

A： Nothing serious. The right one needs some air. 沒什麼大問題，右邊輪胎需要充氣。

B： Thank God it's not serious. 謝天謝地沒什麼大問題。

③ 電梯被困

A： Help! Help! 救命！救命！

B： What happened to you? 你怎麼了？

A： Somebody! Someone is trapped in the elevator. 來人啊！有人被困在電梯裡了。

B： Calm down! 冷靜！

A： It's an emergency! Please get someone to let me out immediately. 十萬火急！請立刻找人來把我弄出去。

B： Sure. Sure. Right now. 當然。當然。馬上。

Scene 56　生 病

Step 1　必 備 表 達

頭痛	headache：have a headache 頭痛，migraine headache 偏頭痛，tension headache 緊張性頭痛，suffer from headache 患頭痛。
流鼻涕	running nose：也可以用 run at the nose 表示相同的意思，nose 的相關搭配還有 bloody nose 鼻子流血，nose bridge 鼻梁。
發燒	fever：fever 的相關搭配還有：brain fever 腦膜炎，enteric fever 傷寒，have a fever 發燒。
鼻塞	stuff nose：stuff 填塞，相關搭配還有：stuff with 使塞滿。
拉肚子	diarrhea：infantile diarrhea 幼兒腹瀉。
便祕	constipation：也可以用 astriction 表達相同的意思。
過敏	allergy: allergic 過敏的，be allergic to 表示「對……過敏」。
心臟病發	heart attack：congenial heart attack 先天性心臟病，coronary heart attack 冠心病。
食物中毒	food poisoning：poisoning 來自 poison 毒物，與「毒」相關的說法還有：poisonous 有毒的，deadly poison 致命毒藥，poison gas 毒氣。
感冒	catch a cold：與「感冒」有關的說法還有：cold cure 感冒藥，freezing cold 非常冷，have a cold 感冒，slight cold 輕度感冒。

Step 2　句 句 精 彩

① 我感冒了。

A： What's the matter? 你怎麼了？

B： I came down with a cold. 我感冒了。

Tips

come down with 染上……病。

I've got a cold. 我感冒了。

My nose is running. 我流鼻涕了。

② 我不舒服。

A： What's wrong with you lately? 你最近怎麼了？

B： I'm under the weather. 我不舒服。

Tips

under the weather 身體不舒服。

I'm not feeling myself. 我覺得不太舒服。

I'm sick. 我不舒服。

③ 我身上出了疹子。

A： I broke out in a rash. 我身上出了疹子。

B： Really? Does it itch? 是嗎？癢不癢？

Tips

rash 疹子。

I think I'm getting a rash. 我身上出了疹子。

I got food poisoning! 我食物中毒了！

④ 我過敏的毛病又犯了。

A： Did you catch a cold? 你感冒了嗎？

B： My allergies are acting up. 我過敏的毛病又犯了。

Tips

My allergies are giving me trouble. 我過敏的毛病又犯了。

It's allergy season for me. 過敏的毛病又犯了。

I'm allergic to pollen. 我對花粉過敏。

⑤ 我拉肚子。

A： Do you have any other symptoms? 你還有什麼其他症狀嗎？

B： I have loose bowels. 我拉肚子。

Tips

- symptom 症狀。
- I have diarrhea. 我拉肚子。
- I don't feel like eating anything. I feel like vomiting. 我什麼也吃不下，就想吐。

⑥ 我頭痛，喉嚨也痛。

A： I've got a headache and sore throat. 我頭痛，喉嚨也痛。

B： Did you take any aspirin? 你吃阿斯匹林了嗎？

Tips

- My head is killing me. 我頭痛死了。
- My throat hurts. 我喉嚨痛。
- My throat is sore. 我喉嚨痛。

⑦ 我一陣一陣地腹痛。

A： I have bouts of abdominal pain. 我一陣一陣地腹痛。

B： You should curl up for a while. 那你應該蜷一會兒。

Tips

- curl up 蜷縮。
- I have pain in my gut. 我肚子疼。
- My belly hurts. 我肚子疼。

Step 3　情景模擬

① 患感冒

A： Are you OK? You don't look so good. 你還好吧？看起來氣色不大好似的。

B： I feel chilly. I came down with a cold. 我渾身發冷。我感冒了。

A： Here, wrap you up in this blanket. 給你，把這個毯子裹上。

B： Thanks. 多謝。

A： You should go to see a doctor as soon as possible. 你應該盡快去醫院看看。

B： I will, but I'm busy recently. 我會的，但我最近很忙。

② 過敏

A： Ah, you are sneezing all the time. 呀，你一直在打噴嚏。

B： My allergies are acting up. I'm allergic to pollen. 我過敏的毛病又犯了。我對花粉過敏。

A： Do you need a doctor? 用叫醫生嗎？

B： No, not necessary. There is some medicine on the table. Can you pass it to me? 不，不用了。桌子上有藥。能遞給我一些嗎？

A： Sure. Here you are. 好的。給你。

B： Thank you. 謝謝。

③ 頭痛

A： What's wrong with you? 你怎麼了？

B： I've got a headache and sore throat. 我頭痛，喉嚨也痛。

A： When did you start feeling like this? 你什麼時候開始有這種感覺的？

B： Um, probably a week ago. Is it serious? 呃，大約一週以前。嚴重嗎？

A： You just have a cold. You need to take some medicine and drink more water. 你就是患了感冒。你需要吃些藥，再多喝些水。

B： I just need to have a good rest. 我只要好好休息就行了。

Scene 57 藥房買藥

Step 1 必備表達

處方	prescription：prescript 藥方。
藥房	pharmacy/drug store：通常來說，pharmacy 中只出售藥品，而 drug store 還會出售一些雜物，類似於雜貨鋪。
ok 蹦	band-aid：band 帶。
繃帶	bandage：這個單字還可以用作動詞，表示「用繃帶綁紮」。
眼藥水	eye drops：drop 此處作名詞，表示「滴劑」。
止痛藥	painkiller：killer 也表示「止痛藥」。
膠囊	capsule：swallow the capsule 吞下膠囊。
藥片	tablet：chewable tablet 口嚼片。
維生素	vitamin：vitamin deficiency 缺乏維生素。
副作用	side effect：還可以說成 adverse effect。

Step 2 句句精彩

① 有治拉肚子的藥嗎？

A：Do you have anything for diarrhea? 有治拉肚子的藥嗎？

B：Yes, we do. It's right over here. 是的，我們這兒有。就在這裡。

Tips

■ Do you have medicine for athlete's foot? 有治療腳氣的藥嗎？

■ I have diarrhea. Do you have medicine for it? 我拉肚子。你們有能治拉肚子的藥嗎？

■ What medicine should I take for I have diarrhea? 我拉肚子，該吃什麼藥呢？

② 我想買點感冒藥。

A：Can I help you? 需要我幫忙嗎？

B：I need some cold medicine. 我想買點感冒藥。

Tips

I need some medicine. 我要買藥。

I'd like some medicine for a cold. 我想買點感冒藥。

I'm looking for cold medicine. 我正在想買點感冒藥。

(3) 這種藥非常有效。

A： These tablets are very effective. 這種藥非常有效。

B： OK. Let me have a try. 好吧。我試試。

Tips

effective 有效的。

Can I stop taking the pills? 我可以停止服藥了嗎？

Does the medicine work? 這藥管用嗎？

(4) 每四小時吃兩片。

A： How do I take this medicine? 我怎麼服用這個藥？

B： Take two tablets every four hours. 每四小時吃兩片。

Tips

How many of them should I take each time? 這藥我每次該服用多少？

One teaspoon, three times daily. 每天服三次，一次一茶匙。

How many times a day should I take this medicine? 這藥每天吃幾次？

(5) 這種藥有副作用嗎？

A： Are there any side effects of the drug? 這種藥有副作用嗎？

B： It may cause drowsiness. 可能會使人犯困。

Tips

drowsiness 困倦。

Are there any side effects I should know about? 有任何副作用嗎？

It's quite harmless. 這完全沒有副作用。

(6) 請按藥方幫我抓藥好嗎？

A： What can I do for you? 我能為您做點什麼？

B： Can you fill the prescription for me? 請按藥方幫我抓藥好嗎？

Tips

■ prescription 藥方。

■ Don't you have a prescription? 你沒有藥方麼？

■ Sorry, sir. I cannot sell it to you because you must get a doctor's certificate or prescription first. 抱歉，先生。我不能賣給你，因為你必須有醫生證明或者醫生開的藥方才行。

⑦ 我聽說中醫療效更好。

A： I've heard that Chinese medicine has better results. 我聽說中醫療效更好。

B： Yes. For this disease, Chinese medicine is better. 是的。這種病更適合看中醫。

Tips

■ Chinese medicine 中醫，「西醫」是 Western medicine。

■ I'll write you a prescription for some Chinese medicine. 我會給你開一些中藥。

■ Let's go to see a Western medical doctor. 咱們還是看西醫吧。

Step 3 情 景 模 擬

① 買藥

A： Can I help you? 需要我幫忙嗎？

B： I need some medicine. 我要買藥。

A： What kind of medicine do you want? 您要哪種藥呢？

B： Do you have anything for diarrhea? 有治拉肚子的藥嗎？

A： Yes, we do. 是的，我們這兒有。

B： Let me have a look. 我看看。

② 詢問療效

A： What do you need? 您需要點什麼？

B： I need some cold medicine. 我想買點感冒藥。

A： OK, just over-the-counter drug? 好，就買非處方藥嗎？

B： Yes. It's OK. 是的。非處方藥就好。

A： Would you like liquid or pill? 你要口服液還是片劑？

B： I have no idea. Can you give me some advice? 我不知道。您有什麼建議嗎？

A：Try this one. These tablets are very effective. 試試這個。這種藥非常有效。

B：All right. I'll take it. 好的。就買這個。

③ 副作用

A：What drug can reduce a fever? 有什麼藥可以退燒？

B：This one. For others, you will need a prescription. 這種。其他藥需要醫生的處方才能開。

A：Are there any side effects of the drug? 這種藥有副作用嗎？

B：Yes. It may cause a loss of appetite. 是的。它會引起食欲不振。

A：Can I still drive after taking this drug? 吃完這種藥後還能開車嗎？

B：Yes. It won't impair your driving ability at all. 可以。一點都不會影響你開車。

Scene 58　醫院就診

Step 1　必備表達

預約門診	make an appointment：appointment 約定。
症狀	symptom：early symptom 早期症狀。
量體溫	take someone's temperature：temperature 溫度。
打針	injection 是動詞是 inject，另外 shot 也可以表示「注射」。
掛號	register：掛號處則是 registration office。
量血壓	take someone's blood pressure：blood pressure 血壓。
檢查	check-up：check over 查看，檢查。
糖尿病	diabetes：juvenile diabetes 青少年糖尿病。
驗血	take a blood test：blood 血液。
全身檢查	thorough examination：thorough 全面的。體檢則可以用 physical examination 表示。

Step 2　句句精彩

① 你有什麼樣的症狀？

A：What symptoms do you have? 你有什麼樣的症狀？

B：I am exhausted. 我很累。

Tips

■ exhausted 疲憊的。

■ Do you have any other symptoms besides headache? 除了頭痛之外，你還有沒有其他症狀？

■ Could you describe your symptoms? 能描述一下你的症狀嗎？

② 你以前有過這種情況嗎？

A：Has this ever happened to you before? 你以前有過這種情況嗎？

B：Never. It's the first time. 從沒有。這是第一次。

Tips

When did the symptoms start? 你什麼時候開始有這種症狀的？

How long have you felt like this? 你有這種感覺多長時間了？

Did you have this feeling before? 你以前有這種感覺嗎？

③ 你最好照張 X 光片，看看哪裡有問題。

A： My arm hurts. 我的胳膊受傷了。

B： You'd better take an X-ray and find out what's wrong. 你最好照張 X 光片，看看哪裡有問題。

Tips

There's nothing out of the ordinary on your ECG. 你的心電圖完全正常。

You're completely normal. 你完全正常。

The examination can help you know what the problem is. 這個檢查能告訴你問題是什麼。

④ 我來量一下你的脈搏。

A： I think my heart has been beating strangely lately. 我感覺我的心臟最近跳得很奇怪。

B： Let me feel your pulse. 我來為你把脈。

Tips

pulse 脈搏，feel the pulse 是「把脈」的意思。

■ Let me listen to your heart and lung. 讓我聽聽你的心肺。

I'll give you a general check-up. 我給你做個全身檢查。

⑤ 感冒正在流行。你有發燒及噁心的症狀嗎？

A： The flu is going around. Do you have a fever and nausea? 感冒正在流行。你有發燒及噁心的症狀嗎？

B： Yeah, I think I might throw up. 是的，我想我會吐的。

Tips

Do you feel ill? 你覺得噁心嗎？

Do you have a stomachache? 你覺得胃疼嗎？

⑥ 拿這張處方到藥店去買些藥。

A： Take this prescription to a pharmacy and buy some medicine. 拿這張處方到藥店

去買些藥。

B： All right. 好。

Tips

■ pharmacy 藥店。

■ Here's your prescription. 這是你的處方。

■ You must take a tonic. 你得吃些滋補藥。

⑦ 請給我開一份醫生檢查報告，我提交給保險公司。

A： What do you want? 您想要什麼？

B： Please write a medical report for my insurance company. 請給我開一張醫生檢查報告，我提交給保險公司。

Tips

■ Could you give me a certificate for sick leave? 你能給我開一張假條證明嗎？

■ I need to have a medical report to make insurance claim. 我需要一份醫學檢查報告，用於向保險公司理賠。

Step 3 情 景 模 擬

① 詢問症狀

A： What's the matter? 你怎麼了？

B： I don't feel very well. 我覺得不太舒服。

A： What symptoms do you have? 你有什麼樣的症狀？

B： There's fluid coming out of my right ear. 我右耳在流膿。

A： Let's have a check. I can't tell right now. 我們來檢查一下吧。我現在還說不好。

B： OK. 好的。

② 病情狀態

A： What's wrong with you? 你怎麼了？

B： I've been having trouble with breathing lately. 我最近呼吸有些問題。

A： Has this ever happened to you before? 你以前有過這種情況嗎？

B： No, it starts probably about a week ago. 沒有，大約一週以前開始的。

A： OK, let me examine your chest and listen to your heart beat. This way, please. 哦，我來檢查一下你的胸部，聽聽你的心跳。請走這邊。

B： All right. 好的。

③ 進行診斷

A： The flu is going around. Do you have a fever and nausea? 感冒正在流行。你有發燒及噁心的症狀嗎？

B：Yes. I feel awfully hot and I'm sweating a lot. 是的。我感覺非常熱，出了很多汗。

A： Let me take your temperature. Stick the thermometer under your arm. 讓我給你量下體溫。把體溫表放在腋下。

B： OK, for how long? 好的，要多長時間？

A： About five minutes. Oh, you have a fever. 大約五分鐘。哦，你發燒了。

B： Oh no! What can I do? 哦，不！我可怎麼辦啊？

Scene 59　在郵局

Step 1　必備表達

郵票	stamp：stamp collecting 集郵。
郵費	postage：postage due 欠郵費。
平郵	regular mail：regular 常規的。
掛號信	registered letter：register 掛號。
郵編	zip code：zip 是 zone improvement program「郵區改進計畫」的縮寫，因此 zip code 是美國郵政管理局所使用的編碼。
保險費率	insurance rate：insurance expense 可以指「保費」，相關的 claim for compensation 是指「索賠」。
超重	overweight：weight 是「重量」的意思，因此這個合成詞表示「超重」。
賠償額	coverage：full coverage 全額承保。
快遞	expressage：express 也可以指「快遞」。
匯款單	post order：在銀行匯款給某個人時，需要填寫匯款單。

Step 2　句句精彩

① 運費要多少？

A： How much is the shipping cost? 運費要多少？

B： Let me weigh. Please wait for a moment. 讓我稱稱。請稍等。

Tips

■ shipping cost 運費。

■ How much does this weigh? 這個郵件多重？

■ How much is an airmail letter to UK? 寄往英國的航空郵件的郵資是多少？

② 這個寄海運要多久？

A： How long does it take to ship this? 這個寄海運要多久？

B： About a week. 大概一週。

Tips

If I send this by air, how long will it take to get to America? 航空信寄到美國要花多少時間？

It will get there on Monday. 週一就到了。

They will probably receive it on Monday. 他們週一就能收到。

③ 您要航運還是海運？

A： Would you like to mail it by air or sea? 您要航運還是海運？

B： By air. It would be quicker. 航運吧。這樣能快點。

Tips

I want to send the registered package by sea. 我想海運這個掛號的包裹。

I want to send this by boat. 我想寄海運。

I'd like to send this package by air. 我想用航空的方式寄這個包裹。

④ 我想要取包裹。

A： I want to pick up my package. 我想要取包裹。

B： OK, can I see your ID card? 好的，可以出示下你的身分證嗎？

Tips

Can I pick up a package? 我可以取包裹嗎？

I'd like to pick up my package. This is the notice. 我想取我的包裹。這是包裹到達通知單。

Has my package arrived? 我的包裹來了嗎？

⑤ 這封快遞郵件的郵費和附加費是多少？

A： What's the postage and surcharge on this express letter? 這封快件的郵費和附加費是多少？

B： 18 dollars in total. 一共 18 美元。

Tips

surcharge 附加費。

How many stamps do I need to paste? 我需要貼幾張郵票？

All prices include postage and packing. 全部價格包括郵資和包裝。

⑥ 我有必要寫上回郵地址嗎？

A： Is it necessary to put my return address on? 我有必要寫上回郵地址嗎？

B： Yes, it is necessary for a registered letter. 是的，掛號信需要寫上。

Tips

■ return address 回郵地址。

■ It's not necessary. 沒有必要。

■ You'd better write it down. 最好寫上。

⑦ 想投保的話，保險費要多少？

A： How much would it cost to insure it? 想投保的話，保險費要多少？

B： That'll be $20. 保險費 20 美元。

Tips

■ Would you like to put insurance on it? 您想為它上保險嗎？

■ What's the insurance fee? 保險費是多少？

■ You should insure this, just to be safe. 為了安全起見，我認為您應該預先投保為好。

Step 3　情景模擬

① 運費

A： What does it contain? 包裹裡面裝的是什麼？

B： Some books and clothes. Is this packing OK? 一些書和衣服。這樣的包裝可以嗎？

A： I think you need some more tape. 我想你還需要再纏些膠帶。

B： How much is the shipping cost? 運費要多少？

A： Five dollars. 五美元。

B： Here you are. Thank you. 給您錢。謝謝。

② 郵寄方式

A： I'd like to send this package back to America. 我要把這個包裹寄回美國。

B： OK. Would you like to mail it by air or sea? 好的。您要航運還是海運？

A： I'd like to send this parcel by airmail. 我想用航運寄。

B： Alright. I need to weigh it first. It's 1 kilogram. 好的。我需要先稱一下。包裹是

一公斤。

A： How much is the postage? 郵費多少錢？

B： 180 yuan. 180 元。

③ 保險費

A： You should write 「do not bend」 on the envelope. 您應該在信封上註明「不能折疊」。

B： Good idea. I don't want it to be damaged. 好主意。我可不想把東西弄壞了。

A： Do you want it insured? 您想給它上保險嗎？

B： Yes, the contents are very valuable for me. How much would it cost to insure it? 是的，這裡面的東西對於我而言很貴重。想投保的話，保險費要多少？

A： 15 dollars. 15 美元。

B： OK. 好的。

Scene 60 在銀行

Step 1 必備表達

外幣兌換	currency exchange：currency 貨幣。在旅遊景點，經常會看到兌換外幣的地方，寫著 currency exchange 的牌子。
匯率	exchange rate：exchange 兌換可以用 exchange 表示。
提款	withdraw：「存款」可以用 deposit 來表示。
手續費	commission charge：commission 手續費，傭金。
餘額	balance：check the balance 查詢餘額。
儲蓄存款帳戶	savings account：account 帳戶。
活期存款	current deposit：「活期帳戶」則是 current account。
自動提款機	ATM(Automatic Teller Machine)：teller 出納員。
年費	annual fee：annual 每年的。
定期存款	fixed deposit：fixed 固定的。

Step 2 句句精彩

① 手續費是多少？

A： How much is the commission? 手續費是多少？

B： It's totally free. 這完全免費。

Tips

■ Is there a service charge if I open a checking account? 如果開支票帳戶，有手續費嗎？
■ Is there any extra fee? 有什麼額外費用嗎？

② 請問今天美元兌換日元的匯率是多少？

A： What is the exchange rate between the US dollar and the yen today? 請問今天美元兌換日元的匯率是多少？

B： 1:98. 1 比 98。

Tips

How many yens to the dollar today? 今天一美元可以換多少日元？

If I change it to US dollars, how much would I get? 我想換美元，能換多少？

③ 我可以從你們銀行的自動提款機取款嗎？

A： Can I withdraw money from the ATM of your bank? 我可以從你們銀行的自動提款機取款嗎？

B： Sure. It's over there. 當然。在那邊。

Tips

withdraw 取錢。

Is the ATM available? 自動款機能用嗎？

You need to pay trans-system service fee. 你需要付跨行手續費。

④ 定期帳戶的存款利率是多少？

A： What's the interest rate for the fixed account? 定期帳戶的存款利率是多少？

B： It's 3.25%. 是 3.25%。

Tips

What's the interest rate per year? 存款的年利率是多少？

The interest is added to your account every year. 每年的利息都加到你的帳戶裡。

⑤ 請填一下申請表，然後去三號窗口排隊。

A： I'd like to make a withdrawal. 我想取錢。

B： Fill in this application form and line up at Window 3. 請填一下申請表，然後去三號窗口排隊。

Tips

application form 申請表。

I'd like to open a deposit account. 我想開個儲蓄帳戶。

Could you tell me how to open a deposit account? 能告訴我怎麼開儲蓄帳戶嗎？

⑥ 我忘了我的信用卡還款日了。

A： I forgot the payment due day of my credit card. 我忘了我的信用卡還款日了。

B： Don't worry. Let me check it for you. 別擔心。我幫您查查。

Tips

■ credit card 信用卡。

■ What should I do if I lose my bankbook? 我的存摺丟了該怎麼辦？

■ My certificate of deposit reached maturity yesterday. 我的定期存單昨天到期了。

⑦ 這個帳戶有最低存款額嗎？

A：Is there a minimum deposit for the account? 這個帳戶有最低存款額嗎？

B：Yes, it's 20 dollars. 有，20 美元。

Tips

■ What's the minimum amount for the first deposit? 第一次儲蓄的最低限額是多少？

■ Our minimum deposit for a savings account is 100 dollars. 我們儲蓄存款的最低存款額是 100 美元。

■ Ten yuan is the minimum original deposit. 最低起存款額是 10 元。

Step 3　情景模擬

① 兌換匯率

A：What notes do you want? 您要兌換什麼貨幣？

B：I want to change US dollars for yen. By the way, What is the exchange rate between the US dollar and the yen today? 我想將美元兌換成日元。順便問一下，請問今天美元兌換日元的匯率是多少？

A：Let me just check the rate. It's 1 ： 98. 我確認一下匯率。是 1 比 98。

B：OK. I want to change 200 dollars. 好的。我要兌換 200 美元。

A：OK, do you have your passport with you? 好的，您帶護照了嗎？

B：Sure. Here you are. 當然。給您。

② 自動取款

A：There are so many people in the queue. Can I withdraw money from the ATM of your bank? 這麼多人在這兒排隊。我可以從你們銀行的自動提款機取款嗎？

B：Sure. It's just around the corner. 當然可以。就在轉角處。

A：Can you teach me how to use it? 你能告訴我怎麼用嗎？

B： Of course. This way, please. 當然可以。請走這邊。

A： Thank you. 謝謝。

B： It's my pleasure. 不客氣。

③ 存款利率

A： I'd like to make a deposit, sir. 先生，我想存錢。

B： OK, give me your passbook. 好的，給我您的存摺。

A： Will I receive interest on this account? 當然。這種類型的帳戶有利息嗎？

B： Of course. 當然有。

A： What's the interest rate for the fixed account? 定期帳戶的存款利率是多少？

B： 5%. 5%。

旅遊英語必備指南

作　　者：金利 主編

發 行 人：黃振庭

出 版 者：崧博出版事業有限公司

發 行 者：崧燁文化事業有限公司

E－m a i l：sonbookservice@gmail.com

粉 絲 頁：https://www.facebook.com/sonbookss/

網　　址：https://sonbook.net/

地　　址：台北市中正區重慶南路一段六十一號八樓
815 室

Rm. 815, 8F., No.61, Sec. 1, Chongqing S. Rd.,
Zhongzheng Dist., Taipei City 100, Taiwan (R.O.C)

電　　話：(02)2370-3310

傳　　真：(02) 2388-1990

總 經 銷：紅螞蟻圖書有限公司

地　　址：台北市內湖區舊宗路二段 121 巷 19 號

電　　話：02-2795-3656

傳　　真：02-2795-4100

印　　刷：京峯彩色印刷有限公司（京峰數位）

國家圖書館出版品預行編目資料

旅遊英語必備指南 / 金利主編 . -- 第一
版 . -- 臺北市：崧博出版：崧燁文化發
行 , 2020.10
　　面；　公分
POD 版
ISBN 978-957-735-994-0(平裝)
1. 英語 2. 旅遊 3. 會話
805.188　109015792

官網

臉書

定　　價：340 元

發行日期：2020 年 10 月第一版

◎本書以 POD 印製